BEST
INTERESTS

A NOVEL

Best Interests

Copyright 2021 Maureen Pollard
Cover image copyright 2021

Print ISBN: 978-1-9991742-3-1
Epub ISBN: 978-1-9991742-2-4

This book is a work of fiction.

Names, characters, places and incidents are products of the author's imagination or are used fictitiously. Any resemblance to actual events or locales or persons, living or dead, is entirely coincidental.

For Dad, who was a great storyteller.

Chapter 1

"Amy, I need you to go check on a family out at the edge of town. Jennifer was supposed to go today, but since she's not back, you'll have to pick it up. The seven days are up today." The woman's voice was brisk.

"Rhonda, I had planned to do some recording."

"The recording can wait. This visit needs to be made today. After the auditor's comments at our last license review, I don't want to be out of compliance again."

"Fine, I'll go now." Amy grabbed her battered briefcase, checked it to make sure she had a notepad and a few pens, then glanced at the files stacked in front of her computer. She held back a heavy sigh as she turned to leave the team room.

She paused at the administrative assistant's desk near the team room door to take a muffin from the pretty plate on the corner of the desk. Amy always brought fresh muffins on Mondays, and it looked like a muffin might be her only sustenance today with this change in plans.

"Amy, you check those kids closely. This family's been on our radar before. Jennifer probably shouldn't have closed the file," Rhonda called from the corner office. She positioned her desk so that she could see everyone as they passed into and out of the team room.

Amy thought about her colleague. Jennifer finished a trial last week where she had been eviscerated by the parents' lawyers and then in the judgement, and she hadn't been back to work since.

Once Amy was in the car, she followed the GPS directions to the edge of town, where the farmland began. She slowed as she saw that the produce stand coming up on the right belonged to the family she was looking for.

A driveway disappeared into a yard hidden by a tall, scraggly cedar hedge. There was barely room for a car to get through. Amy debated parking on the shoulder of the road beside the farm stand. There was just enough space for two cars beside the wooden structure; three walls, topped by a roof that sloped down to the back wall, sheltered shelving along the walls and a table in the centre, all filled with colourful fresh vegetables. A hand lettered sign directed customers to place their payment in a locked box with a slot in the top. More signs listing prices in the same block print were propped around the table.

Looking down the country highway, Amy saw that the next neighbour was about three kilometers away. No, it was safer to take the car in, where it would be closer if she needed to escape in a hurry. She pulled past the driveway and backed in, looking over her shoulder and trying to avoid the overgrown branches.

The hedge hid a rundown house. The shingles were peeling, and a few lay on the ground. The old cement walkway was crumbling. The porch had window frames, but the screens had long been torn or blown out of place. A screen door hung on one hinge, open and banging against the porch frame in the breeze. The porch was bare except for a stack of beer cases.

Amy could hear yelling inside the house.

"You get out of that! Right now! I told you to leave it alone, or we won't have any left for supper! Now, go get the shovel and clean up the dog shit in the yard." After a silent pause, Amy heard a crack, like the sound of flesh meeting flesh, and the front door flew open just as she stepped onto the porch.

A boy, about eleven, ran onto the porch. He froze when he saw Amy. His hair was long and shaggy. It hung down over one cheek but did not cover the bright red mark forming there. The other cheek was pale, smudged with what might be peanut butter.

"Hello." Amy stopped her progress toward the front door. "My name is Amy. Are you Josh?" Amy waited as the child looked over his shoulder through the open door. No one came.

"Yes," he said as he wiped at his eyes with the back of his hand.

"Is your mom home, Josh?" Amy stayed still.

"Yes. Who are you?"

"I'm Amy. From CAS, Josh. Do you know what CAS is?"

"Yeah, you take kids and stick 'em in foster homes so they can't see their families anymore."

"Sometimes we take kids to foster homes for a while, yes, if it's not safe for them at home."

Josh crossed his thin arms over his chest and tilted his chin up.

"Sometimes we help parents find ways to keep their kids safe at home," Amy continued in a quiet voice, without moving. "And sometimes we help families solve problems when they're having trouble getting along."

Josh snorted and spit on the stair beside Amy's boots.

"Ha." He raised his chin higher.

"Joshua Robert Flindall! What the hell are you doing? I told you to go get the sho..." A large woman with ruddy cheeks stopped in her tracks at the door as she caught sight of Amy on the porch. She looked from Amy to Josh, who looked at his shoes and kicked an imaginary pebble on the porch floor.

"Who are you?"

"Amy Malloy. Children's Aid Society. You must be Jane."

"You're new." The woman looked closely at Amy, who knew she was being measured.

"I've been around a while. Mostly working the other end of the county. I need to come in, to talk to you about why Josh has been away from school for the last several days and nobody's been able to reach you." Amy waited, without taking a step forward.

"The phone's out," Jane said. "Jackass left us with no money and the bills aren't paid. I need Josh here to do the extra chores. We've got to keep the house running." The woman crossed her arms over her substantial chest and leaned against the door frame. "He gets sick at school, anyway. He gets terrible headaches and stomachaches when he has to go. He'd rather work the farm with me, so what does it hurt if he stays home with me, at least for now?"

"Well, the law says Josh is too young to leave school for work yet, so there's that. I'd like to talk to you about the situation, so I can understand where you and Josh are coming from. May I come in?"

"Hmpff." The tall woman stepped aside and back into the house, extending one arm to hold the door open as Amy passed her, moving over the threshold and into the front hall.

"Might as well, but I got bread to make. You can talk to me while I work."

She looked at Josh. "You can go get the yard cleaned up, like I said."

Amy followed Jane through the hall to the kitchen at the back of the house. There was an old cast iron woodstove with four burners and an oven was fired up. On a back burner a large pot of water sat, and another pot holding what looked like diced vegetables and barley jostled in a simmering, rich brown broth. On the table sat a large bowl of yeasty dough, risen well up into a puffy curve above the bowl's edge. Jane opened the iron door, threw a log onto the fire in the stove, closed the door, and then wiped her hands on a damp cloth before turning to the bowl. She began punching her fists into the dough, beating it back down. Her shoulders were tense and her eyes narrow as she worked.

"So, Jane, when did Bill leave you and the kids here?" Amy was seated at the far end of the harvest table, with her notebook open on the only unfloured space available.

"A month ago. I've been running like crazy to get the vegetables in, the bread and tarts made, and keep the self-serve stand running out on the highway. Good thing the little ones are back in school, so I don't have to chase after them all day, too. August was hell, just after he left." Jane pounded the dough harder. "What with the squash and the pumpkins all coming on ripe at once, I needed Josh's help to bring it in, get it cleaned up, and put it up to the stand. He don't like school anyhow, like I said."

"You have it pretty tough right now," Amy said. "Josh has been a big help."

"You bet. He's a good worker." Jane glanced out the window facing south, where she could see Josh standing beside a wheelbarrow. "Well, as long as you don't ask him to write anything. Ask him to write something and he'll dawdle until the cows come home. That's true even if he's not sitting in front of a screen, getting distracted."

The dough was flat in the bowl and still Jane pounded as she spoke. The woman looked tired, her expression serious. Amy knew the action of punching the dough was helping Jane calm her nerves.

"Not that we got any screens on right now, with no power. Wouldn't have no water if we didn't have a well and it wasn't hooked up to the gas generator. My folks bring me gas every few days to keep it running and we just turn it on twice a day to get water."

"Sounds like you're working hard to keep things going." Amy made a few notes, then looked up. "I'd like to talk to Josh out in the yard. Mind if I do that now?"

Jane looked at her for a moment.

"Whatever," she said, turning her eyes back down to the dough in the bowl. "Nobody can say no to you people, anyway."

"I'll come back in once I've talked with him." Amy didn't respond to Jane's statement about the power a CAS worker held. There was nothing to say, since it was essentially the truth. If Jane said no, Amy would have to return with police to finish her investigation.

Amy stepped out of the kitchen into the backyard where she had followed Jane's gaze as she'd watched her son through the window. He was using a shovel to scoop the dog's mess into a wheelbarrow, which he then pushed to the edge of the yard and dumped in a pile of debris. The space was otherwise tidy, with a long vegetable patch stretching the full length of the big yard, from the cedar hedge that stood like a shield along the roadway to the back of the property where a pasture was fenced off. Some of the vegetables had clearly been harvested and raked over, but there were still several rows of pumpkins and a row of squash. Another wheelbarrow stood sentry at the end of these rows, half-filled with ripe vegetables.

"Hey, Josh. It looks like you've been working hard here. Those pumpkins are ready for the stand, I guess?" She watched the thin arms deposit a small, round pumpkin on top of the others.

"Yep." Josh bent to pick a tall, oval-shaped pumpkin and placed it in the barrow.

"Josh, what happened to your cheek? It was red when I got here and it's still red now."

Josh looked at his shoes. His left hand twisted the stem of the pumpkin he held. He looked up at Amy, who could see that the red area was turning purple.

"I banged my face on the cupboard door in the kitchen. I was getting a bowl."

Josh furrowed his brow and spit on the ground a short distance from Amy's boots. He put the pumpkin in the barrow and turned to pick another.

"Mmhm. So, what about school?"

"School sucks. It's a stupid waste of time. I don't know why I hafta go. There's work here that needs to be done if we're gonna make enough money to pay the bills." Josh bent again to the row of pumpkins.

"Okay, Josh. I'm going to have to talk with your mom, about the mark on your cheek and about school."

Amy turned to walk toward the house. She felt a tug on her arm and looked down to see a grubby hand on her sleeve. Amy turned back toward Josh.

"She's just doing the best she can," he said, looking into Amy's eyes. "Jackass left us with almost nothing and the little ones need everything."

Amy looked at the boy's discoloured cheek. She looked back into his eyes.

"I know she's trying hard, Josh. I bet you're a big help to her."

Amy turned again and this time she made it up the steps and into the kitchen, pausing to look back at the boy bent over in the pumpkin patch.

"Well, what did he tell you? He mouthed off at me, so I slapped him. I've got enough to worry about without him getting too big for his britches."

"I heard a sound when I was at the door. Tell me what happened."

"I slapped him across the cheek with the palm of my hand. That's why it's red."

"Darker now. It's starting to bruise." Amy watched as Jane gripped the edge of the kitchen table at the news the injury she had caused was worsening. Jane looked at Amy, her face pale and tight. Amy didn't keep her in suspense about what would have to happen next. She knew that not knowing could be more painful than the facts, whatever the facts might be. Besides, it was Jane's right to know.

"I'm going to have to call the police, Jane. I've got to follow the procedures now. I've also got to call my supervisor, and then I'm going to have to talk to the younger kids."

"I know. We went through this before with that other one from your office. The skinny one with the curly hair. That time Jackass hit Chelsea with a belt while I was putting some vegetables out at the stand. It was a few years ago, now. I thought we were done with you when Jackass left. I guess he left more of himself than I thought. Seems like I'm repeating some of his worst mistakes."

"Well, why don't we get started. I'm going to make those calls. Jane, will you agree to bring the kids in for interviews once I get an officer?"

"Yeah, I'll bring them in." Jane set the bowl of dough on the stove to rise again. She wiped her hands on a damp cloth and rubbed her forehead with the back of her arm.

Amy went out to her car and called her supervisor. Rhonda Selleck answered her extension and Amy confirmed her plan to call and request an officer. She'd see if they could do the interview at the CAS office instead of the police station. The interview rooms at both places had video and audio recorders, but the rooms at CAS had a softer environment, with couches instead of a steel desk and hard chairs. Amy avoided taking people to the police station if at all possible. The hard, bare interview rooms seemed to have a way of making situations harder than they had to be.

Amy called the police next. The dispatcher agreed to have an officer call back in a few minutes. Amy made some notes in her book while she waited. When her cell phone rang, she answered with her usual greeting.

"Amy Malloy speaking."

"Hey Amy, it's Evan. I hear you've got something for us?"

Amy blew out a sigh of relief. Evan Grant was one of the good ones.

They had worked together often since Evan arrived in Green Valley from Toronto the year before, and their friendship had grown. After spending several days driving around the county to interview a number of children at different schools about allegations involving a hockey coach, they realized they had a lot in common and started meeting for lunch once in a while.

And now, over the last few months, they had been meeting at the YMCA once a week to play squash. Each week, they played hard for about an hour, then showered and went to Cocoa's Café in Green Valley's busy downtown for dessert. They always sat on stools at the bar in the window, so they could watch as people strolled or hurried by, depending on the weather. They were in the habit of ordering two different selections and sharing them. Whoever lost at squash paid that night's bill.

Over tea and sweets, they would talk about their week. Amy found Evan easy to talk to. He understood her work because it wasn't that different from some of the work that he did himself. He never minded if she had to cancel because of an investigation that kept her after hours, because it sometimes happened to him, too. It was the nature of the job, and just as Evan understood that, Amy appreciated his approach to his own work. He didn't lose compassion for people, even in the midst of serious, difficult circumstances where he was called to use all of his investigative skills and training. He didn't have the same hardness as the furniture in the police interview rooms, or some of their colleagues, who'd grown cynical after years on the job.

"Yes, I've got something for you." Amy told him what she'd witnessed and mentioned the bruise that was forming on Josh's cheek. "There are two younger kids, Tyler Flindall, age eight, and Chelsea Flindall, age six. They're at school right now. Mom is co-operating and says she'll bring the kids in for interviews. Are you available to come to the CAS office?"

"CAS office? You just want to sit on your cushy furniture."

"Yep. As always," Amy said. She could laugh easily at the comment. She could always trust that Evan was on the same page when it came to thinking about the children's comfort.

"All right. I can be over there about eleven thirty. That give you enough time?"

"That should be good. I'll see you then."

"Ok, I'll bring the identikit camera."

"Good idea."

Amy hung up the phone. She stepped out of her car and went back up the porch steps. She knocked on the front door.

"Yeah, just come in," Jane called from the kitchen.

Amy went through the hall and back to the kitchen. Jane was peeling potatoes and setting them in a pot of water on the back burner of the stove. Amy briefly admired Jane's ability to tend to the duty of caring for her family despite the stress of the situation, then realized the woman really had no choice. No one else was going to feed her family.

"Okay, we are going to meet Constable Grant at the CAS offices at eleven thirty. Do you and the kids need a ride, Jane? I can drive you to the school to get them."

"Yeah, that would make it easier. Jackass took the car."

Jane wiped her hands again on the damp cloth and turned from the counter.

"Josh! Wash your hands in the bucket and come in and change your shirt. We're gonna go get the kids at school and go to CAS."

Josh paled as he stood up. He walked to the porch and stuck his hands into a bucket there. He put some soap on his hands from the pump container sitting by the bucket, lathered them up and then dunked them in the bucket again to rinse. He dried them on a worn towel that lay on the step, then came in the house and headed upstairs.

A few minutes later, Josh returned to the front hallway, wearing a clean shirt and jeans.

"Let's go, then. Josh, grab Chelsea's booster seat from the mudroom." Jane grabbed her purse and they headed out to the driveway together.

Once they were settled in Amy's car, neither Jane nor Josh said anything. Amy put the local pop radio station on to fill the silence. She was fine with not having any more discussion until the more formal interviews with the police officer were over with.

Amy pulled up in front of the elementary school. Jane glanced at her.

"I'll wait here. Josh can stay in the car and listen to the music if he wants while you get the kids, Jane."

Jane looked back at Josh. Amy saw the boy nod at his mother. Jane nodded in turn at Amy, and then stepped out of the car. She headed up the long walkway to the front door of the school, her head held high.

Several minutes and a few pop songs later, Jane came out of the school with a child on either side. Their small hands enveloped in hers, the trio didn't speak as they walked toward Amy's car. Jane opened the back door and the smaller children climbed in. Josh helped his younger brother buckle his seatbelt while Jane clipped the girl's seatbelt together around the booster seat.

"Josh? Mama said we gotta go to CAS. What for?"

"Josh! What happened to your face?"

"You two, hush," said Josh. "Listen to the music until we get to the CAS. You'll get your turn to talk then."

Amy pushed in a CD and the car filled with the sounds of a popular children's trio. Chelsea sang along while her brothers sat stone faced. Jane looked out the window until Amy pulled her car into the long driveway beside the two-story brick office building.

Chelsea sweetly chanted the repetitive phrases of the chorus and sang along with the rest of the lyrics. Amy let the music play until the song ended then turned off her car, signaling that it was time to go into the imposing brick building in front of them.

Maureen Pollard

Chapter 2

A logo on the side of the building proclaimed it the "Green Valley Children's Aid Society" in bold letters, with a stick-figure family in a huddle beneath the words. The driveway was lined with maple trees that had mostly turned colour with the recent cold weather. They hadn't yet started to fall into the great heaps of oranges and reds that would be thrown playfully by some of the young children who visited this place.

Amy was parked in a spot near the middle of the lot. The closest spots were always full of people who wanted to walk as short a distance as possible across the span of asphalt. The farthest spots were taken by the staff who still smoked. Out they would trudge at break time to sit, writing case notes, with the car stereo on as they chain smoked. When the notes were finished, they'd return to a desk stacked with the filed details of the lives of families in need in the community.

"Here we are," Amy said on the sidewalk in front of the big brick building. "We'll go in together. Inside, we're going to use two rooms today. The playroom is where we will all sit together to wait for a police officer to come. The interview room is where the police officer and I will interview you, one at a time." Amy made eye contact with Jane and each of the children, smiling slightly to try to reassure them, yet knowing there was little she could do to calm the anxiety caused by the situation.

"Police?" Chelsea's brown eyes grew wide, and she stepped closer to her mother.

Amy bent down beside her on the sidewalk. She kept herself a distance away but looked into the frightened child's eyes.

"Yes, Chelsea, the police officer has to come and help me talk to each of you to figure out what happened to Josh's cheek." Chelsea did not look at Josh or the darkening bruise. She locked eyes with this strange woman with the quiet voice who was squatting in front of her.

"We need to figure out what happened, and the police are good at that. The one who's coming is very good. I've talked to lots of kids with him before."

"Okay." Chelsea's response was hesitant, and she gripped her mother's hand.

"I don't want you to take me to live somewhere else!" Tyler suddenly shouted. He kicked his foot toward Amy, narrowly missing her knee.

"Well, Tyler, I don't want to take you to live somewhere else either," Amy said, tilting her head toward the agency door and giving a small smile she hoped was reassuring. "Let's go inside and see what we can do to figure this out."

Amy stood up and stepped over to the door. She held it open as Jane and the children walked through and into the lobby where a woman with short red hair and glasses perched on the end of her nose sat at a desk facing the door. From behind a pane of safety glass, she smiled at them over her computer screen as she answered the busy phone lines.

Brightly coloured children's drawings were framed and hung on the walls. A low coffee table held a variety of colouring pages and a container of crayons. A small shelf was lined with children's books. A rack on the wall held a few parenting magazines. Two low couches and two matching armchairs formed a semicircle around the low table.

A woman holding a gift bag sat on one of the chairs, with a bag of fast food on the coffee table in front of her. She sat up straight in her chair when Jane and the children walked into the lobby, as though she had been watching the door. When she didn't recognize them, she slumped back in the chair with a heavy sigh.

Amy stood beside the open door of a ten-foot square room. "We're going to go into this room on the left," she said. There were three doors on the same wall. One door was open, waiting for the woman with the gift bag and fast food to enter with her children. The third door was closed, giving the family inside a sense of privacy for their visit, despite the cameras and microphones in the room that allowed staff to observe every interaction.

"I have to pee!" Chelsea announced as she looked around the lobby.

"The bathroom's right over there." Amy pointed toward a door with a sign that read Family Washroom.

"You two wait here," Jane said. "Josh, keep Tyler out of trouble."

"Okay." Josh took Tyler's hand and led him into the room Amy stood beside.

"Tyler, you want me to read you a story?" Josh looked down at Tyler, whose eyes lit up when he spotted some toy trucks on a low shelf.

"No. Hey! Look at that! Dump trucks! THREE of them!" Tyler dropped to the floor beside the toy dump trucks and a mat that looked like a town map. Amy watched as he studied the mat, then began driving the trucks along the roads. Amy thought of the trucks that must drive by the farm stand on the highway and smiled as the little boy made rumbling engine noises as he played.

Josh looked at his brother playing, and then all around at the room. There were two couches along the walls, with an end table between them to form an L shape. Along with the toys, there was a shelf holding books and magazines.

"Where does all this stuff come from?" Josh asked as he waved a hand toward the bounty of toys.

"Well, some of it was chosen by the people who work here. They bought furniture and toys to make these rooms comfortable for children and their families. And some of it was donated by people who wanted to make this place bright and cheerful even though it can make people nervous to be here."

Josh nodded as he grabbed a comic book from the bookshelf beside the door and sat down on one of the couches to read.

Jane and Chelsea came back into the room. Chelsea was wiping her hands on her pants. She stopped in her tracks and looked over at the corner of the room across from the couches.

"Mommy, look!" Chelsea darted across the room toward a hand-painted, wooden kitchen centre, complete with a basket of plastic food and another holding plastic dishes and utensils.

"You can play with it if you like, Chelsea," Amy said. "A man built it for his granddaughter. His daughter works here, so he knows families sometimes come for visits. When his granddaughter grew up, he brought it in here for children to play with when they visit us."

Chelsea pulled out one of the bowls and pretended to pour ingredients before dipping her hands in and beginning to knead imaginary bread dough. Jane sighed as she watched her daughter play. She looked at each of her children, and then over to Amy.

"Can I get you a coffee or tea, Jane?" Amy looked at the children. "Can the kids have a juice box?"

"Sure, might as well. We're probably gonna be here a while, I'm sure. Coffee. Black, please."

"Orange or apple juice, guys?" Amy turned to the children.

"Orange!" Chelsea and Tyler called at once.

"Manners!" Jane reprimanded them.

"Please," they said in unison.

"Can I have apple juice, please?" Josh asked.

"You sure can. Jane, go ahead and have a seat."

As Jane settled on the couch beside Josh, Amy saw her watching her children reading and playing in this cheerful room. Her hands moved in her lap, folding together, then smoothing her clothes, then clasping tightly once more.

"There are a few magazines on that shelf if you want something to look at," Amy said. "I'll be right back."

Amy reappeared a few moments later with the juice and coffee. "Okay, two orange and one apple. Josh, can you take these?" Once Josh took the juice boxes and distributed them, Amy closed the door and handed the coffee mug to Jane.

"Constable Grant will be here soon. I'm going to go make sure the interview room is ready."

Amy left the room and closed the door to give Jane and the children privacy. She approached the busy woman at the reception desk, who knew just what information Amy needed.

"You're in room two. That'll do?"

"Yes. Thanks, Maeve. I'm just going to go check the audio and video now."

"Sounds good."

Amy turned away from the reception desk as the front door opened. The woman on the chair sat bolt upright again, and when two small children ran through the doorway she jumped out of her seat.

"Hey! Hello! I miss you guys!"

The boys ran toward her and nearly knocked her over as each latched onto a leg.

"Mommy! Mommy! Mommy! We got new coats and hats and we had chocolate milk for snack!"

"Okay, okay! You can tell me all about it, but maybe let's get into that room and get your coats off first. We don't want to bother the other people here with all of our noise."

The mother looked over the children's heads at the woman who had brought them in. She nodded, eyes narrowing even though her smile didn't waver. The woman in the doorway nodded back.

"See you at one o'clock, then. Boys! Have a good visit!"

"We will, Lisa, don't worry! Look! Mommy brought us burgers and fries!" the oldest child replied.

"I see that. Aren't you lucky?" The foster mother said, a small, tight smile on her lips as she turned and headed back out to the parking lot.

The mother herded her two children into the room beside the one where Jane and her children sat. Amy was relieved when the door closed, and the lobby was quiet again. The tension could get quite high in the exchanges between parents who had been deemed unable to care for their children, or even visit them independently in the community, and the people who were choosing their children's clothes and tucking them in at night. The subtle, silent tussle over fast food burgers was the tip of an iceberg built of judgment and insecurity.

She walked into the interview room. There was a low table with four armchairs. One chair was placed at each end and two were on the side of the table that faced the wall with a one-way mirror, a camera, and a microphone. Amy flipped two switches on the wall and set a metronome in motion on the table. She walked into the recording room, a long narrow room with a built-in shelf below the monitors, and one or two chairs in front of each monitor and window. There were four stations for four interview rooms. This morning only one other room was in use.

Amy nodded at her colleague Phil Davis as he watched a new worker interview a child on the other side of the mirror. Phil was a veteran, like Amy, but he'd been at the agency almost ten years longer. His hair was greying at the temples, and his beige pullover sweater had a dark coffee stain on the sleeve. Phil made notes on a yellow legal pad, and in a few minutes the young social worker he was training would come into the recording room to ask if he had any suggestions, or any other questions she should ask. The recording rooms were great for such a mentoring opportunity, and they were used just as often in the training of new workers as they were in the type of interview Amy was about to have with Evan Grant.

Amy went down to station three, where she could see and hear the metronome ticking back and forth as she had left it. She pressed 'record' and after a minute, she pressed 'stop,' reset the image, and replayed the scene that she had just filmed. Good. Everything was working. She headed back into the interview room and stopped the swinging arm from producing the regular clicks she had used as a test recording. As Amy finished, the door opened, and a uniformed officer strode into the lobby. He turned and saw Amy and a grin broke across his face, displacing the serious look she knew he usually wore when in uniform.

"Hey, Evan. How are you today?"

"That's Constable Grant to you, Ms. Malloy!" Evan gave her a mock-stern look for a moment. Amy grinned, appreciating their easy rapport. It made a difficult job feel just a little more manageable.

"I'm glad it's you today," she said. "I told the kids you're a good guy. They're nervous, so it was nice to be able to tell them that."

"Well, I try, anyway," Evan said, smiling at Amy. "Now, have you got everything set up in the interview room?" Evan asked.

"Just tested it. Everything's working. We're in room three today."

"Good. Where's the family? I thought you were bringing them." He looked around the lobby.

"I put them in visiting room A. The kids are playing, and Mom's having a coffee."

"Well, we might as well get to it." Evan headed toward the closed door.

Amy ran ahead and stepped in front of him to open the door so the children would see her face before noticing his uniform. Jane looked up, but Josh kept reading and the younger children continued their play with the toys.

"Jane, Josh, Tyler and Chelsea, this is Constable Grant." Amy gestured at the police officer standing beside her, who offered a small smile and nodded his head.

"Constable Grant, this is Jane." Amy paused as Evan shook Jane's hand.

"And this is Josh."

The officer also shook Josh's hand.

Amy moved to stand between the younger children. "This is Chelsea, and this is Tyler." She put a hand on each child's shoulder as she said their name.

Evan knelt down between the younger two children and looked at their toys. Neither child moved.

"Why, that is an awesome kitchen set-up. What are you cooking?"

"I put the bread in the oven and now I'm making oatmeal. There's no milk so we have to have it with water, but it's good for our bones."

"Ah. Very good for your bones, no doubt." Evan nodded. He then turned toward Tyler.

"What are all these dump trucks carrying? They must be working on an important project."

"They're carrying away dirt from the hole where the new houses are going to be. Their boss is building houses, with new kitchens, just like that one there." Tyler jerked his thumb toward the play centre where his sister was busy. "He's gonna give them away to families, like in the big lottery for the hospital."

"Ah. What a good idea!"

The police officer stood back up.

"Josh, I think we'll start with you," Amy said. Come on across the way to the interview room." She turned to Tyler and Chelsea. "Do you two want to see the room before we get started?"

"Yeah. I guess." Tyler stood up, eyeing the dump trucks.

"Okay, let's go take a quick look. Then you can come back here to play until it's your turn."

Amy led the way to the interview room. Evan took up a chair at one end of the table. He pulled a leather-bound notebook out of his pocket and a black pen. He set these items on the low table and looked up at the children.

"Josh, where do you want to sit? In the middle, or at the end?"

Josh came in and sat at the chair farthest from the policeman. He stared at his hands.

"When it's your turn, you can each choose your own chair, too," Amy told Tyler and Chelsea.

"Okay. Can we go play now?" Chelsea eyed the door of the visit room where her mother waited.

"Yes, go ahead."

"Josh, I am going to flip these switches on the wall to turn on the video camera and microphone. Then I am going to go switch on the recording equipment. When I come back, we'll get started."

"Okay." Josh continued to stare at his hands, sitting silently with the police officer as they waited for Amy.

Amy came back into the room, closing the door behind her before sitting in the armchair beside Evan.

"So, Josh. It is Thursday, October fifteenth, 2019 and it is eleven forty-five a.m. I am Constable Evan Grant, and we are at the Green Valley Children's Aid Society. With me is Amy Malloy, a child protection worker, and Josh Flindall. Josh, can you tell me your full name?"

"Joshua Robert Flindall."

"And your date of birth, please."

"January fourteenth, 2001."

"Okay. Josh, you have a mark on your left cheek. Tell me what happened."

"I was home this morning helping with the chores for the farm stand. My mom got mad because I hadn't gone out to clean up the dog shit...er...dirt...with a shovel like she told me to. I told her just a fuckin' minute, and she slapped me on the cheek."

"So, you were home from school, helping with the chores?"

"Yes."

"And your mom was mad because you hadn't cleaned up the dog dirt yet."

"Yes."

"And when you told her 'Just a fuckin' minute' she slapped you on the cheek."

"Yes."

"What did her hand look like when she slapped you?"

Josh held out his hand, open and raised, palm toward the officer.

"Like this."

"Okay. And where did she slap you?"

"Here." Josh pointed to his left cheek, where the rounded purple bruise was clear against his pale complexion.

"On your left cheek."

"Yes."

"Then what happened?"

"I went outside to do what I was told. Amy was there, on the porch. She asked to talk to my mom. She said CAS might help." Josh looked up at Amy, as if he were checking to see if she would question his account. "She talked to my mom in the kitchen while I went out back."

"Then what happened?"

"She came out and talked to me. I never said my mom hit me. I said I hit the cupboard door in the kitchen."

Josh glared at the officer now.

"What did you say that for?"

"She's trying hard. She's not perfect, but she's trying hard. It hasn't been easy since Jackass left. I should've done what she told me, and I shouldn't've mouthed off to her like that. She has it hard enough."

Josh finished the speech, half angry and half pleading. He stared at his hands again.

"Who's Jackass?"

"My dad. He left in the summer."

"Ah. Okay. Josh, what usually happens when you get in trouble at home?"

"Don't get in much trouble. If I don't listen, I can't watch TV. Don't have any TV now anyway. No electricity. If I'm mouthy, I get sent to my room until I'm ready to apologize."

"What else happens when you get in trouble?"

"That's it. She never hit me before today. Jackass used to hit us. He'd use the belt, like I said last time we were here. But she never did."

"Okay. What about Tyler and Chelsea? What happens if they get in trouble at home?"

"Same thing. No TV or sent to their room. They might have to stand in the corner. That's it." He paused, looking up at the corner of the interview room. "Maybe no dessert if they don't eat their dinner."

"Okay. Josh, how is school going?"

"Goes fine when I get there. I haven't been much this month because harvest is on. We've gotta get the eggs to the market and the vegetables to the stand. Otherwise, we aren't going to have enough money to fill the oil tank for winter. We can go without electricity, and I can cut wood in the neighbour's bush they said, but we need the oil too. Otherwise, we all hafta sleep in the kitchen."

"Okay. Is there anything else you think we should know today, Josh?"

"Yeah. My mom's a good mom. She's doing a good job." He gestured at his cheek. "Today was just a bad day. Everybody has a bad day."

"Okay, Josh. This interview is concluded at twelve ten p.m. We're going to take some pictures of that bruising now." Evan got out the camera and a small ruler. He explained to Josh that he was going to place the ruler beside the bruise to show the size accurately. Josh stood still while the police officer worked. He refused to make eye contact though, keeping his eyes trained on the picture of a sailboat on the wall instead. When Amy said he was done, he jumped up to follow her across the lobby.

"Okay, who would like to go next? Tyler or Chelsea?" Amy asked when they reached the playroom.

"Me! Can I bring a doll?" Chelsea clutched the baby doll she'd been feeding with a toy bottle.

"Sure. Come on with me."

They crossed the lobby and Chelsea chose the same chair Josh had chosen. Amy explained she would be right back after she turned the recorder on. Chelsea showed Evan her doll, thrusting it toward him so he could examine it. When Amy returned, Evan handed the doll back to Chelsea, who put it in her lap as the interview began.

"This is Constable Evan Grant at twelve twenty-two p.m. on October 15, 2015 at the Green Valley Children's Aid Society. With me is Amy Malloy, child protection worker. We are interviewing Chelsea Flindall. Chelsea, what is your full name?"

"Chelsea Rose Flindall."

"When is your birthday?"

"June sixth."

"Do you know what year you were born?"

"No."

"Chelsea, do you know the difference between the truth and a lie?"

"Yep."

"Okay, if I say I am holding a ball in my hand, is that true?" Evan held out his pen.

"No!"

"What is it?"

"That's a pen!"

"That's true Chelsea, this is a pen, and I'm going to use it to take some notes while we talk. Chelsea, it's important that we talk about the truth today. When we ask you a question, please be honest, even if your answer is 'I don't know'. Okay?"

"Okay! Mama always says to tell the truth, or no one can trust you."

"Your Mama's pretty smart. Chelsea, do you know what happened to Josh's face?"

"No. He didn't have a bruise at breakfast. I asked him in Amy's car, but he wouldn't tell me."

"Okay. What happens at home when Josh is in trouble?"

"Well, Daddy would hit him with the belt, usually. But Josh hardly ever gets in trouble since Daddy left. Sometimes Mama sends him to his room if he's mouthy. But Josh is hardly ever mouthy. Josh says we gotta do what Mama says. Since Daddy left, she needs our help."

"What happens when you get in trouble at home?"

"Well, Mama used to say no TV, but we don't even have TV at all anymore. Now I have to go to my room. Or stand in the corner for six minutes. Because I'm six, so that's how many minutes I have to stand."

"What happens when Tyler gets in trouble?"

"Well, if he has to stand in the corner, he gets eight minutes. He's eight. His birthday is in the summer."

"Does anything else happen when Tyler gets in trouble?"

"Sometimes he has to go to his room. But he likes it there because he plays with his Legos and builds cars and trucks. Mama makes him stand in the corner more."

"How do you like school?"

"I love school! My teacher is Mrs. Roland, and she has the prettiest sweaters! She has a whole collection. Her sweater today had a pumpkin on it! Because Thanksgiving is next weekend!"

"That sounds nice. Chelsea, is there anything else you think we should know today?"

"Yes. I would like to have a kitchen set, just like that one in the room we're playing in. I just love it!"

"It is a great kitchen set," Evan said. "Okay, thanks, Chelsea. This interview is concluded at twelve thirty-seven p.m. Amy will take you back to play and it will be Tyler's turn next." Evan nodded across the lobby. Amy didn't bother to turn the recording equipment off this time. She walked Chelsea back to the room where her family was waiting. She called Tyler to come next.

"Fine," the boy said, keeping one hand resting on the largest truck as he stood up to follow her. "Can I play with the trucks more after?"

"Yes, you will be able to play while we talk with your mom. Josh will stay in here with you and Chelsea then."

"All right." Tyler stood up and looked over his shoulder at the trucks as he crossed the room.

Amy took Tyler into the interview room. She suggested he choose a chair. He sat in the chair beside Evan and looked up at the officer.

"I want to be a policeman when I grow up."

"Do you, now?"

"Well, if I can't get a job driving a dump truck or a front-end loader, anyway."

"Well now, those are all good choices, Tyler. Okay. I'm going to say a few things for the camera over there now." The officer pointed at the wall where the recording equipment was mounted.

Tyler's answers echoed the statements Chelsea had made. When Evan ended the interview, Amy stood up and smiled at Tyler.

"Can I go play now?" he asked.

Amy nodded and led the way across the lobby and into the visit room. Tyler dropped to the floor where he'd left the dump trucks.

"Jane, come on over to the interview room, please. Josh, you know where the bathroom is if the younger kids need to use it?"

"Yeah, I know." Josh didn't look up from his comic book.

"Good. We'll be back soon."

Jane didn't say anything as she crossed the lobby with Amy. Her lips were tightly closed, and her knuckles were white as she clutched her handbag.

"Come on in and have a seat." Evan gestured to Jane to take her pick of the armchairs. She sat in the one closest to the door. He sat in the far chair and Amy sat in the middle once more.

"The recording equipment is on, Jane, so I'm going to introduce us for the video now."

Evan stated the necessary details as he opened the interview. Before he began questioning Jane, he pulled a card from his pocket and read Jane her rights. When he finished, he asked if she wanted to talk to a lawyer.

"I don't have any money," Jane answered.

"I can put you in touch with duty counsel and you wouldn't have to pay," Evan said.

"That will just take more time. Let's just get it over with. I don't have anything to hide."

"All right. Ms. Flindall, your son, Josh, has a mark on his face today. Please tell us what happened."

"Well, this morning I kept Josh home from school to help with some of the chores. There's supposed to be a hard frost this weekend and we've gotta get the squash and pumpkins in off the ground before then. So, I told him to go out and clean the dog dirt out of the back yard while I finished making the bread, then I was gonna come out and we'd finish the harvest together. I was hoping we would get the whole thing done today so he could get back to school tomorrow, maybe."

"So, Josh was home from school, and you told him to go clean up the yard. Then what happened?"

"Well, he was standing there in the kitchen, takin' his time getting his boots on. I hollered at him to get out of the soup pot and get the dog's mess cleaned up and he looks at me with a smirk and says, 'Just a fuckin' minute'. Well, I didn't even think about it, I just hauled off and slapped him on the cheek."

"Which cheek did you slap?"

"The left one. The one that's got the bruise." Jane shook her head. A tear threatened to spill, but she tilted her head up and kept it from running down her cheek.

"Okay Ms. Flindall. I'm gonna have to caution you. I am going to have to charge you with assault for slapping Josh and bruising his face. Do you understand?"

"Yes." Jane stared stonily at the police officer across from her.

"Do you want to talk to a lawyer now?" he asked.

"I still don't have any money."

"You can talk to duty counsel, Ms. Flindall. It doesn't cost you anything."

"Well, I guess I better then."

"Okay, we'll need to go over to the station. I need to process your charge there. Is there anyone who can pick up the children?"

"Am I going to jail?"

"No," Evan said. He paused his notetaking to meet her nervous gaze with kind eyes. "I have to get the paperwork done at the police station, you're going to make a call and talk to duty counsel and if you promise to appear at the court date, then you will be free to go."

"Can the little ones go back to school? They won't be done until four." She looked from Evan to Amy.

"Let me talk with my supervisor, Jane," Amy said. "Give me a few minutes." Amy looked at Evan and he nodded.

Amy walked to Rhonda's office and knocked.

"Come in," the supervisor replied in a clipped tone. Amy took a deep breath and tried to focus on what she hoped to achieve by the conversation.

Amy's supervisor, Rhonda, was a tall, thin woman with straight blonde hair that parted in the centre and fell to her shoulders in a long bob. When she was annoyed or impatient, she would push out her lower lip and huff out her breath in a way that made her bangs rustle and resettle over the frown lines etched in her forehead. In the seven years they had worked together, Amy had learned to ignore the dismissive gesture in order to advocate for her plans. She clamped down on her personal reactions to Rhonda as soon as they arose, so they wouldn't get in the way of what was best for the families. Now, Amy sat down across from her supervisor to explain the situation with Jane and the kids.

"Well, if you look at the history, there are three previous openings." Amy consulted her notes. "Two are for Bill Flindall using physical discipline with the children, once hitting Josh with a piece of scrap wood, and once using a belt. The third one was Bill hitting Jane when she stepped between him and one of the children. Jane Flindall was appropriate and protective each time, removing the children from the home and staying temporarily at the shelter."

"Sure, then running straight back to him for more." Rhonda rolled her eyes.

"Well, he's gone now. It's just Jane and the children. She's admitted to what happened, and Evan's going to charge her with assault. She needs to be processed and talk to duty counsel, but she'll be out by dinner time. Josh can go home."

"Amy…" Rhonda tried to interject, but Amy pressed on.

"He wants to go home. If I drop him off at the house, he'll be there when Tyler and Chelsea get home on the bus, which is what they would do most days if their mother is out at the farm stand."

"If you take him somewhere without his mother, you're apprehending him."

"No, I'll have Jane with me. She doesn't have a car. We'll drop the little ones back at school, Josh at home, and then I'll drop her at the police station last. I have to make a stop that's just a few blocks from the station anyway."

"Fine. You're going to burn yourself out one day, all this running you do for people. They need to be responsible for solving their own problems, you know. They'll never learn if you just keep fixing things for them."

Like Amy, Rhonda didn't have children. Just after Amy moved to this team, Rhonda once opened up to Amy in her office at the end of a long afternoon as they were wrapping up a difficult file.

"You know, sometimes I think part of why I can do this job is because I don't really like children that much," she'd said, putting her hands on her hips and shifting her weight as she spoke. "I have a clearer thought process because I'm not mired in the muck of raising children myself. Parenthood just seems to fog people's minds." Amy remained silent and Rhonda continued. "Of course, there's also the reality that child welfare is one of the few jobs in social work with a decent salary and good benefits."

"Well…" Amy hesitated to reply, "I don't have kids either, but I feel differently about it." Amy was still trying to understand Rhonda's approach at that time and hadn't yet learned to expect this type of callous statement from her. Amy had since learned that it was better to ignore the commentary and use each moment of their consultations to try to convince Rhonda that the details of her plans made sense.

Now she focused on the facts, as she tried to explain the benefit of helping to get Jane's family home.

"I'd hardly call giving someone a ride fixing their problems, Rhonda. My small efforts to help aren't that powerful."

"True enough. Just as well, or we'd all be out of work here," Rhonda agreed.

Amy bit her tongue, as she had learned to do when Rhonda made such flippant remarks. She left her supervisor's office. It didn't matter. She had permission to follow her preferred plan. She would have to settle for that. She knew she and her supervisor would never agree on their basic beliefs about the families they served.

Most of the families Amy met were either struggling with a developmental stage, a family crisis that was taxing their resources, or they were struggling because they didn't know how to fix something in their family relationships. Though she wasn't a parent, she knew that parenting is hard work at the best of times. Amy figured if you hadn't had a good example or if you didn't have anyone in your corner, it made the job that much harder. Rhonda just didn't seem to see that. She seemed to see people either as pitiful victims, or as the creators of their own problems.

Amy walked out of the secured office space and across the lobby. The visit room door was open, and Jane was sitting on the couch beside Josh. Tyler and Chelsea continued to play.

"Jane, we can drop Tyler and Chelsea back at school, and then drop Josh off at home so he'll be there to look after them until you get there. Then I can drop you off at the police station before I head to my next appointment. Will that work for you?"

"Yes." Jane stared at Amy. "Thank you, I guess."

"Sure." Amy shrugged. "It's all on my way, anyway." She turned toward the children. "Okay, Tyler and Chelsea. I hate to break it to you, but we've got to go! I know you're going to miss the toys, so even though it's not much, I brought you each one of the books we like to give out to kids who visit us here."

Amy held out a book with a purple cover for Chelsea and a green one for Tyler. Although they each took a last longing look at the wonderful toys, they came over to collect the books.

"We're going back in my car. Did you guys want to say goodbye to Constable Grant?"

"Sure."

"He's still in the interview room."

Amy followed them over to the room. Through the open door, they could see the police officer bent over his notebook, reviewing what he had written.

"Goodbye, Const-Consta-Constabule Grant," Chelsea said.

Tyler raised a hand and said goodbye to the police offer, who told the children to be good for their mom. Amy filled him in on her plan for delivering Jane to the police station.

"Great," Evan said, smiling. "Then I can go ahead and get started on the forms. Jane, I'll see you there. When you arrive, I'll give you the number so you can call duty counsel. The sooner we get this all squared away, the sooner you can get home. Maybe in time for dinner with the kids."

"Okay." Jane opened her mouth again, but when no words came, she closed it.

"Let's go. You two need to get back to class!" Amy herded the younger two out to her car and opened the back door for them. She buckled Chelsea into the booster seat and watched Tyler fasten his own seatbelt. Josh got into the back seat last, while Jane lowered herself into the front seat.

They dropped Tyler and Chelsea back at school, and then dropped Josh off at the house.

"I'll get the pumpkins in at least, Mom," Josh said. He rested his hand on her forearm.

"Do what you can, son," Jane said. "I don't know what time I'll be home. There's some stuff for sandwiches for you and the kids."

"Okay." Josh leaned down to hug his mother in the front seat. Then he stood and watched until the car backed out of the driveway before he went up the steps, through the house to the back yard and the pumpkin patch.

Once the two women were alone together in the car, Jane turned to Amy. "Am I going to go to jail?"

"I don't know, Jane," Amy said. "I don't do the criminal work. It's your first time. It's hard circumstances you're in. Judges take it all into account when they make decisions about someone. I can't give you any legal advice though, and I won't pretend to know what to expect from the criminal court process, never mind the outcome. You need to have that talk with duty counsel."

"Maybe I'll just get probation." Jane's voice cracked on the last word.

"I don't know, Jane. They may want you to get some counselling, too. Josh said this was the first time you've ever hit him. You'll need to figure out what to do so that it's also the last time. See whether there's anything in the system that can help you do that, and you'll take something good out of this."

They arrived at the station and Jane got out of the car. Amy came around to Jane's side.

"You don't have to walk me in like I'm some runaway. I'll go straight in." Jane's mouth closed in the firm line that was becoming familiar.

"I know. I've just got to touch base with Constable Grant before I head to my next home visit."

"Oh," said Jane, the tension in her face easing slightly. "Sure."

The women walked into the police station's public entrance together. Amy approached the counter, noticing a man holding a wooden clipboard sitting in one of the hard, plastic chairs of the waiting area. Amy glanced at the clipboard and saw that he was filling in the form to receive a police record check. Probably for work, although maybe to volunteer somewhere.

"We're here to see Constable Grant please, Shirley."

"Oh. Hi, Amy! How are you doing today?" The middle-aged woman in a navy cardigan smiled as she stood up from behind her desk, which was covered in stacks of papers.

"Not bad. You keeping busy today? Looks like lots of paperwork, as usual," Amy said.

"As always. Full moon coming, you know."

"Of course. If it doesn't get us coming, it gets us going. We can count on that, can't we?"

"You bet. I'll get the officer for you."

Amy waited until Evan came out to collect Jane. The two women stood in silence, but only for a few minutes.

"Hi Jane. Thank you for coming. Please come this way." Evan opened the door to the back of the station and gestured for Jane to walk through.

"Amy, I'll catch you later? I think we'll see each other again later this week, right?"

"I'll be there." Amy knew he meant their squash date. "And I've put in an order for a copy of today's tapes to be delivered here to your attention. They should be here Monday."

"Great. See you later." Evan winked and tipped an imaginary hat toward Amy as he closed the security door behind Jane Flindall. The stranger filling in his form in the police waiting room had no idea that Jane was about to be charged with the assault of her child, and Amy smiled with satisfaction. That was the way confidentiality should be handled. People made mistakes, but they still deserve dignity.

In her car, Amy paused to make some notes about the situation. She reached into her lunch bag and rummaged around. After a moment, she stopped making notes and looked into the bag. Huh. She must not have packed a lunch today. That must have been yesterday. Judging by the containers, it might have even been the day before that.

Chapter 3

Amy drove across town for a routine stop at a home where the Rhodes family had been working to clean up their house and address some safety concerns. She pulled into the driveway right on time. That was a rarity in this work of home visits. Amy had learned to schedule her visits with a caveat. She told people that she would be there at a specific time "give or take about twenty minutes, depending on weather or traffic that day." Of course, traffic in the county could include a tractor she couldn't pass or waiting for a farmer to finish herding his cows across the street to the pasture.

After a quick walkthrough, she was satisfied with the state of the house. The parents had dealt with the risk issues, fixing a broken window and cleaning up the glass, and getting rid of the backlog of garbage. They'd maintained their housekeeping for a few months now and it was time to think about closing the file.

Once she pulled out of the driveway, Amy pulled over down the street and took out her notebook. She glanced at the clock on her dash and figured she had about twenty minutes before her next home visit. It would take about ten minutes to get there if she hit all green lights on her way. She had time. She opened the notebook and made her notes about what she had seen in the house. Just the facts.

Attended at 43 Sycamore Street unannounced. Yard and driveway were clear of debris and garbage other than two full garbage bags beside the side door, ready for garbage day tomorrow.

When she finished the summary, Amy put her notebook and pen away in her bag, put her car in gear, carefully pulled out into the street, and headed to her next appointment. Her car was like a roving satellite office, tethered to her cubicle at the CAS office by an internet connection and her laminated identification card. It was quieter than her team room, but sometimes the quiet left her with too much space to ponder how she had gotten to this point in her career in this complicated system.

As she drove to the next home, Amy thought about her work. She'd started as a young woman. Before she was even done school, her first field placement had been with the Children's Aid Society in Toronto. Amy remembered her supervisor. A smart, funny lady named Roberta, with curly auburn hair and a toothy grin, who really understood the needs of families. On the first day of her third-year placement, Amy sat in the supervisor's office and listened to the speech the woman had obviously repeated many times. She had a sturdy reusable bag holding props that she pulled out on cue.

"In this job, you must always be empathetic and understanding. The work we do impacts people's lives, and we have an obligation to consider their point of view and their right to make decisions for themselves." Out of the bag came a tissue box, to be set in the centre of the table between Amy and the supervisor.

"This job also requires you to make use of authority and to enforce the law in order to protect the best interests of children."

On the word authority, she pulled out a dog-eared copy of the Child and Family Services Act.

"A child protection investigation requires us to use every tool at our disposal. Never forget this and go in unprepared, with only one item or the other in your kit bag." Roberta also made it clear to Amy that as she developed her own skills, it was critical to seek out mentors in the field. Experienced workers who would take the time to answer her questions and offer suggestions.

"Choose the ones who aren't bitter. The ones who can still have hope for families in dire circumstances. Don't imitate the ones who see our clients only as victims of the system. Listen to the lunchroom conversations and choose the ones who have balance. From them, you can learn to find your own balance."

Amy wondered if she still fit that bill herself. Sure, she wasn't surprised by much during home visits anymore. She was busy looking for the reasons behind people's behaviour. She didn't think she was bitter. On the other hand though, she wasn't sure she still held out much hope that the system would change.

One last stop, then she'd be done for the day. Amy tried to clear her mind as she drove down the narrow lane, made narrower by the cars parked along the south side of the street. She pulled her car into a dirt driveway and shut the engine off. She took a deep breath and closed her eyes for just a moment.

A loud bang came from the front of her car. Amy's eyes flew open and she looked out through her windshield. A grinning boy stood with the palm of his hand flat on the hood of her car. His curly brown hair was long, hanging over his forehead. His green eyes were full of mischief.

"Hi, Amy!" he shouted.

Amy opened her car door before responding.

"Hi, Justin. How's it going today?"

"Gotcha good that time! You almost jumped right outta the car!"

"Yep. You're lucky you didn't give me a heart attack. You shouldn't scare people like that."

"Nah, you're the lucky one. I don't know CPR." The boy laughed and followed Amy as she went around to her trunk. Amy smiled sadly at this little boy who knew enough about life and death to make such a joke.

"What've you got for us today, Amy?"

"Same old thing, Justin. Here, you take this one."

Amy handed him a cardboard box. It was full of dry goods. Justin quickly scanned the box.

"Rice Krispies! No way. I told you, if they don't have Corn Pops, we don't want cereal. Rice Krispies. Blech. Those are practically healthy." Justin frowned at the box.

"You get enough sugar, Justin. You need the good stuff and you said you liked these better than Shreddies. Besides, this is what they had this week."

"Yeah, yeah. Whatever."

Amy followed the boy up the steps, carrying a second box in her own arms. The door opened for them, and a small, frail woman stepped aside to let them pass.

"Amy, you went for us again? I thought they said you couldn't go for us anymore." The few words caused the woman to start coughing, and once she started, she hacked and coughed for several long moments. Amy and Justin, used to the coughing jags, took the boxes into the kitchen, and set them on the table, giving her some time to get over the fit.

"Hey, Mom! Look! Amy got you some of that soup you like so much. You said this soup is expensive and people only donate cheap stuff." Justin sorted the food in the two boxes into groups on the table.

"I think it was on sale again last week. They must have trouble moving it because it's expensive, so they put it on sale a lot. People like to donate sale items to the food bank," Amy said.

"Lucky us." Justin's mother joined them in the kitchen, wheezing, but no longer coughing.

Amy glanced around the room. The yellow paint on the walls was faded, and the countertop was worn but clean. Amy remembered her first visit to the house, when the call had come in to report that Justin's behaviour had been escalating and he was out of control at school. When he was sent home one day with a note, he hadn't returned to school and there was no response from the parent. When no one answered her calls either, Amy had shown up at the house to meet Faye. It was clear right away that the woman was ill, and Amy was touched as she watched the young boy steady his mom as she walked from the door to her chair at the kitchen table. He fetched her inhaler from another part of the house, then stood beside her as mother and son looked at Amy.

Faye had been pale, and her chin quivered as she explained that she'd been diagnosed with terminal cancer. Justin had crossed his arms over his chest and tilted his chin up defiantly as he eyed Amy. It hadn't taken long to figure out that Justin's aggressive behaviour at school had been his way of getting himself suspended so he could stay home and care for his mother. Faye, in turn, had been too weak from her treatments to enforce his attendance. Amy connected Faye with a volunteer from a nearby church, who would stop in mid-day when Justin was in school. Once he believed his mom would be okay, he was back to being the well-mannered young man the teacher had read about in his past report cards.

"How are the treatments going, Faye?" The tumour growing in the woman's torso was inoperable because of the way it was wrapped around some of her organs. It was crowding her lungs, which didn't help her breathing.

"Not so good," Faye said, shaking her head. "The doc says the tumour isn't shrinking at all. He says if the next round doesn't work, the chemo might kill me. I don't know how much time I've got."

"Well, you've got to keep your strength up, Faye. How are you eating? Looks like you've lost some more weight."

"Well, the only thing I can get down is that soup. It's damn lucky they keep getting it in at the food bank."

The woman glanced at Amy and for a second Amy feared that Faye might challenge her on just where the soup came from, but instead, she walked gingerly to the table where Justin had laid out the food from Amy's boxes. Amy watched Justin sort the food by container, placing cans to his right, boxes to his left, and jars in the centre of the table. She reflected on his situation. Faye had once told her that Justin's father died young, in a motorcycle accident, when Justin was just a baby. Now his only living parent was gravely ill, and there was no extended family around as far as Amy knew. It was a frustrating gap in the system that Faye didn't qualify for government funded care because she was still able to dress, bathe, and feed herself. Since she'd had to leave her job at a local factory, Faye couldn't afford the cost of private in-home care, which left Justin carrying the burden of responsibility.

"I can't get out at all, now that the air's turning cold." Faye said, gazing out the window then turning back to Amy. "I can hardly breathe anymore. They have a volunteer pick me up to take me to the clinic for my treatments. She keeps the car hot, and I put a scarf over my mouth and wrap up with a blanket over my head just to get out there." The long disclosure started another coughing fit. Looking at the woman in this moment, Amy felt the full weight of the terribly sad routines that shaped the days for Faye and Justin. Faye was bent over, and as Amy searched her mind again and saw the limits of what she could do to help this family, Amy suddenly felt like she might need to sit down herself. Instead, she put a hand on Faye's shoulder and guided her to sit in a chair at the table.

"Justin, besides what I brought, how many cans of this soup have you got left?"

"None, Amy. It's all Mom will eat. A can in the morning and a can at night. Doesn't last long that way."

"Okay. Do you have enough of what you need? Milk?"

"Yeah. I get the vouchers from school and I pick milk up twice a week on the way home from school."

"Good. Let me know if anything changes, or if you need something. Okay?"

"Yeah, yeah. I'll call you if we need something, Amy."

The boy punched her in the shoulder, then ran away to the back of the house where his bedroom was.

"He means thank you," Faye croaked, her voice raw from the coughing. "We're both grateful for you making these stops. He's a good boy and he does a good job. He microwaves my soup when I can't get up myself. Makes his own meals and keeps the house tidy. He's still keeping up in school, too." A tear traced down Faye's cheek, and she wiped it with the back of her hand. "Don't know how I got so lucky with that one."

"Well, he's got a good mom who taught him well enough, I guess."

Faye smiled, but she didn't laugh. It would just set off another coughing fit.

"I'll be back next week with another load."

"Thought you could only go to the food bank once a month."

"They're making a special exception because of your circumstances." Amy didn't look the woman in the eye as she spoke. She picked up both boxes, empty now. "See you later, Faye."

"Right. See you later, Amy. Thanks again." Faye began coughing again, and Amy made her own way out of the house.

On the way home, Amy stopped at the grocery store. She went to the soup section and picked out several cans of Faye's favourite soup. She started to walk away, and then went back to the shelf and put the rest of the cans in her cart. She wandered the aisles, picking up some peanut butter and jam, some microwavable rice, and some canned vegetables. She threw in a box of granola bars and some puddings. Butterscotch, which Faye said was Justin's favourite. As Amy walked down the cereal aisle, she passed the low sugar, high fiber cereals and went straight for a box of Corn Pops.

Amy got into the car. She didn't need to make any notes this time. She'd closed the file on Faye and Justin several months ago. There were no protection issues here. Just poverty, isolation, and a dying mother trying to take care of her son. It had been true that there was no food in the house. Amy had arranged the milk vouchers through the school, and they included Justin in their hot lunch program with a subsidy from the school council. Amy had been to the food bank a few times for the family, who had no car and no way to pick up the supplies. Faye was too ill to go, and Justin was too young to be given food without a guardian present. Food bank policy.

Amy paid for the groceries and took them to her car. She opened the trunk and transferred the groceries from the bags into the two empty boxes that sat in her trunk. Ready to go again the next time she had time to stop into Faye's place. She knew keeping the boxes stocked was her way of coping with how much she worried about them. It was something she could do, though as she closed the trunk, she again found herself wishing she could do more. Sometimes it felt endless, like she just went from house to house, trying to make things a bit easier for people and a bit safer for children. Yet terrible situations continued to happen, and children continued to be at risk in so many ways.

Amy caught a glimpse of herself in the rearview mirror. Her eyes were bright with unshed tears, and her cheeks were red with the effort to hold them back. She wondered what would happen to Justin when his mother died. Faye was an only child, and both her parents were dead. Amy sighed heavily as she imagined Justin, grieving, and maybe acting out, ending up in foster care.

Amy wished she had a supervisor she could talk to about this situation, but she knew the unwritten rule. If you needed to talk about whatever difficult thing you had just done, you were weak. You just did the job, day in and day out. You found your own way to deal with the stories of abuse, suffering, and neglect, to cope with the images that burned into your brain. Amy had been doing this a long time, and she had good enough coping skills, she supposed. Sometimes that meant she just moved through the days, almost on autopilot as she followed the rules and checked off the tasks on a to-do list. Then she went home and immersed herself in distractions and comforts to protect herself from feeling it all too much. She put the car in gear and headed home.

Maureen Pollard

Chapter 4

As she drove home, Amy considered which container she would pull from the freezer for dinner, as a way of beginning the mental shift from work to her evening at home. She'd made a batch of meals a few Sundays ago. It had been one of the first fall days when it was cool enough to have the oven and stovetop on all day. She'd cooked spaghetti sauce, lasagna, pot pies and shepherd's pies, as well as soups and stew and chili. Her favourite recipes were well-represented.

All of it was frozen in individual servings, ready to pull out and microwave on a night like this, when she was tired, hungry, and late getting home. Which was almost every night.

Amy's self-sufficiency was a trait built over many years, as she had been on her own since seventeen. Her parents divorced when she was fifteen and then spent two years fighting over her.

"Amy, I'll take you to Florida for March Break, but you have to tell your mother you want to live with me at least fifty percent of the time," her dad once offered.

"Amy, if you go to your dad's this weekend, I'm going to get rid of your records. You play that damn music too loud anyway, so you just give me a reason and it's gone," her mom threatened.

"Amy, don't you love me?"

"Amy, can't you see how much I need you?"

"Amy, can't you see what this is doing to me?

By seventeen she'd had enough. She worked as a waitress in a diner and saved all her money until she had enough for rent. She moved into a room in a boarding house of sorts, downtown, where the buildings were a little more worn-out and the rents were a little cheaper. She quickly learned to keep to herself, to lock her door whether she was in her room or out, and to mind her own business. The widow who owned the house had a room on the main floor and rented the three upstairs bedrooms as well as the one in the basement to anyone who could pay the rent. Neither parent called nor visited, angry with her for not choosing them.

As soon as she turned eighteen and could serve liquor, Amy spent her evenings and weekends working in the dark, dingy bar off the lobby of the local hotel. During the week, she dealt with the regulars. They didn't often tip much, saving their pennies for the next round. It was on the weekends when live bands played that Amy made really good money as she hustled drinks to the thirsty crowds. She didn't date. She declined the many drunken proposals and propositions she received at the end of most shifts. She became known at the bar as the snooty waitress who preferred to be alone, and earned the nickname "Princess", a moniker often offered with mocking, exaggerated affection.

She got up early to finish her homework most days and still made it to class on time. She was not going to be at anyone's mercy. That meant she had to get the grades to get away to school and out of the town where she was cast as a one-dimensional character.

Amy maintained straight A's all through high school, which earned her the scholarships she needed. The guidance counselor had been the one to suggest that she live in residence in Toronto. He told Amy that would be the best place to make friends and be part of campus life. Ha. Amy had nothing in common with most of those naïve, immature girls whose main goal seemed to be studying the drink menus at local pubs while they shared pitchers of cheap draft beer. She was a serious student, and she immediately had a job as a server in one of the chain restaurants on Yonge Street. She had no time for anything else.

She did meet Rachel, and that was great. Rachel was a business student, and they were next door neighbours on the third floor of the residence. Amy came home from a late shift one night and found Rachel alone in the lounge, fretting over her dwindling bank account. Amy told her the restaurant was hiring. Rachel applied and once they started working together it didn't take long before they were practically inseparable. The girls studied together in their off hours even though they were in different programs. They both liked to listen to classic rock while they studied, and that sealed the friendship.

Amy worked hard to survive in Toronto while she finished school. She maintained honours-level grades, despite working long nights. She had to keep up her grades to keep her scholarship, so she did. There was no other choice in her mind.

It worked. When she graduated at twenty-two years old, she went to work right away at the Children's Aid Society where she had completed the field placement that would launch her career. Toronto's density and size allowed Amy to learn a lot about child protection as she made her way into run-down highrises and rickety rowhouses, and sometimes, into fancy, well-kept single-family homes.

Amy dated a little in those days, sometimes progressing past the first few awkward coffee or dinner dates into what seemed like the beginnings of a comfortable relationship. They didn't last though.

There was Aiden, a colleague on another team at the same agency. He'd broken up with her to date a supervisor.

Then there was George, the probation officer who broke up with her because she liked to go out once in a while and he preferred to stay in so he wouldn't run into any of his clients. George didn't even shop for his own groceries, opting for a delivery service instead, even though it cost almost twice as much.

Jim was the last man Amy had dated. A young Toronto police officer, he was smart, talented, and witty. She could still feel his strong fingers massaging the tension out of her neck muscles, and those same fingers stroking and caressing her more intimately through the long, wonderful evenings they shared together.

They'd been dating for just over a year when Jim made an announcement over dinner one snowy evening.

"I've got some good news."

"What's that?" Amy smiled at him.

"I got hired to work on the Emergency Response Team with the provincial police. I'm going to start out at the detachment in your hometown!" he said, grinning.

Amy stared, silently willing him to declare it a joke.

"I start next month. We have time to pack up our places, get you a job at the CAS there, and find ourselves a home we both like."

Amy still couldn't answer.

"Amy? Aren't you excited?"

When Amy didn't respond, Jim's enthusiasm dimmed.

"Amy. This is your chance to fix things up with your parents. I know you know how I feel about that."

"I do know. It's hard to understand when you come from such a close family, as we've talked about before," Amy said slowly. "But we've never talked about you applying to the provincial police. Or moving anywhere, let alone *there*."

"I wanted it to be a surprise."

"Oh, it's a surprise all right…" Amy agreed.

"Hey, you're the one who said I should start looking at other regions when we were talking about my career goals," Jim countered. It was true, she knew that promotions in policing sometimes required movement from one detachment to another, or one service to another and they had talked about it. But they'd also talked about her determination never to return to the town she grew up in.

Amy tried once more to explain why she couldn't move back to her hometown. Why it would feel like failure. Why she didn't really want to try to reconnect with her parents, neither of whom had even sent her so much as a Christmas card since the final time she told them over the phone that she would not take sides.

Jim was disappointed with her. He thought she could do better as a support to him and as a person herself. She packed up a box with the belongings he kept at her place, included her key to his apartment, and dropped it all off at the office of his building manager, sealed and clearly marked with his name. She didn't need the few toiletries she had accumulated in his bathroom. She'd never left anything else of hers there, and she'd never given him a key to her place, so that was that.

After Jim, Amy declined invitations to date. She occupied herself with more work and distracted herself with hobbies. Writing in journals, painting on dollar store canvases with cheap acrylic paints, and learning to sew baby quilts when Rachel announced she was pregnant.

After a few years, Amy was tired of city life. She didn't like the noise. She hated the fact that it was never truly dark. Not even on the longest night of the year could you see the stars beyond the glare of the streetlights. She was tired of feeling crowded inside the buildings and out on the streets.

After the baby was born, Rachel started saying she was too busy when Amy asked her to meet for dinner. She eventually stopped even meeting Amy in the city for coffee, as she immersed herself in the world of new motherhood. As Amy's other friends got married and started families, she didn't bother deepening any new relationships with colleagues. She built a reputation for making beautiful wedding and baby quilts for her colleagues, but she didn't get too close. It was too painful to be left behind.

Ready for a change, Amy started looking for another job. She found one at Green Valley Children's Aid Society. A small agency in a rural county. No city within the county boundaries. The biggest town had a population of fifteen thousand people. The schools were small, the stores were pleasant, and traffic moved freely on the streets and highways. The perfect place for a fresh start.

Amy's crash course in budgeting gained during her early days on her own had served her well. She'd lived frugally during her years in the city—staying in a tiny apartment while she earned a big city salary. That lifestyle had allowed her to save enough money for a down-payment on a house in the country.

At twenty-six years old, Amy bought her first home. It was a small house on a wooded lot. The place had three bedrooms, an old stone fireplace, a country kitchen, and a fire pit in the back yard. Amy loved it. She loved that no one could see her house from the road and that she could hole up here for a week at a time when she was on vacation and not see another soul. Over four years, she'd made it cozy, painting the walls bright colours and making one of the bedrooms into an art room, with a big writing desk against one wall and an easel by the north facing window.

Amy pulled into her driveway. She considered the temperature and decided to leave the boxes in the trunk. They wouldn't freeze. Not yet anyway. She grabbed her black leather bag and headed up the stairs of her porch, pushing thoughts of her past out of her mind.

Amy smiled as deep barking greeted her. She opened the door and stepped aside just before the wolfhound came bounding out.

"Well, hello there, Wiley. I'm happy to see you, too."

Amy petted the big dog, set her bag inside the door, and walked out into the yard. She threw a stick and Wiley happily chased it, returning it several times for another round. Amy threw it one more time and the dog looked first at her, and then at the stick, before turning to climb the porch stairs.

"Had enough, then?" Amy laughed. "Okay. Let's get supper." She followed the dog onto the porch and opened the door again. They went in together and Amy filled the dog's food dish, then refreshed his water.

"So, how was your day, Wiley?" Amy paused as if the dog would answer. She put a portion of frozen lasagna in the microwave.

"Mine was all right. The usual. Dirty house, physical abuse investigation with police." Amy rattled off the files as if they weren't people, just problems. "And a stop to see Justin and Faye." Amy's breath hitched as she said Faye's name.

Wiley nudged Amy's hand with his nose and pushed his shoulder into her hip. Amy dropped to her knees beside him. She wrapped her arms around his shoulders and buried her face in his neck. The dog sat patiently as she cried, waiting until her sobs subsided before he licked the salty tears from her cheeks.

"I know. There's not a damn thing I can do about it. I don't know what will happen to Justin when she goes, Wiley. I just know it's coming. That woman has the look of death about her." Amy heaved a sigh. She turned her microwaved food onto a plate and took it over to the couch. She turned on the television and sat down to watch the evening news as she ate.

The news of the day didn't really register as Amy thought about her cases. She planned to spend the next morning in the office, where she would sit in her cubicle and try to block out the sounds of her co-workers as she plodded through the required paperwork to prove she was doing what the agency paid her for. What the government paid the agency to do. In eight years, the paperwork had changed, and changed again.

It was supposed to be easier for workers. That's what they said each time management rolled out a new paperwork package. What it really did was make it easier for management to take a quick look at a file and see what a worker had done or hadn't done. Easier for the auditors who came to check up on them every year, and easier for the supervisor to blame the worker when something went wrong.

Amy had a few file reports due. One was for Amanda and her two children. That file kept Amy from falling asleep some nights, worrying about what might happen. Other nights it woke her up with nightmares.

Chapter 5

A few days later, Amy woke up early. It was her thirtieth birthday. She looked around her room, which was the same as any other day. It was just another morning at the start of another day of work. It was hard not to take stock of where she was in her life. There was no sign of the partner or family she had once thought would be part of her future. She really wanted to be content and not let it bother her, but if she was honest with herself, it felt a little heavy this morning.

On her way to work, she tried to shift her mood by getting into the Happy Birthday playlist she'd made just for the occasion as she drove to work. She didn't really want to be young forever, but she did like the first three songs on her playlist that celebrated eternal youth. The opening strains of the next song, with a rich male voice singing about his funeral, followed the closing notes of a vibrant young woman's voice singing about dying young. Amy spent a quick second questioning her judgement about music and mood but proceeded to belt out the lyrics anyway.

She'd always had a slightly morbid sense of humour, even before her job made this a survival mechanism.

As she sang, though, she felt her mood turn one shade gloomier. She knew neither parent would send her birthday greetings. She also wondered who would come to her funeral if she died. Some of her co-workers, probably, but that might be it. She hit the button to switch the music off as she pulled into her usual spot in the parking lot. She slammed the car door a little harder than necessary and strode purposefully toward the building, through the entrance and past reception.

"Hey, hey! Good morning, birthday girl!" Maeve grinned.

"Thanks, Maeve," Amy said.

"Well, you look sour. What's the matter?"

Amy stopped beside Maeve's desk, her foul mood receding just a bit as she saw the concern in her co-worker's eyes.

"Ah, not much really. Just a mini pity party."

"Well, chin up. Turn that frown upside down! It's your birthday, and a pity party is not allowed." Maeve grinned.

"If you say so." Amy gave Maeve a small smile.

"That's better!" Maeve cheered.

Amy moved through the building toward her team room. It was early yet, so she didn't run into anyone else. She might make it to her desk without having to smile again, and she could try to pick up where she left off feeling sorry for herself.

As she rounded the corner by her desk, her eyes widened. Her cubicle was decorated with brightly coloured streamers, a few taped-up balloons, and a big sign that said "Happy 30th Birthday, AMY" in silver Sharpie ink.

"Surprise!" Janet Ramsey, the team administrative assistant grinned from inside Amy's cubicle as her teammates Rosa Lopez and Ella Aird popped their heads over the cubicle walls. Emma Labelle and Jyoti Patel came around the corner together, giggling and holding out a muffin with a candle in it. They sang happy birthday to Amy, who felt tears well up as she looked at these women who were celebrating her.

"Surprise, indeed," Amy said when they finished singing.

Best Interests

"Blow out the candle!" Ella called out.

"Make a wish, Amy." Emma lifted the muffin up closer to Amy, who blew the candle out.

"What did you wish for?" Jyoti asked.

"You're not supposed to tell, or it won't come true," Emma said with a grin. "But I bet she wished for a boyfriend!"

"No woman needs a boyfriend!" Ella cried as she peeked over the cubicle wall.

"Now, that I can't deny," Matt Feltz said as he appeared from around the corner. "I think we all know that men need you more than you need them."

"Well, in a healthy relationship, I think that both partners can rely on each oth..." Amy didn't get the chance to finish speaking as Emma pushed a piece of the muffin into her mouth.

"Mmmm." Amy finished chewing before speaking again. "That's delicious. Apples and cinnamon. Who baked my favourite?"

"I made them. I found the recipe on that pioneer woman website Janet's always talking about. I didn't burn them!" Emma grinned as she passed a container of muffins around.

"Nice work. Maybe you can take over Muffin Mondays?" Amy teased her younger colleague.

"No way! I'm not ready to displace the queen of Muffin Monday. Everyone likes your baking best, Amy." Emma was blushing.

"Hmm. Maybe we'll have to start having guest muffin makers. You can be the first, Emma. We'll pick a day, and you can bring the muffins. What about the first Monday next month?" Amy asked.

"Sure. I can do that." Emma grinned.

"Okay, that's enough. Time to get to work." Rhonda clapped her hands a few times as she came around the corner. Emma held out the muffin container, but Rhonda held up her hand to refuse the gesture.

Ella and Rosa's heads disappeared below the cubicle walls. Emma put the lid on her container and went back to her desk.

Janet straightened her skirt as she stood, tugged the balloon that had been taped to Amy's computer monitor to take it with her, and went back to her workstation. Jyoti had already silently escaped Rhonda's stern gaze.

"Well, Amy, happy birthday," Matt said, winking. "Don't forget to keep lunch free and meet us in the parking lot just before noon."

"Sure, Matt," Amy agreed. It was tradition for the team to go out for lunch to celebrate a birthday. Her teammates' fussing and Matt's reminder had her feeling a little lighter. She wasn't completely alone in the world with her dog, after all.

The morning went by quickly as Amy filled in digital forms and wrote reports. She had another office day coming up, where she would spend the whole day completing paperwork, but it was good to get it started, and being at her workstation meant she was more likely to remain available for her birthday lunch.

Amy was startled by a knock on her cubicle window.

"Hey! It's noon. We're all waiting, Amy. Let's go!" Emma, perpetually excited, stood at the opening of Amy's workspace.

"Right. I'll just save this file." Amy hit the button on her keyboard, then stood up and stretched before following Emma out to the parking lot, where Janet organized them all into cars. She'd made the reservation for lunch, too.

As they settled into their usual seats around the corner table at the Sly Fox Grill, Amy smiled. She enjoyed the banter of her team, and she was grateful that Janet had included Phil. He'd been her first friend here. Already an old hand at this agency when she started, he'd shown her around the county, letting her shadow him on several home visits and at court so she could adjust to an environment that was so different from the city she'd trained in.

Lunch flew by, with plenty of light-hearted chatter and no talk of work. Rosa and Phil commiserated over the challenges of raising teenagers, while Janet shared parenting wisdom with Jyoti and Ella, whose young children were close in age to Janet's grandchildren. Emma leaned in to reassure Amy that being thirty wasn't so bad. Her oldest sister turned the big three-oh six months ago now, and as far as Emma could tell, it wasn't that different from being twenty-nine.

They had a new server that day. She said she'd just started that week.

"Well, you'll get to know us soon enough," Amy said. "We come here for lunch whenever one of us has a birthday, and sometimes we come after work, too."

The woman had just finished clearing their dishes when several of the wait staff came to the table together and began singing as a chocolate cake with a burning sparkler was set down in front of her.

When the song ended, another server set down a stack of dessert plates and forks beside the cake.

"You all sound like you have a lot of fun together. Where do you work?" The new waitress asked. There was a moment of silence.

"We work at Green Valley Children's Aid Society." Amy's voice was quiet, but clear.

Anytime she was asked, Amy generally announced her profession with some pride. She was mindful that not all of her co-workers felt that way. As far as Amy was concerned, it was better to know right away if people were going to be afraid of her because of her job. It was better to know, rather than invest in any sort of relationship and have the prospect of friendship ripped away when someone discovered what she did for a living and snapped their mouth shut, suddenly fearful. Or, sometimes worse, bitched to her about how terrible the Children's Aid Society was, ripping helpless children away from their loving parents and letting other children die at the hands of monsters. The agency could never get it right, in the public's mind. As a worker, you were held to account if you admitted that you worked for CAS.

She wished people would realize that child welfare was just like any other field. Sure, there were people like Rhonda, bitter, judgmental and disengaged. But there were also people like Amy, trying to do the right thing in a system that was often difficult to navigate.

Subtle tension changed the woman's face, her lips pursed and eyes narrowed before she spoke again.

"Ah. I see." The waitress turned abruptly and left them. She didn't come back. Another server collected the dessert plates and brought them the bill. Amy told Matt she'd be out to the car in a minute after a stop at the restroom. When she was sure her co-workers were gone, she popped back by the table where the new waitress was wiping up their crumbs.

"What's your name?" Amy asked quietly.

"Joan," the woman said.

"Well, Joan. Thank you for excellent service today. It made my birthday special," Amy continued as she placed a ten-dollar bill on the table.

"Your friends already left a tip."

"This is from me, since I didn't have to chip in because it's my birthday. I'm sorry if it was awkward today. We really appreciated your service. I'm sure we'll see you again since we come here often. Have a good afternoon."

Amy didn't wait for a response. She knew people had a broad range of experiences with the child welfare system, and she knew this woman's response was nothing personal. She did want this woman to know Amy was a caring, professional who also worked from the heart. Maybe it would soften this woman's impression of what a CAS worker is.

Amy headed out to the parking lot where Matt was waiting with Rosa and Ella. Once he'd delivered them all back to the office parking lot, she'd head out for her afternoon appointments, starting at the school with Amanda's children, Rex and Angel.

Chapter 6

As she sat in the plastic desk beside the round table in a small room that was usually used for remedial reading classes, Amy let her mind drift back to the beginning of her involvement with the family of the little boy she was waiting for. Amy had worked hard to gather the details for court, and they were stuck in her mind, sometimes playing automatically like the film clips on social media do, as though with a mind of their own.

Amanda was a young mother, giving birth to Rex when she was just seventeen. He was a happy baby, healthy and lively, which Amanda claimed made up for her derailed plans to attend art school in Toronto. The father went away to college that September and never came back, happy to escape the small town he'd been born and raised in. Amanda kept Rex, and with her parents' support they did okay.

Amanda stayed with her parents, Jim and Lila, in their three-bedroom bungalow in a subdivision on the edge of town. She returned to the high school to upgrade her math mark and repeated art class for pleasure. Lila took care of Rex for a few hours each morning before going into her shift as a personal support worker in a senior's residence where she worked steady afternoons. This all worked pretty well until Amanda met Jake. The details of the file Amy assembled showed how Amanda's troubles had gained momentum at this point forward despite her relatively supportive family.

Jake was twenty-five when Amanda was eighteen. He was a musician, playing in the downtown dive where the underage kids could still get a drink. He introduced Amanda to drugs. Marijuana mostly, and then a few party drugs, like ecstasy. He'd been charged with possession a few times, but nothing much came of it, and he kept landing back on the street and getting up to his usual bad habits.

Amanda found Jake compelling, with his dark blue eyes and black hair, such a contrast to his pale skin. She liked his band's moody music, and she liked to ride in his souped-up old Jeep with the top down, leaving Rex with her mother and taking off for road trips with Jake. Amanda craved the feeling of freedom that came as the vehicle flew down the highway. She liked the feeling of relief she got, too, when she used marijuana. A dreamy, relaxed state filled her mind with wild creative images, although she was so relaxed she didn't manage to capture many of them on canvas.

Amanda soon got pregnant. When he found out, Jake ditched her. She spent the pregnancy morose, but essentially drug free, since Jake was out of the picture and she didn't have another source.

With Amanda spending more time at home, without drugs, her parents started to notice something different about her. She was vague at times, not sure what she was doing or where she was when they came across her pacing in the house. She was nervous, afraid that the neighbours were watching Rex. She told her parents that she believed the neighbours, a retired couple, wanted to steal his youthful energy.

Lila woke with Rex and spent each morning with him. She took Rex to daycare on her way to work in the afternoon and Jim picked him up on his way home from the factory where he worked in management. This left Amanda to her own devices, but at least everyone felt assured that Rex would be fed and safe during the day as Amanda seemed to drift further into her own world. Lila and Jim made polite conversation with her. Sometimes they challenged her irrational statements, but this upset her too much. Eventually they gave up the challenges and just nodded, making small neutral sounds when she said something odd. They took her to the doctor and told him that she seemed a bit unlike herself, but not much more than that. The doctor said sometimes pregnancy and its after-effects can do this.

When the baby girl was born, Amanda named her Angel. She cradled the infant close to her breast and eyed the nurses and her parents suspiciously, refusing to allow it when they tried to take the baby to give the new mother some rest.

Amanda resisted pain medication. She then started hiding the baby when she knew the nursing staff would be coming to check on them. Once, she swaddled Angel and tucked her in the closet in a nest of the flannel blankets from her bed. She was certain the infant was at risk of being abducted.

The nurse had called CAS and an investigation had determined that the children were in need of protection due to Amanda's unusual behaviour. Amy remembered her growing sense of worry as she interviewed people, and the details of Amanda's concerning beliefs and bizarre behaviours were uncovered.

Although she didn't see her son often, Amanda was protective of Rex, but in a manner that was stifling and restrictive. Lila and Jim continued to care for Rex while Amanda and the baby remained in the hospital. From her hospital bed, Amanda argued with her mother against Rex's continued attendance at daycare. She was certain that his youthful energy was vulnerable to theft by an aging crone she sensed was nearby. When asked,

Amanda declared that anyone over thirty could be the aging crone looking to steal her children's life force.

It was hard for the medical staff to gauge Angel's growth, since Amanda wouldn't let them weigh her or watch her nurse. On the third day, the obstetrician called in a psychiatrist for a consultation when Amanda reported that she had to protect the baby and explained that was why she'd hidden the baby in the closet the other day, and why this morning she'd wrapped the baby, including her little face, with bandages she found in an unlocked storeroom. Fortunately, a nurse had come in to check on the baby before Angel's mouth and nose were covered with more than one layer of the gauze.

Amanda was given a sedative, and when she finally slept, the nurse on duty slipped Angel from her arms and took her to the nurse's station where Angel was weighed and examined. She was a good weight and appeared perfectly healthy.

Amanda was wheeled to the locked in-patient psychiatric unit, where she spent the obligatory seventy-two hours mandated by the legal form that was signed when the doctors felt she might be a risk to herself or someone else. When that assessment period ended, Amanda was diagnosed as having had a psychotic episode and she was held for further treatment. She was prescribed medication and the hospital staff tried to convince her to take the pills as they worked to get the dose right. The doctor met with her regularly and asked her all the same questions. Eventually, she determined what the psychiatrist wanted to hear.

No, she was not hearing any voices.

Of course, there are no evil crones nearby trying to steal her children's life force.

Yes, she must have just been overtired.

Yes, she would take her medication and yes, she would stay with her parents.

She was discharged after two weeks and joined Rex and Angel in her parents' home. She was able to manage for a little while, but the fact that she had stopped swallowing her pills meant that it wasn't long before her symptoms returned, and Amanda resumed talk of trying to protect her children.

Frustrated that she wasn't allowed to be alone with her children, and annoyed that her parents didn't seem to take the threat of evil seriously, Amanda spent more and more time alone in her room.

One evening, Amanda beckoned Lila to her room, her eyes red-rimmed and her face tear-streaked. She told Lila she had dreamed that she herself was the crone who might steal her children's life force. She realized that she and no one else was the most risk to her children, in the end, and now she understood why they were all keeping her from being alone with her babies. Amanda said they were right, and it was for the best that they be kept apart. Her mother watched, unable to stop Amanda as she gathered a package of baloney, a loaf of bread, some underwear, a few changes of clothing and a pair of sneakers. The last item she added to the duffle was a plastic rosary she had picked up somewhere. Even though she'd never even visited a Catholic Church, she touched it reverently.

Picking up her bag, Amanda turned to her mother, smiling through her tears as she walked out the front door without saying a word. They didn't see her for three years, although Amanda called them on Angel's first birthday to say she was safe, living in an apartment in the city with a roommate who was helping her get counselling. She wouldn't give them her address and didn't call again. Eventually, Amy worked with Jim and Lila to seek legal custody of the children, and the file was closed. There were no protection concerns if Amanda wasn't around.

But all that changed last year. Amanda had shown up on her parents' doorstep one evening. She had a bag of gifts in one hand and a suitcase in the other. She said she'd spent several months in a supported living program after she had been hospitalized on a locked psychiatric unit for almost two months. She was taking her medication daily, as prescribed, and she was working with her psychiatrist to manage the symptoms of her psychosis and maintain stability. She seemed well enough, but

Lila and Rick had called Amy anyway. Amanda wanted the children placed back in her care, and they wanted CAS involved.

That was eight months ago. Amanda had signed releases of information. Amy gathered the hospital records, the reports from the supported living program. She tried to talk to the psychiatrist, but the doctor had a policy that he would not provide any information to any third party without the patient present during a conference. Amanda refused to consent to such a conference, saying that she needed one safe place to talk about her mental health without being threatened by CAS every time she turned around.

Amanda hired a lawyer. Amy didn't know where she got the money, but it didn't matter. The lawyer did his job. He filed an application to have the children returned to the care of their mother, filing Amanda's affidavit stating that while she recognized that she had not made adequate plans for her children when she was unwell, she was now stable and ready to resume full-time care.

Amy thought there might have been a trial, but Rhonda and the agency lawyer agreed with Amanda's lawyer that the evidence they had gathered showed Amanda's dedication to taking her medication and staying well so that she could provide a home for her children. She had enough money to rent the upstairs unit in an older house that had been divided into apartments. This place was a few blocks from her parents' home, so at least they would be nearby. She made connections with the staff at her children's school, she involved herself in the children's daily care under the watchful eyes of her parents. Amy had no indication that there was a current risk to the children. Except that the psychiatrist wouldn't confirm or deny his opinion of Amanda's current mental health status and prognosis. What he did do was write a letter that said most people with major mental health diagnoses, including psychosis, do not present a risk to the public. He stated that more often, they are a risk to themselves.

The judge was pleased when an agreement was made to return the children to Amanda's care. Amy worked with Amanda, Lila, and Rick to develop a plan that would enable the children to gradually move houses. They would begin with overnight visits to Amanda's apartment. It was clear to Amy that the converted home had received only enough maintenance to allow it to continue to be habitable for rent. The main floor was occupied by the owner of the home, an elderly woman rarely seen by Amy during her weekly visits with Amanda and the children.

Amy called Lila and Rick weekly, to see how they thought things were going. She checked in with the school staff every other week for an update about the children's adjustment.

Aside from Angel's occasional absence from pre-school, and Amanda's occasional tendency to be dramatic during interviews, every report and each visit produced evidence that Amanda was mostly fine, and the children seemed to be adapting well enough to their return to their mother's care. It was normal for children going through such a change to have some regression after all, and to show some anxiety.

Amy watched, and waited, as the term of the supervision order neared an end. There was a one-year court order to allow CAS to stay involved with Amanda and the children, in a nod to the significance of the risk to the children at the time of Angel's birth, when Amanda was wrapping newborn Angel to hide and protect her, and because they were still quite young. In four more months, the agency would be looking at terminating the supervision order. At this point, the evidence showed that Amanda was stable, and the children were settling.

But Amy remembered Amanda's eyes. The flashes of impatience when no one would agree with her that Rex and Angel were at risk because of evil forces. The desperation that Amy had seen reflected in the young mother's eyes during their intense interviews over the weeks before Amanda had packed that bag with her rosary and left her children behind. When she remembered those eyes, Amy worried about what the future might hold if Amanda's health deteriorated again.

Amy blinked, putting the past back where it belonged, staring at the picture of a yellow star with the letters "st" printed in bold black letters underneath as she waited. In a few minutes, the door burst open, and the little boy darted into the room, pulling out a chair and dropping into it.

"Hi, Amy," the boy said. "Mr. Mahood came to my class to get me, so I knew you were here."

"Hi, Rex. I guess it's kind of unusual for the Principal to come to get you from class. How are you?"

"Good. Mom gave me cheese and crackers in my lunch, and the teacher said I could bring them since you came during snack time again."

"Ah, I'm sorry. I'll try to come during math next time, instead."

"It's okay." Rex was sitting in his own plastic chair, putting a piece of cheese between two round crackers, swinging his feet as he took the first bite and waited for Amy's questions.

"How are things going at home?"

"Fine. Mom says we might have to move. She thinks the neighbour is too nosey. She didn't pack any boxes yet, so I don't know if she means it. I like my room. Mom painted my windows for me."

"Ah, what colour is your windowsill now?"

"Black, like the Silver Surfer's clothes. He was one of the Titans Three who saved the world from new technology."

"If his clothes are black, why is he called the Silver Surfer?" Amy asked.

"Because his *cape* is silver!"

"I see. Did you get some new superhero comic books?" Amy smiled when Rex nodded enthusiastically.

When it was Angel's turn, the girl sat very still, as she usually did, with her hands clasped in her lap and her small legs dangling over the hard edge of the plastic chair. Angel would stare at Amy with big round eyes, but she would never say much when Amy asked questions.

Amy left the school and drove to the home where Amanda, Rex, and Angel lived. Up the stairs, in the living room of Amanda's apartment, Amy sat on an upholstered wingback chair. Amanda didn't sit across from Amy on the overstuffed couch this time, instead pacing back and forth across the length of the room.

"Why do you need to know that?" Amanda demanded, her eyes narrowing when Amy asked about the details of the children's care.

"Well, I'm just curious about how Angel's doing. The school said she missed a few days of school last week, and she was a bit pale and quiet this morning. I wondered if she was getting a cold or something," Amy said.

"She's fine. That child is just fine. I'm watching her closely, ready to act at the first sign of any risk to her." Amanda eyes flashed as she glared at Amy.

Amy remembered the spark in those eyes, so different from the tired, heavy-lidded eyes through which Amanda stared out at the world with when she was taking her medication.

It was the image of those bright eyes, the signal Amy worried might mean that Amanda's psychosis may be returning, that would wake Amy up at night. She would dream that Amanda was in her room, determination shining in her eyes as she began to wrap Amy's face in a heavy gauze, Amy lying there, inert, unable to reach up and push her away. Always powerless in these dreams, Amy would wake sweating and gasping, as if her face had really been covered, her breath blocked.

Amy could see that light flicker again in Amanda's eyes today as the young woman paced back and forth across the living room, impatiently answering questions.

"No, I haven't been hearing voices."

"Angel is fine. I have to keep a close eye on her, of course, because she is only four. The young ones are so vulnerable. So, I always make sure she is safe."

"No, I don't have any concerns about the landlord. She's no trouble at all, now."

These answers were all just fine. She couldn't just apprehend children based on a look in a parent's eye. Tomorrow Amy would add another report to the file.

Chapter 7

In the morning, Amy let the dog out as soon as he'd devoured his breakfast. Wiley wandered around the garden and made his way to the side yard where he did his business. Amy sipped her coffee and absently chewed her toast as she watched the dog lope after a rabbit. He had no chance of catching the creature despite his long stride. He was too big to get into the thicket where the animal disappeared.

When Wiley came in and settled down on his bed by the fireplace, Amy took her shower and got dressed. She slipped into her boots and gathered her bag. She threw Wiley a chew toy before she locked the door behind her.

As she drove over the hilly country roads, Amy registered relief that the snow wasn't flying yet. She didn't like the roads in winter, but it was the price she paid for privacy. Her cozy house was wrapped in woods that shielded her from the rest of the world, which was just what she needed after intense workdays travelling across the county.

Amy liked the mornings. Every day offered a fresh start. She let the music of her Life is Good playlist roll over her. Two of her favourite songs about letting things go played back-to-back, one a soulful ballad of encouragement and the other a melodic call for release. Different lyrics and completely different sounds, but a solid sentiment from both musicians. She wanted to focus on the things that were the best in her life, and the songs she chose reflected this.

Amy pulled into the parking lot at the agency and parked at the far end. She was humming as she walked.

She entered through the main door of the building. Many of her colleagues used the employee entrance at the rear, choosing to settle into the office space before facing anyone who may be waiting for them in the reception area. Amy preferred the front door. She arrived ready to go and so she might as well begin. She swung the door open and stepped into the lobby.

"Well, well, well. Look who's finally decided to show up." A short, wiry man with spiky brown hair and flashing brown eyes stepped in front of Amy.

"Hello, Andrew. How are things?" Amy looked at the clock. The building had been open for about three minutes now.

"You know how I am. You're the one who took my kids last week."

"What's happening this morning, Andrew?" Amy kept her voice low.

"I missed my visit yesterday. I want to see my kids. I tried to call but I couldn't get through." Andrew was pacing in the small space of the lobby.

"Finally talked to that blonde woman. She called me when the visit was supposed to start. Said I wasn't going to get to see them this week since I didn't show up. Well, that's not good enough!"

Andrew was clenching his fists and his face was red as he stopped before Amy. Maeve waved to get Amy's attention. She pointed to the panic button, the one that would summon police immediately. It rang directly into the station, and the rare times it was used it generated an immediate police presence.

Amy shook her head as if she were shifting her bangs out of her face. Maeve nodded and took her hand away from the panic button. She let it rest on the counter next to the button as she watched the scene continue in the lobby.

"What happened yesterday afternoon, Andrew? Why did you miss the visit?" Amy stood her ground and spoke quietly.

"My mother was supposed to drive me here. Only she showed up drunk. I couldn't let her drive and my license is still suspended. No one else would come that far." His voice took on a pleading tone. The trip to the agency's office from Andrew's home took just over an hour.

"I tried to call. I really did. I couldn't get through, and I finally gave up. Then that blonde one—Tina, or Tonya?—called me to ask where I was." His fists were clenching again.

"Okay. Andrew, let me talk to the supervisor, and to Tanya. I'll need to check out what was happening yesterday and what the schedule looks like today and tomorrow. I don't know if we can schedule another visit, but I will look into it right now."

"Fine. I'll wait."

"Sure. Now, if the schedule does allow another visit to be arranged this week, how will you get here?"

"I'm staying with my friend in town. He came and picked me up when he finished work yesterday so I could come in here this morning to get this straightened out."

"Great. We'll need to talk about what your plan will be. It's a long trip, and if you have a hard time getting here, a missed visit is a big deal. Especially with no call. The kids end up waiting here and no one comes to see them. It's hard on the kids."

Amy knew she was pushing it, but she figured she'd better find out what this guy was going to do. The family wasn't known to the agency, so she was still in assessment mode, looking for clues about the strengths and issues in the family as she had no history to take into account.

"I know it's hard on the kids. That's why I tried to call." Andrew stared at the floor.

"Okay. Let me see what I can do, Andrew. Will you wait?"

"Of course, I'll wait. I need a smoke, anyway, so I'll wait outside."

"Sure. You've got to go out to the corner of the lot. There's a picnic table, a bench and a bucket of sand for butts."

"Fine." He stepped around Amy and headed out to the parking lot. He already had his cigarette pack open and was plucking a smoke out of it as he walked through the door.

Amy went through the security door into the area where Maeve sat. She smiled as she watched the woman adjusting the photographs of her grandchildren so that each of the freckled faces would grin at her throughout the day.

"Good morning, Maeve! Business as usual around here, I see."

"Well, that's another job well done. You're good with people, you know." Maeve nodded toward the door closing behind Andrew.

"Ah, people just want someone to listen when they're upset. If you take the time to listen, they'll surprise you with their ability to move on. Speaking of which, Maeve, what was happening with the phones yesterday?"

"Power outage from about two until about three forty-five. No calls in or out. It's a stupid system that way. Power goes out and all you social workers walk around here like there's nothing to do because your phones and computers don't work."

"Hmm. That would have been around the time he said he was trying to call in."

"Well, he wouldn't have got through. Not yesterday."

"Okay. Thanks, Maeve."

"Right. That's what they pay me the big bucks for." Maeve laughed as Amy headed deeper into the office building.

Amy headed first into the team room where the men and women who observed the access visits sat. There were four on that team, and they were always busy. Between the four of them, they had three visit rooms, plus community visits, that all needed someone to watch and take notes and intervene if things got out of hand.

"Hey, good morning. Is Tanya in yet?" Amy asked the worker in the first cubicle.

"Hey, Amy. She just got here. Went to get a coffee, so she should be right back."

As if on cue, an athletic-looking blonde woman came into the room, holding a mug in her hand.

"Hey, Amy. That Andrew Sonnen didn't show up yesterday. No call to cancel and then he's all mad on the phone because I said it's against policy to reschedule a no-show."

"Ah, yes. He said he tried to call. Tanya, what were you doing in the time slot before his visit?"

"I was booked in back-to-back visits from ten yesterday morning until the Sonnen visit was supposed to end. Had about twenty minutes for lunch at one and then I was back at it in the viewing room the rest of the day."

"Okay. Well, the phones were out for about an hour and a half. Did the monitors work?"

"Now that you mention it, when the power went out, I had to go sit right in the visit room for the last one. It was loud, too, that family with the five kids all under seven." Tanya paused.

"You know, I never even thought about the phones being out. By the time I thought about the Sonnen visit, the kids were here, and he wasn't. The power was back on and there were no messages. So, I called him and that's what I said. No rescheduling for a no-show."

"Okay. So, he has no license, and he said his mom showed up drunk to bring him for the visit, so he had no ride. Says he tried to call, and the phones were down."

"Well, that could be. And it's a long drive from up there. Lots of folks have trouble getting in from there, even in good weather."

Amy watched Tanya's eyes narrow, and her lips form a thin line as she considered this new information.

"So, are there any time slots when the visit room is open, and you could facilitate a make-up visit today or tomorrow?"

"How's he going to get here?" Tanya's brow furrowed as she pulled up the visit room schedule on her computer screen.

"He's here already. His friend went to get him last night and told him he could stay over when he has a visit, so he can walk and be here on time."

"Ah. Okay, then. The visit room is open this afternoon. Hmm. If we had Sally bring the kids in right after school, they could be here by about three fifteen. I could fit in a one-hour visit before my next one scheduled at four thirty."

"Okay. Let's do that. I'll let Rhonda know, and I'll write up the case note. Thanks, Tanya."

"All right. I'll let you know if he misses again."

"Good enough."

Amy left the room and walked to where Andrew was pacing in the lobby. He slowed, then came to a stop an arm's reach away from her.

"Turns out the power was out when you were trying to call yesterday. Our phones don't work when the power's out, and Tanya was booked in back-to-back visits all day, so she didn't notice before she called you. Tanya says she's got space in the visit room schedule for an hour this afternoon, if you can make it."

"I can be here. Absolutely." Andrew released the words in a sigh of relief. "What a mess. I felt like I was going crazy. I thought I'd never be able to convince you that I really tried. I even had their after-school snacks ready to bring. What time should I come back?"

"We're not quite done yet. My supervisor has to approve it. Can you wait around while I go check?"

"Oh, I'll be here. I'll just go have another smoke." Andrew turned and walked out the door, pulling another cigarette out of the pack in his hand.

Amy headed up the stairs to her own team room. She glanced over at Rhonda's office, but the door was closed. Amy turned the corner around an empty cubicle and hung her bag on the hook on the wall of her own cubicle.

Amy once again considered the empty cubicle. They had been trying to get another team member for several months. The Board would only approve a contract posting and no one wanted to move to Green Valley for a contract. It was too far away from the city and a contract held no appeal for many of the droves of social workers graduating each year. For that matter, child welfare held no appeal for many of them. It was going to take someone who really needed a job to fill a twelve-month contract that only had seven months to go in it before the next budget took effect.

Amy switched on her computer and grabbed her coffee mug. She headed over to the team coffee machine and brewed herself a single serve coffee that would smell more like a cinnamon bun than it would taste. As she was stirring in sugar, Rhonda's door opened. Her colleague, Emma, came out of the office looking unhappy. She headed straight for her cubicle without saying good morning. Amy knew better than to interrupt that mood with a cheery hello.

"Hi, Rhonda. Do you have a minute? I just want to touch base on the Sonnen case. Dad missed his visit yesterday, but I've got it rescheduled for this afternoon, if you're okay with it." Rhonda nodded, and Amy stepped into her office.

Amy stood with her coffee and Rhonda sat in her padded leather chair. Amy filled the supervisor in, and Rhonda agreed it was best to give him another chance today. They would wait and see if he made good on his promise to be in town well ahead of future visits, but with the problem with the agency phones it was better to give him the benefit of the doubt.

"The judge won't like it if it looks like we didn't give him a fair chance at a visit. If he misses another one, though, we've got him," Rhonda said.

"Sure, Rhonda. Thanks," Amy said as she moved to the door.

Amy headed back downstairs and through reception into the lobby. Andrew was waiting for her, sitting on the couch that faced Maeve, flipping through the pages of one of the parenting magazines that lay on the coffee table in the lobby.

He stood up as Amy came into the lobby.

"We can fit in a make-up visit this afternoon at three fifteen."

Andrew sighed and appeared to relax.

"It will only be an hour. I know your visits are supposed to be two hours long, but the room is only open for one hour, and that's the only time Tanya is available."

"Okay. It's better than nothing. I'll be here. Can I bring them something?"

"Like what?"

"A snack or something. They usually eat after school. That's what I was planning when I missed the visit."

"Yes, a snack is fine. No peanut products, please. We try to keep the building peanut-free."

"Doesn't everywhere now? I don't know why they even make peanut butter anymore."

"Okay, Andrew. Be here about three o'clock please. The kids will come in with Sally as soon as school is over, and you can have a one-hour visit. Next week, the visit will be on Tuesday, as usual, from four to six. I will call you Friday to check in after today's visit."

"Fine. That's fine. I'll be here at three." Andrew took a few steps toward the door, stopped, and turned back toward Amy, his eyes narrowed. "I suppose I owe you a thank you."

"No. This is my job. A visit with your kids is your family's right. This is a visit you're entitled to under the circumstances. You made the right choice not to allow your mother to drive here drunk, and not to try to drive yourself while your license is suspended. It was not your fault our phones weren't working. If you don't show up next week, we will be unlikely to schedule a make-up again."

"Oh, I'll be here all right. Every visit, from now on," Andrew said. His chin tipped up and he smiled tightly as he spoke.

"Good. Your children look forward to seeing you." Amy nodded at Andrew and he nodded back, then spun on his heel and headed out the door.

Maureen Pollard

Chapter 8

Amy headed back to her cubicle. She sat down at her desk and typed the case note into her computer file. She entered some notes about her home visits the day before, and then checked her emails. Nothing pressing jumped out from the screen. A lot of committee meetings. New policy needed to be drawn up for health and safety since the incident last month where a staff member had slipped on the kitchen floor because someone hadn't bothered to wipe up spilled milk. That email was followed by one reminding people that the fridge was being cleaned out on Friday, so if they valued their containers people should take them home because EVERYTHING was being tossed so the fridge could be scrubbed once again.

Amy scanned the rest of the emails, then closed the window so she could concentrate on her file documents. She pressed the button that would put her phone in "do not disturb" mode. She opened her family file program and focused on the first of three reports she needed to complete.

In the cubicle next to her, Ella was on the phone with her mother, making arrangements for a late pick up of her children after an evening home visit. Matt and Emma were bantering about who was in line to get the next dreaded parent-teen conflict file assignment. Jyoti was already on the phone, using her best professional voice to request a report from a doctor. Rosa was humming in her cubicle, probably already well into writing reports since it was a recording day for her, too.

Amy put headphones on and listened to the soft sounds of an instrumental music playlist to help block the noise of her teammates.

It was a good team. Rosa and Jyoti were older and more experienced. Matt, Ella, and Leigh Ann were all knee-deep in babies and toddlers outside of work. Emma was single, like Amy, but at twenty-five she was the baby of the team, energetic and keen.

Amy often felt like the odd one out, but she didn't really mind. There were a handful of folks in the agency she felt close to. Phil Davis, for one. He'd been here for years, but he was still working investigations. Most of the other old-timers were either working in the foster care department, where life was supposedly easier, or had moved into supervisor jobs that paid more. As far as Amy could tell from the investigations she'd done, the foster care department had almost as many heartbreaking stories as the protection department. And the supervisor salary came complete with supervisor-size headaches.

While she waited for the next file to open on her slow computer, Amy reviewed the latest colourful flyers offering training opportunities for professionals. Amy was keen to learn new approaches to child welfare, and she looked forward to one training event of her choice each year. The agency training budget allowed every staff member to choose one training each year relevant to their work. Last year, Amy had gone to a two-day workshop about using mindfulness to help clients who are struggling with trauma. She found, to her surprise, that while the mindfulness techniques sometimes seemed to help clients, they were probably most helpful in her own life. She used one of the breathing techniques she learned to calm her anxiety when she approached new houses. It also came in handy as she waited in tense crowds for her case to be called into the courtroom. She knew, too, that her music playlists helped her regulate her emotional state, whether she needed to calm down or lift herself up.

Amy considered the trainings offered so far this year. She knew that Rhonda would not approve another mindfulness training. Amy had fought hard to get it approved the first time, since Rhonda thought it was all nonsense. Her background was in nursing, rather than social work. She'd been at the agency a long time though and had been promoted to supervisor before the child welfare field started to align in hiring primarily social workers. Rhonda didn't believe in anything that wasn't science, and she didn't consider mindfulness to be scientific. Nothing else appealed, but Amy kept looking at the flyers that came in each month anyway.

Amy opened the file on Rex and Angel. She began the process of documenting the activities of the last six months of work on the file in the required form. She started with the list of contacts, including every time she had a telephone call, email, or personal interview with anyone involved with the family. She listed them in chronological order and made sure to identify the contact person.

Next came a summary of the activity. Amy wrote about her home visits. Her fingers paused on the keyboard as she realized she had not seen either child's bedroom in the past month.

"I'd like to see the kids' rooms today," Amy said to Amanda at the last visit.

"Oh, Rex said he would rather no one go in his room when he's not here. Why don't you come back after school tomorrow and ask him to show you then?" Amanda had replied.

"Okay, I'll come about three thirty and the kids can show me their rooms then," Amy agreed. Except the next day Amanda had canceled the appointment, and Amy hadn't been back yet.

Amy wrote a summary of her interviews with the children at school and her conversations with Lila and Rick. She wrote about the update the doctor had provided and the report by the school principal on behalf of the teachers. Amy wrote that once again she had contacted the psychiatrist to ask for a summary of Amanda's current mental health status and treatment plan to no avail. He had written a brief email that his position on disclosure of a patient's personal health information had not changed.

Amy wrote the plan for the next six months. This was easy because it would be the same as the previous plan.

Monitor the situation through home visits.

Conduct interviews of the children at school.

Contact the maternal grandparents for updates.

Consult other professionals involved with the family about progress.

These steps would provide the information that Amy would use as she prepared for the case to return to court, when the judge would be expecting to make a termination order based on how this year had gone. Amy wished she felt confident that the apparent progress was the true picture. She sighed and finished the report with her electronic signature.

Amy opened another file to begin the same process. She glanced at her watch and realized it was almost eleven. She stretched her shoulders and took off her headphones. Today, like many other days, she would go to the lunchroom early. It would be quiet still, with just a few staff wandering in.

On this day, Amy heated up a bowl of her velvety butternut squash soup and sat down at the table.

One of her co-workers rummaged in the fridge. "What are you sitting here in the dark for? "You got a headache or something?" she asked.

Amy smiled at the back of the short woman wearing a peacock blue pantsuit, the back of the jacket riding up as she rummaged.

"Hey, Kiyana," Amy said.

"What a mess this is. Good thing we're cleaning it on Friday. There're a few science experiments in here. Again." Kiyana turned toward Amy, running a hand over her cropped black hair as she continued. "So, how are things going on your team? We're barely keeping up. We've got three workers off sick and the other three are running ragged trying to cover off all the emergencies."

"We seem to be hanging in there," Amy said. "They can't find someone to cover Leigh Ann's maternity leave. At this rate, she'll be back long before they find anyone who'll come here for a short contract. Other than that, everyone seems to be holding their own. Busy of course, but that's the way it usually goes," Amy answered.

"Well, that's true enough. It's always busy, whether you have a full team or not."

Amy stood up and took her bowl to the sink. She washed her bowl and spoon and placed them in the rack to dry. She washed up the rest of the dishes sitting in the sink and on the counter, mostly coffee mugs people had just left sitting there as if by magic they would be dealt with.

"Why do you always do everyone's dishes?" Kiyana asked.

"Not everyone's. I don't mind. I find the soapy water soothing, and if I'm filling the sink to clean my own it only takes a few minutes to do up the rest."

"Girl, you're nuts. You're part of the problem, you know. People leave their stuff there because they know someone like you will just take care of it."

"Maybe." Amy shrugged.

"I think we should just throw the mugs out. You leave it dirty, and it's gone. I bet that would stop them."

"Oh, I doubt it would stop dirty dishes from being left here. Might make a few folks mad though. Some of these are personal mugs, probably with some sentimental value."

Amy thought about a mug she had brought to work with her when she was young, the last gift given to her by her grandmother. It had helped her feel connected to her history, despite the problems she had with her parents, and she wanted to focus on that family connection in this work. One day during lunch she had set it on the table between sips. An ever-dramatic intake worker, Thomas, was telling a wild story about a home visit where he had been chased. He was waving his arms around and he knocked the mug off the table. Everyone turned to stare as the mug shattered on the floor and the coffee splashed up the cupboards. Amy got up to clean up the mess and a few people bent to help her. As Thomas returned to his story without any acknowledgement of his mistake, Amy felt her cheeks start to burn as tears welled up. It was just a mug, but it had mattered to her.

The next morning, Amy had brought in a cheap, plain mug to use at work, and when it broke, she replaced it with another cheap mug. She left her sentimental mugs at home, and she didn't sit down at a full table during breaks anymore.

"Anyway, I don't mind." Amy dried her hands on a paper towel. She grabbed her bowl and spoon and headed to her workstation.

"Another short lunch, eh? Well. See you later, Amy."

"Yes. Have a good afternoon, Kiyana."

Back at her desk, Amy left her headphones off. The team room was quiet. She'd heard the others talking about going out for lunch again today. That would buy her some time to work in peace.

Amy checked her voice mail. There was just one message, from Evan. He'd picked up the interview tapes and wanted to know if Amy wanted to review them with him at the beginning of the week. He was getting them transcribed. He was on days Monday and Tuesday. Amy called back and left a message on his voice mail that she could come in Monday first thing. They would meet at the police station for the review. When they were done, she knew he would talk to his Sergeant about the charges.

Amy turned her phone's "do not disturb" function back on and opened her next file.

The afternoon passed quickly. When Amy took her headphones off, she was not surprised that the team room was silent. The younger staff had kids to pick up at daycare, and on the days when there were no crises they left promptly. There were enough days that they worked late throughout the year.

Amy headed downstairs and prepared to leave through the lobby. The front door would be open for another two hours yet, while the late afternoon visits were held, giving parents and children a weekly chance to reunite around the kids' school schedules.

As she entered the reception area, she heard shouting. Amy stopped in her tracks, trying to make out the words before deciding what to do.

"He's not breathing! The baby's not breathing!" A frantic female voice rang out throughout the lobby.

"What have you done now, woman? I leave the room to take a piss and all hell breaks loose. What are you shouting about?"

"He's not breathing!" The woman sounded near hysteria.

"Well, don't just stand there. Call 911!" the man roared.

Amy stepped through into the lobby. An infant hung loosely in the woman's grip. The lips were blue, and the eyes were vacant.

Tanya came out of the observation room and headed directly to the infant.

"I know first aid. Can I help you?"

The woman wheeled to face her.

"Yes! Please! My baby isn't breathing!" The woman held the baby toward Tanya.

Amy looked at the man, tall and muscular with a long ponytail and a leather vest.

"Go ahead!" The man was still yelling.

Tanya took the baby from the woman. As she cradled the baby, she bent so that her ear was over the baby's mouth to listen for any breath, while she tried to find a pulse on the upper arm under the baby's T-shirt. Tanya looked up at Amy, then glanced at the parents. Amy could tell by her expression that she was finding neither breath nor pulse.

"Tanya," Amy said, "I'll call 911 from the land line and tell them we need an ambulance for an unresponsive baby. One of you go over to the window there and answer any questions the dispatcher has about the baby's name and age and what happened." Amy went to the phone at Maeve's desk and dialed, keeping her eyes locked on the unfolding scene as she did.

The man waved for the woman to go over as he stood guard, watching as Tanya set his child down on the floor. She bent over the baby to begin CPR.

"How old is this child?"

"Ten months last week," the man answered. His arms folded and unfolded as he stood helplessly watching.

"I'm going to do CPR now. I want you to stand back. When Amy gets off the phone, I want you to tell her to get the AED and first aid kit. Okay?"

"Sure." The man took a step back, keeping his eyes on the child.

Tanya began chest thrusts with two fingers on the baby's chest. She counted aloud to thirty thrusts, then looked in the baby's mouth. Nothing. She bent down and put her mouth over the baby's mouth and nose. Her first breath didn't go in. It sounded as if she was blowing a raspberry on a baby's belly. She adjusted the baby's head and tried again. It still didn't go in.

Tanya started chest thrusts again. She concentrated on her movements, and when she reached thirty thrusts, she once more looked in the baby's mouth. She saw something at the back of the baby's mouth and reached in with her pinky finger. She pulled out a small rubber tire, from a toy vehicle in the visit room. Tanya bent down and breathed into the tiny mouth.

This time her breath went in. She waited as the chest fell, then breathed in again.

Tanya concentrated on the next series of thirty chest thrusts and as she breathed in again, the baby's stomach heaved. She lifted her head and turned the baby on his side just in time, as he emptied the contents of his stomach onto the tiled lobby floor. She kept him on his side, rubbing his back as he cried.

With the baby breathing and crying, the man stood with his arms at his side. Amy could see his hands shaking as she approached from the reception desk.

"An ambulance is on the way. Someone should wait on the steps for them and bring them in." Amy sent a young worker who had come into the lobby out the door to watch for the paramedics.

The woman dropped to her knees beside her baby and tried to pick him up, but Amy put a gentle hand on hers.

"It's best to keep him on his side right now. Just rub his back." Amy guided the woman's hand to a spot between the shoulder blades, and the mother rubbed her child's back.

"The paramedics will come and take a look at him. They'll want to be sure he's okay after the CPR. If you keep rubbing his back and talk to him, it will help him stay calm while we wait."

The woman moved her hand on her baby's back and began to sing.

"Hush little baby. Hush little baby." She sang just those three words, over and over again, as if she had forgotten the rest of the song. The baby calmed when he felt his mother's touch and heard her voice in his ear. The man knelt down and placed his large hand on the baby's brow. He put his other hand on the woman's shoulder, and she glanced up at him briefly, without pausing in her singing.

The paramedics arrived and checked the baby over. He was pink and his vital signs were good. They suggested the baby be seen at the hospital, just to be sure everything was fine. He had been unconscious and not breathing, after all, and had

CPR performed. Amy suggested Tanya go with the baby in the ambulance, and she would bring the parents over in her car.

"It's usually a parent or guardian that comes in the ambulance." The younger paramedic said. "Usually the mother, if she's present."

"Yes. This may seem a bit unusual, I'm sure. Please accept that Tanya is acting as the guardian at this moment."

The younger paramedic furrowed his brow.

"This is the CAS," the older paramedic said, speaking for the first time. "The kid's probably in foster care for whatever reason and here for a visit with the parents because he's not living with them right now." The younger one looked at the parents, this time narrowing his eyes.

"I'll bring the parents along in my car then. Thanks." Amy brought a quick end to the conversation and Tanya prepared to go with the paramedics by ambulance.

"I'm Amy Malloy." Amy extended her hand to the mother first, then to the father.

"Shelley Brown," the mother said. Her grip was soft, and her hand was damp.

"Jim Horner," the man said. His grip was firm and steady.

"Let's gather up your things, and we'll head over to the hospital. I'm just going to let the other staff know, so they can have the foster parent meet us there."

Jim and Shelley picked up their bags from the visit room. Amy popped her head into the monitoring room to ask the staff there to call the baby's foster parent and have them head over to the hospital.

Amy grabbed some paper towels and cleaned up the floor. She washed her hands in the public bathroom off the lobby, then headed out into the parking lot with Jim and Shelley.

They didn't speak much during the drive to the hospital. It was a short trip as the agency was only a few blocks away. Amy escorted the worried parents into the emergency room. She confirmed that Tanya had already called a supervisor on her cell phone to make the report of this serious occurrence.

The foster parent arrived within moments. When Amy was sure that things were under control, she said her goodbyes and headed out to her car. She was late getting over to check on Faye and Justin.

In the driveway at Faye's, Amy took a moment to compose herself as she collected the box from her trunk. It was a lot, sometimes. Life really was fragile. Amy was glad the agency valued first aid training for staff. That baby could easily have choked to death if Tanya hadn't known CPR. She took a deep breath. Working in child welfare meant sometimes coming close to death, and today's experience left her feeling raw. Now, here she was at the home of a family confronting mortality in another form. She prepared herself to be present with Faye and Justin with a deep slow breath.

Amy didn't have to knock. Justin answered the door, and she took note of his long, sad face.

"Hey Justin, what's up today?"

"I got in trouble at school again." He ducked his head as he said this. "I'm suspended for three days."

"What happened?" Amy asked, concerned that Justin was once again on the school's radar.

"I was fighting with another kid. Punched him right in the nose." Justin seemed matter of fact about it, and it just didn't settle with Amy.

"What did the other kid do?"

"Nothing. I didn't like how he looked at me, I guess."

"Hmm," Amy said.

"So, I have to stay home for three days. At least I can look after Mom and make sure she eats lunch while I'm here." Justin looked up at the social worker, his brow furrowed. "Since Cindy moved, there's no one to check on Mom now."

Amy nodded, beginning to understand what might have happened. Last week, Justin had been in a scuffle with another student who'd made a comment about his mom. He was sent home for the day. He must be back to his trick of behaving bad enough they'd keep sending him home.

"You know, we should have a talk about that," Amy said. "Maybe we should see if there's another volunteer from the church who can visit and make sure your mom gets some lunch, like Cindy was doing. Then you can stay in school."

Justin looked up then, surprised. He looked ready to argue, but when he saw the soft look on her face, he set his mouth in a resigned pout and nodded his head.

"Yeah, maybe."

Amy helped Justin put the food into the cupboards and checked in on Faye. The frail woman lay under a faded patchwork quilt. Two pictures hung on the wall. In one, a much younger Faye stood in her wedding dress beside a handsome young man in a suit against the backdrop of a park somewhere Amy didn't recognize. The second was a photo of Faye with Justin that must have been taken when he was about a year old. Amy wouldn't have recognized the woman in the picture as the same woman in the bed.

Faye was sleeping and had a peaceful look on her face. Justin stood beside Amy, and when he crept a little closer to her side Amy put her arm around him and gave him a squeeze. She wished she could tell him it would be all right, but it just wasn't true.

Amy stayed long enough to play a card game with Justin, and by the time they were done, Faye roused enough for a few words with Amy.

"Justin's got a few days off school." Faye said. "He said they told him he could work from home and hand in his homework."

"Did they?" Amy asked, her eyebrows raised as she glanced at Justin, standing beside his mother's bed with a pleading look on his face. "Lucky you, to have such good company for a few days."

The tired woman smiled and patted her son's hand, nodding.

Best Interests

When Amy headed out and got in the car, she didn't bother to select a playlist for the drive. Sometimes there were just no songs that would ease the ache. It was time to go home.

Maureen Pollard

Chapter 9

Instead of music, Amy tuned into the talk radio station on the way home. It was the only news she would listen to, and she only left it on long enough to make sure she hadn't missed any big event, whether local or beyond. Once she got home, she would immerse herself in her soothing post-work routines.

Turning into the driveway, Amy smiled when she saw Wiley waiting patiently on the porch, his tail wagging furiously. The large pet door that allowed him to easily let himself in and out through the day and night and the invisible fence system that kept him safe at home had been some of her best investments. The bit of draft she occasionally felt from it on a windy day was worth it.

Though she lived alone, Amy made a point of eating most meals at a properly set table. Even if they were microwaved more than half the time, like the chili she heated up and carried to the dining room that night.

Her chair faced out the large picture window in the living room, giving her a beautiful view of the woods that surrounded her front yard. She chose to eat her meals in this pleasant way to make them as different as possible from the lonely meals of her childhood, eaten on the living room floor with the TV blaring to try to drown out the sound of her parents fighting.

After dinner, Amy worked on a new short story. She had a collection of them. She would never share them with anyone. She was afraid that people would think she was writing about them. She wasn't, really. She was writing about the basic human experience.

What Amy tried to understand and explore through her stories were those human challenges common to everyone. People were always so afraid they were crazy, or that they were the only one who experienced a problem, or who felt like a failure. The more people Amy met the more she recognized the commonalities underneath the suffering. Tonight, she wrote about what it felt like to have a manager who seemed to have no compassion or empathy. Well, she thought, maybe occasionally she was writing with someone specific in mind.

Amy wrapped up her writing session, grabbed her gym bag, and drove back into town. It was squash night. She glanced at the clock on the dashboard. She would be a few minutes late, but Evan would expect it. She was a little bit late for almost everything. Never more than a little late, but never there on the nose. When she thought about it, she guessed it was probably a side effect of the unpredictable nature of travel between home visits that spilled over into her planning of personal activities, too.

Tonight, they played hard, as usual. For several rallies, the only sounds were from the bounce of the ball against the racquets and the walls, and the squeak and the slap of their sneakers on the wood floor. Amy laughed when Evan missed an easy return for the third time.

"What's on your mind, Evan? You never miss those easy ones," Amy said, looking at her friend's face, which had a strange expression on it, both distant and intent at the same time. "And you've missed three now."

"Nothing, really." He kept his eye on the ball as he waited for her to serve.

"Don't give me that. We've been playing together long enough now. I think I can tell when something's bothering you."

"Okay, well, I'll tell you then," Evan said, turning to face her and letting his racquet fall to his side. "You. You're what's bothering me."

Amy's head bobbed up and she stared at her friend. He held eye contact and squeezed the ball repeatedly in his left hand as he waited for her to respond.

"Me? What did I do?" Amy finally said.

"Nothing. Everything. I wanted to tell you in a different way, but what's the point of waiting? Look, Amy, I can't stop thinking about you. I'll say it the simplest way I can, so I don't mess this up." He glanced up at the ceiling, then brought his gaze back to her eyes. "I really enjoy this time we spend together. I really, really like you. And I'd like to see you more often."

"Ah," Amy said quietly, giving him a warm smile. "That's a bad idea."

"Why? You must like me too, or you wouldn't drive all the way back into town like this every week."

"I do like you. That's why it's a bad idea." Amy set down her racquet and touched her friend's arm. "I don't think a relationship would work out for me. I told you about how badly things worked out in the past when I tried to date. I'm selfish, I put my work before anything else, and that will include you. You'll be fine with it for a little while. Maybe longer than some guys because you actually get it. But it won't last. You'll get angry when I cancel because I have to place a kid. You'll be annoyed if I answer my cell phone when we're together because I took another on-call shift. Then, I'll get frustrated with your impatience, and we'll break up, and we won't be friends anymore. I like you too much to let that happen. I need a *friend*, to tell you the truth."

"I love all of those things about you. I am not those other guys you dated in the past. I won't get angry or annoyed, and you won't have to get frustrated and break up. I know it. Look how well it's worked these past few months."

"Sure, for hanging out once a week as friends. If we were having sex and I answered my cell phone you'd change your mind."

"If we're in bed and you notice your cell phone is ringing, I'm not doing my job." Evan's eyes twinkled as he grinned at her. They'd been trading grins and cathartic jokes for months now in moments like these that sparked with humour but also a slight edge of something more. Amy realized their jokes had been charged with a new kind of energy for a while now. She couldn't believe that she hadn't seen it for what it was until now. Or maybe she'd been afraid to look closer and risk their friendship.

"Seriously!" Amy said. She couldn't keep from laughing, though.

"All right. Let's forget it for tonight. I'm going to beat you at this next game, and then we'll go and enjoy dessert."

"You're on, Constable Grant," Amy said, sighing with relief that this conversation was over. She really liked Evan, but she wasn't much good at romantic relationships or even conversations about them.

They finished the next game, and Evan did win, so it was Amy's turn to pay for dessert. But when they got to the cash register at the café, he paid anyway.

"Consider it a belated birthday present. I didn't find out about your big day until I was out with Phil the other day after your team lunch. So, happy birthday, Amy." He bent down and touched his lips gently to hers, then straightened up and opened the door for her.

"Thanks, Evan."

"Next year, I'll be ready."

"Good night, Evan." Amy smiled as she closed her car door, turned the key in the ignition and gave her friend a wave before pulling away.

Chapter 10

The next morning, refreshed and feeling pleased that she had caught up with her recording yesterday, Amy headed into her team room with a smile. She set down a basket of fresh, warm muffins and half a stick of butter on a saucer. She put out some flowery serviettes and a note card that said, "Surprise, it's Muffin Thursday! This week's bonus muffins are Banana Oatmeal with Chocolate Chips. Help Yourself." She went to her own desk, where she hung up her jacket and bag, then sat down to check her messages.

"Amy? Can you come in here for a minute?" Rhonda's voice called over the cubicles.

"Sure. Be right there." Amy finished making a note about the calls she would need to return, hung up her phone, and headed into her supervisor's office.

"What's up?"

"I wanted to talk to you about Amanda. I read your recording last night. It's a good report, but I think you're hovering over her too much. We have six months to go on the supervision order. I want you to start to back off. We don't have grounds to continue the order. You know we're going to be closing it. Weekly visits are too much now. You need to reduce the visits."

"I'm not convinced Amanda's doing as well as it appears. I think the psychiatrist knows that she's had some challenges and isn't talking." Amy watched Rhonda roll her eyes.

"I know, I know. You've got another gut feeling. Well, Amy, we can't build a court case on your gut feelings. It's not in anyone's best interests. You've been around long enough to know that. Visit them twice a month for the next three months, and then only go once a month for the last three months of the order."

"Fine. I suppose that if something's going to happen, it's more likely to be when the training wheels come off anyway."

"Sure. And by the way, no more unannounced visits. You've been going to the house unannounced every other visit, and there has been nothing out of order, so stop it."

"Fine," Amy said, keeping her expression bland.

"You don't need to mother them, you know. Sometimes I just don't understand the way you work."

Amy didn't bother to reply. She just went back to her desk where she put her headphones on and pulled up a playlist with soothing songs. She would hit the gym at lunch though, where she would put on angry songs and pound out her frustration on the treadmill.

After several songs and a lot of deep breathing, she was calmer. She opened the calendar function on her phone and checked for appointments and reminders. She knew anything could change her schedule in a heartbeat. It was the nature of the job, and probably a part of what had kept Amy so interested in it all these years.

Amy deleted next week's unannounced visit she had planned to make to Amanda.

Amy thought about Amanda's concern that she might pose a risk to her children. Through her research she learned that the chances of someone in a psychotic state becoming violent were actually quite low. If it did happen, it tended to make sensational headlines, making it seem like violence was more of a risk than it really was. The risk increased with the use of psychoactive drugs, which may well have been a factor for Amanda. She was so closed to sharing information that Amy just didn't know. But usually, people with this kind of mental health problem were more likely to attempt suicide than to try to harm someone else.

Maybe Rhonda had a point. Hovering over the family wasn't going to solve anything. In fact, if she was hovering, it was harder for them to demonstrate whether the seemingly positive change was real. She had to let go of this. She wasn't helping anything this way. She deleted the following week's visits with the children at school and her planned call to Lila and Rick.

Amy considered the rest of her week. Tomorrow was Friday. She needed to go back and check on the state of that house that had been unsafe, to see if the parents had managed the clean-up tasks she had left them. That was the only item she had booked, and it wasn't until one o'clock in the afternoon.

Amy looked up at her computer. With her screen open to her case list, she considered what other tasks needed to be done. She decided to work on a recording that was due next Tuesday. Things had been going well with that case, and she would have the closing summary done by coffee break. It was a family that was working with her voluntarily to sort out some concerns the parents had about disciplining their twin toddlers. Amy smiled at the thought of the chubby baby boys.

It was the type of case that workers look forward to but don't get assigned very often. The parents, recognizing that they were overwhelmed and struggling, had called the agency to ask for help. Amy worked with them over a three-month period, offering some tips and suggestions. She gave them contact information for the multiple-birth parents' group in a nearby city and with that link, the parents felt connected to other families coping with similar parenting challenges.

Amy finished that recording and saved it. She would submit it to Rhonda for approval on the due date, leaving it open until then just in case something changed. It was a lesson every child protection worker learned very quickly—not to try to predict what would happen next.

Amy stood up and stretched her arms over her head. She walked over to get a coffee and took one of her own muffins. She chatted with Janet, the team secretary. Janet's grandchildren were coming to visit for the weekend, and she was full of plans for their time together. Amy listened and smiled at the thought of this serious, efficient, professionally-dressed woman, changing into jeans and a T-shirt after work to throw a glow-in-the-dark bowling ball, or changing into a swimsuit to jump from the high-dive board at the community pool.

Back at her desk, Amy found herself thinking about Rex and Angel again, and her recent interviews of the children at school. Rex was wearing his silver cape over black clothes to school every day now. The teacher didn't mind. She had another student who insisted on wearing the same princess dress every day for two weeks after the family trip to Disney World, much to that mother's mortification.

Last week, Rex had told Amy he had superpowers.

"I can stop radio signals." Rex had puffed out his chest and explained that by moving the radio wires just so, he could make it stop playing the music his mother hated.

"Rex, you should leave the wires alone. It could cause you to get a shock. Wires are best for grown-ups to fix."

"Mommy says I'm a big boy and a good helper. She made me my cape. I have another one at home."

"You are such a big boy. I know Mommy wants you to be safe too, so be very careful around the wires, please."

Angel was home from school that day, but she had seemed physically fine. Amy figured the child must be getting enough to eat, because when she was offered snacks, she was just as likely to refuse them as to eat. She was growing. But she didn't seem happy. She often stood beside Amy's chair, staring intensely as the social worker spoke with her mother. Sometimes, the little girl would reach out and touch Amy's arm.

"Don't mind her. She's just checking to see if you're real," Amanda had said as though this was nothing out of the ordinary.

Amy wondered what would make Angel question her reality but hadn't considered it further at the time.

Amy called Amanda's number. There was no answer. Amy left a message that she would like to plan a home visit next Tuesday at about three when the children would be done school for the day. She asked that Amanda call back to confirm the time would work.

Amy called High Five Developmental Services. She was following up on a referral she had made for a mother whose baby was having some developmental delays. The family doctor noticed that although she was giving the baby basic care, she seemed disinterested, and she hadn't been seen talking to or playing with the baby.

"Hi Sydney, it's Amy Malloy. How are things going with Melissa Simpson?"

"Oh, they're going well. We've been into the home three times, and Mom is really taking it seriously. She's paying attention when the worker's there, and it seems like she's doing well between visits. She's much more engaged with Sierra already."

"That's great. Just what I hoped to hear." Amy made a note in the file.

Once another service was involved, Amy could sometimes take a bit of a back seat for a while. This was a perfect example. Melissa needed a chance to make use of the new ideas and support before Amy followed up. She was pleased that it seemed to be a good connection and they were already making progress. Amy could imagine closing this file if things continued this way for a few more months. Maybe Melissa would agree to stay involved with High Five. That would be so much better than going to court.

Amy viewed the court process as a sort of backup system for her regular plans to work with families. If Amy laid out her information to the court, and the court agreed that there was some risk to the children and that Amy's proposed plan was a good way to reduce the risk, then an order would be made. Usually, an order was made for six months but sometimes for as long as twelve months. At the end of that time the agency and the family would return to court to provide an update on the progress that had been made in addressing the risk to the children. The family would have to answer to the judge if they had not followed the court order, and sometimes this motivated parents to make positive changes for their children's well-being.

Amy knew the court also served as a checkpoint for the agency. Sometimes, it was easy to think one knew best when one spent day after day going into people's houses, judging a parent's ability to care for the children and telling parents what to do. The power of the position could go to a protection worker's head, and a judge would challenge the agency's right to run roughshod over a family without demonstrating that the agency's plan was in the best interests of the child.

'The best interests of the child' was a phrase tossed about liberally at the Children's Aid Society. Everyone was sure they understood the term, but it was complex. Were the best interests of the child served by allowing them to remain living in substandard housing when the parents were on government assistance and could not afford to move into a safe and secure building? Were the best interests of a child served by removing the children from the care of those same parents, who used every penny to ensure the children had snowsuits and boots even as the parents wore threadbare, thin jackets that didn't cut the wind on the worst days as they walked their children to and from school?

Lunch time rolled around, and Amy headed out for a walk. The agency was in the heart of town. It had been built on the site of an old five and dime style department store that had burned down, leaving a big empty lot in town. Having outgrown the small brick building on the edge of town that the Children's Aid Society had occupied for more than fifty years, the board of directors had negotiated with the town to purchase the land at a reasonable price, and the new building was erected soon thereafter.

Amy walked past the small shops and boutiques on the main street of Green Valley. The new location made the agency much more accessible for clients in town. The reality was that a good number of families served by the agency were out in the countryside. Some folks had vehicles, and some did not. Some of those who had vehicles did not have money for gas. The people at each end of the county had great difficulty getting to the agency, with almost an hour's drive in either direction to get to Green Valley, which lay at the centre of this rural county. The agency had toyed with the idea of opening satellite offices, but it was simply not cost-effective to run an extra office space at each of the four corners of the county. It would hardly be adequate anyway, as so many families lived on the long, winding country roads, with their access as limited to any of the villages as it was to the town of Green Valley itself.

Amy popped into the Jumping Beanz Café. She ordered a peppermint mocha and a slice of banana coffee cake. As she waited for her order, she chatted with a table of high school students. She recognized Jackson, a thirteen-year-old boy she had interviewed and put in temporary foster care about a year ago when his mom and dad left him alone, without groceries, for two weeks while they went on vacation in the Caribbean.

The teenagers each had a tablet, phone, or laptop on the table in front of them as they took their caffeine hit, and though they weren't talking much to each other they were friendly with Amy when she asked what was happening over at the high school since the merger into the new building.

Green Valley had a declining student population, just like almost everywhere in Ontario. The school board had been maintaining three old schools in this town for decades, trying to keep up the maintenance on all three buildings with their impressive architecture and rich history. The decision had been made to build one new school that would have room for all grades from kindergarten to grade twelve.

"It has a sick new tech department, with all new machines. There's a gym, a cafeteria and an auditorium," Jackson said. "It's weird being in the halls with the little kids though. Man, they are so small. Some of them can't even do up their coats."

"How is it you end up in the same halls with them?" Amy was curious about this new experiment in education. Kindergarten to twelve, under one roof in one super-school. Would it be the wave of the future? Would the smaller kids be victimized as so many of their parents feared?

"There's a buddy system. They matched us up with the primary kids to help them. The grade eleven and twelve classes take turns. Twice a week at recess we help them get their coats and boots on to get outside for recess during our break between classes."

"Really? How's that working?"

"Those little kids are funny. It's no big deal for us to go down the hall and help them. A couple of days a week we get a pass to be late to class to hang out with them for a bit. You wouldn't believe it. They think we're awesome!"

"One kid told me he wanted to be just like me when he grew up, and I was like 'What?' and he said yeah, he wanted to have blue hair and a diamond in his nose like mine." The youth who spoke had a wisp of blue through the front half of the thick hair that swept across his forehead. His diamond nose ring twinkled in the café lighting, as did the studs on his leather jacket and boots.

He smiled shyly at Amy. "That was kinda sick. Most people are afraid of me."

"Well, people might have trouble seeing the real you behind all your gear. It distracts them, all the colour and glitz."

"Well, yeah." The teen grinned. "I guess that was kinda the point."

"Little kids can see past stuff adults can't sometimes, huh?"

"Yeah, I guess that's what's cool about this buddy thing. I thought it was gonna be a pain, but it's actually pretty cool."

Amy's order was ready. She collected her drink and snack and headed for the door.

"Hey, uh, Amy?" Jackson called after her.

"Yes?" she paused as he approached her, throwing a glance over his shoulder to see if any of his friends were listening.

"I, uh, I just thought you should know. There's this kid. Justin. He's in grade three. I'm his lunch buddy. So, like we go into the kindergarten room at lunch one week every month to help the kids open their containers and stuff like that. Anyway, Justin..." Jackson looked at his feet and then lifted his gaze to meet Amy's. "I think something's wrong at home. He's missed a bunch of days in the last month. Says his mom's sick and he has to help her. And he's been trying to pick fights with other kids. He even tried to fight me. I think he might need help. From someone like you, I mean."

"Do you know his last name?" Amy asked, already aware that Jackson was talking about Faye's son. An image of Faye, how thin she had looked when Amy last saw her, appeared in Amy's mind. She thought of how Faye had said Justin warmed up her soup for her when she couldn't do it and how he'd arranged things so he could be home with his mom. She blinked.

"No." Jackson looked worried. "I could probably find out though."

"That's okay, Jackson, I can check into it with the office." Amy touched Jackson's elbow lightly. "You're a good buddy, Jackson. Keep it up, all right?" He nodded then turned to head back to the table where his friends were still sitting with their electronics.

Amy walked around the block on her way back to the office. She would stop again as soon as she could to check on Faye and Justin, but she couldn't give Jackson any indication that she knew them. If Justin hadn't mentioned her, she certainly wasn't going to let Jackson know Justin had been connected to CAS.

At her desk once more, Amy cleared aside all the paperwork. She called the school and left a message for Rich Mahood, asking him to call and talk about Justin. She put on her headphones and listened to a playlist of random alternative music from her youth. The chat with the teens had her feeling nostalgic and the sounds made her smile.

Amy took out her lunch bag and ate her salad first. Her head bobbed to the music as she sipped her mocha, savouring it along with the banana cake from the café.

As the last notes faded on the refrain of a song by one of her favourite post-punk bands from the 80s, Amy reflected on the lyrics. The vocalist sang about change and Amy wondered if her own life would ever change in a meaningful way. She glanced over at the twelve-month calendar tacked up on her cubicle wall. Month after month, more of the same. Most days, the changes were small and hardly noticeable, with nothing major to tilt her world on its axis. The opening of one file, the closing of another. The gradual increase or decrease of the temperature with the changing seasons. The small lines forming around her eyes and the corners of her mouth.

Eight years ago, Amy would not have imagined herself still working as a front-line child protection worker, investigating allegations of child abuse and neglect, knocking on strangers' doors, and asking them very personal questions in intense investigations. Eight years ago, Amy had considered it possible or even likely that she might have a partner, might have a family, children of her own to love and raise. She would not have imagined herself alone with only the company of a wolfhound.

Her mind turned to Evan's recent disclosure about his feelings, but she didn't know what to do about the fluttering she felt when she thought about him, so she quickly brought her focus back to her home and the reprieve it gave her from the stress of work. She would not have imagined that this would be enough for her.

It was though. It was enough to do a job she loved, to own a comfortable home secluded in the woods, and to be able to enjoy her life as she saw fit, without anyone to answer to. So what if she also had to make all the decisions on her own, to solve all the problems that came up when you owned a home and a car? So what if the house was dark when she got home after an unanticipated investigation went late into the night? She thought of the men she had dated in the past. Their support had come along with compromises and complications, as any relationship does. Her mind turned back to Evan, and she realized again that things between them were nice and uncomplicated. She had it good, just the way things were.

Amy loved her work, and it did satisfy her, despite some very difficult days. Not too long ago, in a low mood one evening, she had pushed herself to do some free writing about the qualities she brought to her work and what was important to her in that work. She called the phrases up in her mind's eye now, as she often did in moments of doubt. She loved the fact that she had an opportunity to help families make their lives better. Her willingness to listen, her ability to set aside judgment and meet people where they were in their circumstances, the possibility that she could offer real help. These were the things that kept her going. It was why she kept cleaning supplies and non-perishable food in her trunk year-round. In the winter, she collected outgrown gently used hats, mitts, boots, and coats from friends and family and tucked them into her trunk as well, so she had something to offer when she came across a family in need. It wasn't the things themselves that were important, but the acknowledgement of the real needs people had, and trying to meet them with compassion and respect.

It wasn't much, really. It certainly didn't solve a family's problems to give them some soup or a mop or a coat. Amy had no illusions that what she was doing would save the world. But what she was doing could help a family. What she was doing might help a child.

Amy's phone rang, jarring her out of her reflections.

"Amy Malloy speaking."

"Hey, Amy. Listen, I'm going on holidays for two weeks," Phil Davis said. "Would you be able to cover a couple of my files for me? I hate to ask, but I'm kind of in a pinch." Amy could hear exhaustion and concern in her friend's voice.

"Sure, Phil. Not enough coverage on your team?"

"No, and these two files need more attention. Everyone who'll be here while I'm off has less than two years on the job and they're up to their eyeballs in it. I'm concerned that these ones might fall between the cracks, and they're both high-risk. I know you're busy, too, but I trust you with these ones."

"Sure. What have you got?"

"I have a baby, Felix. He's four months old, diagnosed failure to thrive. He needs to be seen every three days, but the home is right here in town. Living with Mom and her boyfriend. Sonya Wells is twenty. The boyfriend, Brian Keeler, is twenty-one. He's not the dad. Came on the scene when she was pregnant, and bio-Dad had already taken off. They didn't have a lot of money, so they were trying to stretch the formula. When the baby went for his well-baby check-up, he had lost weight over four weeks instead of the gain that was expected."

"So how is this baby still there? And why every three days instead of every day until he's back on track?"

"The judge said neither parent has any history. The boyfriend's parents are both professionals. The mother's dad died when she was in high school. Her mother works for the government in Ottawa. The Judge felt it was likely these parents are just young and uninformed. Ordered the baby back home at the first court appearance after the apprehension. Rhonda said since the baby's over three months, every three days is often enough for visits. She said there's no time to see them more often because there are other families that need to be seen, too." Phil's voice was flat. Amy understood. Sometimes you just didn't have it in you to fight with the system and the people who directed the work.

"Okay, every three days. Starting what day?" Amy made notes as Phil spoke. She appreciated his ability to get to the facts. They shared a common language, having worked in the field for so long. They understood each other without a lot of extra discussion.

"Start Monday, please. I was just there this morning. They had a case of the premixed formula, full. The receipt they showed me was for the purchase early this morning. The baby should be going through one case about every five days. The doctor specified this pre-mixed formula and the amounts to be sure the baby would be getting enough calories. They shouldn't water it down to last and they don't have any excuse not to mix it properly."

"Right. Did the court order conditions against the parents?"

"Not yet. Mom was tearful and remorseful at the doctor's office. The boyfriend wasn't there but the doctor called him to stress how important it was to feed the baby properly and he agreed to this plan, both on the phone with the doc and when I met with him. This is their chance to get the baby back on track."

"Any relatives around? In case the baby needs a placement?"

"Yes, in a kin search with the mother and the doctor, I found out there is a maternal aunt locally. She lives up in the North end of the county, so she hadn't seen the baby much, but she is willing to be involved. She's agreed to call her niece once a week to see if she needs anything. The maternal grandmother is too far away to be first choice. She has a strained relationship with Sonya and hasn't met the baby."

"What is this girl doing in Green Valley?"

"She moved here for college. Got pregnant by a classmate. She dropped out and when the dad graduated and left to go back to his hometown, she got together with Brian. Moved in with him before the baby was born, and here we are."

"Okay. What's the other file?"

"The other one is a seven-year-old kid. Mom has been in rehab three times. She just got out two weeks ago. So far, so good. The kid stayed with the neighbor all three times. Last time it went really well for about nine months. Then she got the news that her father was being charged with historical sexual assault by her best friend growing up. She stayed in the full three-month rehab program this time and got connected with a counselor. She seems to be hanging in there."

"How often are you visiting there?"

"Once a week, unannounced. Either around five in the evening, or around eight thirty in the morning. Kid needs to be at school for nine and if she's drinking, she doesn't get him up and ready. If she's drinking, she's usually passing out by supper time. Midday she can still be all right, so it's better to go early or late. I've been alternating from week to week."

"Is she in town, too?"

"Yep, right on the edge though."

"All right. Have a great trip, Phil. I mean it. I've got these covered."

"Thanks, Amy. I'd never rest if one of the newbies were covering these two for me."

"I hear you. I remember being fresh in the job and up to my ass in alligators. I wouldn't have known a high-risk baby even if I held one in those days."

"Exactly. Well, I'm off. I have two more recordings to finish and then I'm outta here. My plane leaves at six thirty tomorrow morning and then I'm on a sunny beach with a beverage in my hand for the next seven days."

"Have fun! I'll see you in two weeks."

"Right. Unless I decide to get a job as a cabana boy."

"Sure, Phil," Amy said, a teasing tone in her voice. "Although you might be past your best before date for any job that ends in the word 'boy.'"

"Hey, a man can dream. Even a man with greying hair, a bad back, a comfortable wife and two kids in college he's still paying for."

"Sweet dreams then, Phil." Amy laughed as she hung up the phone and gathered her belongings to head out for a home visit.

Best Interests

In her car, she checked her watch and decided to stop at the sub shop. It was the quickest, sort-of-healthy food option. She ordered her sandwich and was soon back behind the wheel, headed to see the Somani family.

As Amy pulled up in front of a small brick house, she glanced at the clock on her dashboard. Five minutes after three. Good. Not as late as she often was, going from one place to another across the county.

She crumpled up the sandwich wrapper and threw it in a ball on the floor on the passenger side of the car. It joined her bagel wrapper from this morning's breakfast and her empty coffee cup. She downed the last of the milk in the small carton and threw that on the floor too. Some days she felt like she should just get a garbage pail for the floor of the car, but that might make it too easy to buy lunch every day.

It didn't take her long to get her update. The parents both worked shift work, and right after lunch was a good time to meet when they both worked afternoons. They filled her in on the latest developments with their teenager, who was living at home again after a summer of conflict and couch surfing. The parents were relieved that things seemed to be back on track at home and at school. Amy was relieved, too. She wasn't particularly surprised, though. In some cases, conflict between parents and teens was a seasonal affair. The coming of cold winter weather could bring youth back to the warmth of home just as predictably as the warm spring air and sunshine could lure them.

It seemed like things had settled down enough that she could probably close the file. She'd come back once more, just to be sure.

Amy left the home, driving back to the office to make some notes. That was her mistake.

Maureen Pollard

Chapter 11

Amy knew better than to go back to the office on a Friday afternoon. She had barely finished her case note when she heard Rhonda's voice as she walked around the team room looking for someone to go out on a call.

"Who's still here? We've got a one-one-A. Kid with a bruise on his cheek," Rhonda said in a clipped tone. "Anyone still here?"

"I'm here, Rhonda," Amy said, moving to shut down her computer.

"Well, then you're it, Amy. You're the only one in the place right now."

Amy sighed and swiveled her chair to face her supervisor.

"So, the school just called, of course. Eight-year-old Timmy Rankin showed up at school this morning with a bruise on his cheek. Classroom teacher and the gym teacher both asked what happened and he said his dad pushed him into the coffee table.

The gym teacher forgot to call after gym class because she had lunch duty. So now Timmy's bus is loading in thirty minutes."

"So much for our duty-to-report trainings, I see," Amy said.

"You need to get over to the school right now and see this kid. I'll only be here until four thirty, so as soon as you see what the mark is and ask him what happened, call me and we'll make a decision about whether he can go home on the bus."

Amy sighed. Her vision of a cheese fondue with French bread and Granny Smith apples as she read by the fire tonight blinked out with her supervisor's words. Amy grabbed her briefcase, checked to see that she had the child diagram outlines she would need to document any marks on the boy, and stuck two fresh pens in the inner pocket.

"Okay. At Chris Hadfield School?"

"Yes. Thank goodness, the family lives here in town. You can get there in a few minutes. I'll be on standby. Until four thirty."

Amy grabbed a granola bar from the box in her drawer. Pausing, she grabbed two more, just in case. Amy drove to the school, parking in the visitor spot and rushing in the front doors. She stepped into the office and over to the counter where the school secretary was working on her computer. This woman was new to the school and Amy didn't recognize her.

"Hello, I'm Amy Malloy. Children's Aid Society. I'm here to see Timmy Rankin please."

"Oh, we thought you would wait until Monday since it's so late in the day."

"We have to see a child with an injury within twelve hours of getting the call. It's safer to see him here than to go to the home when he gets off the bus."

"Oh, I guess so. I'll call him down. Should I call the parents?"

"No, thank you. I'll take over from here, and I'll follow up with the parents. I'm going to take a look at Timmy and talk to him for a few minutes. If it seems okay, I will make sure he gets on the bus. If I'm concerned and it takes more time, I'll call the parents to let them know he won't be on the bus."

"Oh. Well, I'll have to check with Mr. Mahood."

"Sure, you can do that. Mr. Mahood is familiar with our procedures."

The secretary used the intercom to call Timmy down to the office. Amy headed for the reading room next door and waited in the hallway for Timmy.

A small boy in an oversized sweatshirt came down the hall. He walked slowly. The hem of his pants stopped above the bump of his ankle bone and his shoes were scuffed and muddy. He had a battered backpack slung over his shoulder. As he came closer, Amy could see the mark on his cheek.

"You must be Timmy," Amy said. The boy nodded. "Hi, my name is Amy."

"Come on in here for a few minutes, please. I have a few questions for you."

Timmy shuffled into the room and sat in the chair nearest the door. He kept his backpack on his shoulder and sat on the edge of the chair.

The mark on his left cheek was reddish purple. About three inches across at the widest part, there were three extensions of the bruise trailing up toward his left eye. Amy eyed the mark closely.

"Timmy, I work at the Children's Aid Society. Do you know what we do?"

"Yeah, you take kids, and they never see their parents again."

"Well, not usually. Mostly what we do is try to help parents and kids solve problems. We talk to people and see if we can help them change things in their family so that everything feels better. Sometimes, if kids aren't safe, that means they live somewhere else; that's true. Sometimes it's for a little while and sometimes it's for longer."

Amy paused and nodded toward the boy's left cheek. "I'm here today because I heard you had a bruise on your cheek. I heard there might be a problem happening, and so it's my job to ask you some questions about it. Tell me, Timmy, do you know the difference between the truth and a lie?"

"Yes."

"How old are you?"

"Eight."

"Okay. If I said you were ten, would that be the truth, or a lie?"

"A lie. I'm eight and that's the truth."

"Great, thank you. Now, can you tell me what happened to your cheek, Timmy?"

"I hit the coffee table."

"Ah. Tell me what happened just before you hit the coffee table."

"I was with my dad. We were wrestling, and I hit the coffee table with my cheek."

"You hit the coffee table with your cheek?"

"Yeah, I think." Timmy looked down at his hands as he fiddled with his backpack strap.

"Can I look at the bruise, Timmy?"

He looked up at her and gave his head a toss to flip his hair away from his left cheek.

"See, Timmy, I have been looking at bruises on kids for a long time. When a kid hits a coffee table, usually the bruise is in kind of a straight line, or maybe a triangle if the bruise comes from the corner of the table instead of the straight side."

Timmy's eyes widened.

"Your bruise is not a straight line or a corner. Did something else happen, Timmy?"

He didn't say anything for a moment as he picked at a loose thread on the backpack strap.

"Um…well…"

Amy waited in silence. She kept her distance and kept her hands still as she waited, watching the boy struggle with a decision.

"My dad. My dad…"

"Your dad?"

"My dad hit me. I was playing in the living room and I jumped off the couch. I hit the coffee table and knocked it over. My dad was sleeping in the lazy boy and it woke him up. He jumped up and slapped me on the face." The words tumbled out of his mouth in a rush.

"Ah. You jumped off the couch and knocked the coffee table over. It woke your dad up and he slapped you on the face?"

"Yes." Timmy was breathing hard.

"Show me what his hand looked like when he slapped you on the face, Timmy."

Timmy lifted up a hand and held it open with the palm facing Amy as he raised it over her face.

"Thank you. Show me where he slapped you on the face."

Timmy pointed to the bruise on his face. He looked down at his shoes and his fingers returned to picking at the strap of his backpack.

"Okay, Timmy. We have some work to do tonight. I'm going to have to talk to my supervisor first, and then I am going to call your dad. Before I do that though, who lives in your house, Timmy?"

"Me and Dad and Mom."

"Do you have any brothers or sisters, Timmy?"

"No. Dad says I'm enough of a problem. Any time Mom talks about wanting another baby, Dad says so."

"Okay, Timmy. Here. If you want you can draw a picture while I make the call to my supervisor. I'll be right back."

Amy went into the office. As she approached the desk the secretary looked up and frowned.

"Timmy won't be able to go on the bus. I'll call his parents in a few minutes to tell them, but I need to call my supervisor first. Timmy is in the reading room waiting."

"Oh, I already called his dad. I told him you were here. He's not very happy about it. He said he's coming right over."

"I'm sorry? I thought I said not to call the parents."

"Well, this is my job, and I know it well enough, thank you. If a child is missing the bus, I have an obligation to let the parents know."

"Did you check with Mr. Mahood?"

"I know my job." The woman smiled tightly and turned to her keyboard.

Rich Mahood came out of his office, smiling. Amy had first met Rich when she was a new worker, and he was still teaching in the classroom.

"Did I hear my name taken in vain? Ah, hello, Amy. How are you? Here to see young Timmy, I guess?" He smiled as he greeted her, concern visible in his eyes despite his warm expression.

"Hi Rich. How are you? I've been talking to Timmy, and I'm going to have to take him for a longer interview. He's going to miss the bus. I was explaining to your new secretary that I need to call my supervisor and then I'll let the parents know. Unfortunately, she's already called the father, so I have a problem."

"He's on his way here, Mr. Mahood," she said.

The principal's smile faded. "He's what?"

"He's on his way here. Should be here any minute now."

"Rich, I need to get back to Timmy. I'll make my calls there. You're going to need to head the dad off. Send him over to the Children's Aid Office if he'll go."

"Bring Timmy into my office, Amy. This guy's a hothead."

"Okay."

Amy hustled to the reading room.

"Hey, Timmy, come on with me. We're going to use Mr. Mahood's office instead. He has a more comfortable chair for you to sit in while I make my calls. I'll bring your bag." Amy picked the backpack up from where Timmy had laid it at his feet while he drew.

"Okay."

They walked swiftly back to the main office across the hall. Just as they closed the door to the principal's office, Amy heard a male voice yelling down the hallway.

"Where's my boy? Where the hell is my boy?"

Mr. Mahood stepped out of the office, closing that door behind him, too. Amy could see the secretary through the window in his door, wide-eyed and pale behind her desk.

Amy dialed her supervisor's number. As soon as Rhonda picked up, Amy launched into her explanation, choosing her words carefully as she was fully aware that Timmy was listening closely.

"Something's come up, Rhonda. I met Timmy. He's with me now, in fact. He does have a bruise on his face. It seems he woke his dad up when he was playing, and Dad slapped him with an open hand across the left cheek. There's a reddish-purple bruise and it looks like it might be consistent with a hand because the bruising extends in three lines up from the main round bruise on the cheek."

"Shit. You'll need to apprehend, pending the full investigation. Bring him here, and we'll get him set up with some dinner while you call police and organize the interviews and the medical exam. We'll need to get a kin search started as well."

"Sure, except the secretary called Dad to tell him that Timmy was going to miss the bus. Mr. Mahood is dealing with that now out in the hallway, while we're waiting in his office."

"Dad is there?"

"Yes, that's right." Amy eyed Timmy as he sat in the principal's chair, looking out the window. She would have to be careful what she said. "I think Mr. Mahood is explaining that we have to try to see what's been happening. I told him to suggest to Dad he can meet with me over at the office."

"Well, if he's coming here, I'll put Maeve on alert. You'd better take Timmy to the police station instead of bringing him here, if that's how it goes."

"Yes, that's what I was thinking. I'll see how it's going here, and I will call you back as soon as I know who is going where."

"Fine."

Amy hung up. She called the police station and let them know that she was at the school with a child who had a bruise on his cheek, consistent with a handprint. She was going to need an officer to conduct a joint investigation. The dispatcher said she would see who was available and have them call her cell phone.

Amy was looking toward the hallway as she was giving her phone number, so she saw the fist fly through the glass of the outer office door. The shattering sound could be heard clearly over her cell phone, as could the scream of the secretary.

"Do you need assistance there?" The dispatcher asked.

"Yes, there's a situation in the outer office now. I'm in the inner principal's office with the child. I can't see what's happening. The principal was out in the hallway with the father."

"Okay, just hang on."

Amy could hear the dispatcher call out for police to attend the school immediately. She couldn't hear the responses as they came in from the units reporting their location in relation to the school.

"Hold tight. There are two units on the way. Are there any weapons?"

"I don't know. I'm in the principal's inner office. I can't see or hear anything now. It was a hand that broke the window you heard. I did see that. The principal is still out there, too. I saw his hand grab the one that broke through the window. I could see the sleeve of his jacket."

"Right. Hang in there. Are you okay? Is anyone hurt?"

"I can't see the secretary. She dove under her desk, but she hasn't come up. Some of the glass fell over her."

"Right, I'm going to send an ambulance."

"Yeah, she might need one. That hand that broke the glass might need medical attention as well."

"I'll see what I've got. Stay on the line, please."

Amy could hear bursts of shouting from the hallway. She looked down at Timmy. The child was colouring a picture of a tree, with a complicated crosshatch of lines across it where the trunk split into the tree's many branches. He was colouring in individual leaves, concentrating hard, and did not appear to notice the noise in the outer office or the hall. Amy knew better, though. She knew full well that the boy was keenly attuned to the sounds of his father's voice in the hallway. His white-knuckled grip on the marker gave him away.

"Hey, Timmy. How're you doing?" Amy spoke softly.

"Fine."

"Good. I like your drawing."

"It's a secret tree fort. This is the lock over here. When you go in, no one can follow you. You just have to get the door shut. They can't find the lock, see, because it blends in with the pattern."

"I see. That's very clever. It looks like a safe fort."

"It is."

Timmy bent his head lower over his work and continued adding leaves to his tree.

"Amy?" The voice on the phone was back.

"Yes, I'm here."

"Good. There are two cars on the scene now. The officers should be in the hallway. An ambulance is on the way. Is anything else happening now?"

"Not that I can hear or see. I still can't see the secretary."

"All right. Hang in there. It should be just a little longer now."

"We are."

Amy watched Timmy colour and listened as the voices rose in the hallway again. This time she heard the words clearly.

"He's my son. I demand to see him! You have no right!"

Amy heard another male voice rise in volume, but she could not make out all the words. It wasn't Rich Mahood's voice. She guessed it was one of the police officers, on the scene now and countering the dad's argument.

"You don't need those handcuffs! I'll go with you. But don't you think this is over, Mahood! I'll have your head for letting them get to my boy here!"

Another few minutes passed. The door to the outer office opened and Amy watched Rich step through. He rubbed his face wearily with one hand as he pushed the door open with the other. His grey suit jacket was wrinkled and smeared with dark red streaks near the lapel. Amy supposed Timmy's father had grabbed him with a bloody hand when Rich reached in to move him away from the broken window. He looked over at his secretary's desk.

Amy heard the sirens. Ambulance this time, and they were free to announce their arrival. The police had left their sirens off, Amy realized, to give them the element of surprise.

The principal nodded at her, and she opened the door to his office. Together they looked over the reception desk. The secretary was underneath, having pushed her chair back out of the way so she could fit in the space where her feet usually rested.

"Ms. Lindle. Are you all right?"

There was no response to Rich's inquiry.

"Kim?"

Amy could see the woman's back shaking. A whimper escaped her, but nothing more. She made no move to come out from under the desk.

"Hello. What's happening here?" The paramedics came into the office, carrying gear.

"My secretary seems to be in some distress."

The paramedics looked around the room and one stepped toward Amy.

"No. She's the CAS worker. The secretary is there." Rich pointed behind the desk, toward the floor where the woman huddled.

"She won't answer us, and she won't come out."

"What's her name?" One paramedic was opening a first aid kit and the other walked around the desk."

"Ms. Lindle. Kim Lindle."

"Hi, Ms. Lindle. Kim? My name is Jon, and I'm a paramedic. I'm going to take a look at you and see what's happening." He stepped in beside her but didn't touch her yet.

"Kim, can you hear me?" The paramedic knelt down beside her.

He put his hand on her back and she flinched.

"It's okay, Kim. It's all over now. You can come out. The police are here. That guy's left the school, and he's not going to hurt anyone now. I'd like you to come out so I can take a look at you, please. I need to make sure you're all right."

The secretary slowly backed out from under her desk as the paramedic kept talking, his voice low and soothing. He kept his hand lightly on her back, moving with her as she came out.

When Kim was finally out from under the desk, Amy had a good look at her. A piece of the glass from the door was embedded in the secretary's cheek. It had narrowly missed her eye, landing deep in the meaty part of the left cheek. Kim was pale and her eyes were glazed.

"Great. Now, please have a seat. We're going to do a bit of bandaging here and then we're going to take you over to the hospital so the doctor can have a look at that. You might need a stitch or two. You're going to be all right though."

The paramedic nodded up at his partner, who passed over some rolls of gauze. Jon used them to support the piece of glass in the secretary's cheek, holding it in place so it would not wobble around and cause more damage as they transported her. As he worked, Jon continued to ask her questions. She did not respond, just sat shaking and pale, staring at the broken window in the door as he worked.

Amy looked at Timmy, who continued to work on his drawing, adding yet more leaves. He was varying the shades of green as he drew each individual leaf, and the effect was quite realistic.

A police officer poked his head into the outer office.

"So, is Amy Malloy here?"

"That's me." Amy looked over.

She was relieved to see who it was. She'd worked with Paul Shields on a few investigations in the past two years since he'd been hired by Green Valley Police. He was thorough, and he seemed to have some respect for Amy's skills. That wasn't always the case with cops. They often seemed to expect her to be gullible and incompetent, even though she actually had more training and experience in forensic interviewing now than some of their new hires.

"Hello. I hear we have some work to do this evening?"

"We do. Would you like to come in for a minute to meet Timmy? Then maybe we can step into the hall and talk about our plan."

"Sure." Glass crunched as the officer stepped into the principal's office.

"Hey, Timmy!" The officer stopped near the desk where Timmy was working. "I'm Constable Shields, but you can call me Paul. That's a great drawing. Have you been working on it long?"

"Just since this lady brought me into the office and said she was going to make some phone calls."

"Wow! That's not very long. It looks great. Tell me about it."

"Well, this is the tree trunk. It's a strong tree. An old one. It's a good place to build this secret fort. The branches that make the fort cross back and forth like it's just a part of the tree, but it's really a secret place. Once you're inside you're safe. The leaves are magic. They stay on the tree all year long, and they hide the fort even when all the other trees lose their leaves in the fall."

"That's really cool. I bet everyone would like to have such a great secret fort."

Amy noticed the boy did not tell the police officer about the secret lock. She made no comment. Timmy made no eye contact as he explained his drawing. He kept adding more leaves, methodically alternating colours as he worked.

"Timmy, I'm going to step into the hallway for a few minutes," Amy said. Are you okay to wait here?"

"Yep. I have to finish the leaves."

"Good. I'll be back in a minute."

Amy stepped out into the hallway with the officer. He pulled out his notebook and took notes as Amy reviewed her involvement since the CAS had received the call. Paul had been one of the officers first on the scene. He confirmed that the other officers had arrested Timothy Rankin and taken him out of the building. He was going over to the police station to be held while the police waited for further word from Amy and Paul.

"So, do you want to come and interview Timmy at CAS then? We can use the interview room. My supervisor will have it set up when we get there."

"Why not at the police station? I usually do my interviews there."

"Because he's eight," Amy said quietly. "And because he has a bruise on his cheek that he says his dad caused by slapping him for playing too loud. Because his dad will be at the police station. I think the CAS office will feel safer if he knows his dad is not in the same building." Amy smiled tightly as she calmly recited her reasoning.

"Look, the set up at the police office is safe. The kid won't see his dad."

"Maybe not, but he'll know his dad is in the building," Amy countered.

"I don't see the point. I've interviewed lots of kids at the police station and they've handled it fine."

"This little boy is drawing a picture of a safe, secure tree fort that he can get into and no one else can. It's our job to keep him safe, and that includes making him feel safe. I think that's the point."

"Okay, Amy. You make a good case. CAS it is." Paul said. "Evan was right. You definitely put the kids first."

Rich Mahood joined them in the hallway before Amy had a chance to respond, or even really consider the fact that Evan and Paul had been talking about her. She knew they spent a fair bit of time together since they coached a youth basketball team together on Saturday mornings.

"Hey, Rich. Thank you for holding him out here. I'm sorry about that," Amy said.

"Not your fault. I can't believe she called him without talking to me." Rich was shaking his head as he watched the paramedics finish wrapping a bandage around his secretary's cheek. She was not looking very good. Her skin was very pale, and her eyes were glassy.

"Well, she paid a steep price." Amy looked at Kim as the paramedics lifted her onto the stretcher in the hallway.

"She won't be back. My guess is she'll be off on leave for a while, and then they'll either put her on long-term disability or they'll put her in one of the tiny schools out in the middle of nowhere where they think something like this can't happen."

"Well, we know better. But really, what do we know?" Amy asked. She didn't expect an answer. She and Rich had worked together enough. He'd made a few reports that Amy had investigated. They understood their systems and they understood each other.

"Do you need anything else here?"

"I did leave you a message about Justin again." She paused and Rich nodded to suggest he'd received it. "The volunteer that was coming to help his mother at lunch has moved. I think he's starting fights again so he can stay home and take care of his mother. Home care wasn't approved, so she doesn't have someone to help with lunch when he's at school. He might not be as angry and tough as his act suggests."

"Ah, I wondered about that. I'll follow up. I might know someone who could put a friendly visitor in place around lunch time. I'll make the referral."

"That might work really well," Amy agreed, then glanced around the office. "Sorry about this mess."

"Like I said, not your fault. You're going to take Timmy with you, yes?"

"Yes."

"Well, I better call about replacing the glass. While I wait for them to come, I can get the paperwork started."

"Okay." Amy stepped into the office again. Timmy put the finishing touches on one last leaf, then put the green markers back into the box Amy had given him.

"Hey, good timing finishing that picture, Timmy! Thanks for putting the markers away. We're going to head over to my office for a while."

"Where's my dad?"

"He's going to wait for us at the police station."

"They're going to give him a coffee and a sandwich while he waits there," Paul added.

"He doesn't like peanut butter."

"Oh, it will probably be roast beef or turkey."

"He likes roast beef."

"Well, that will probably work out for him then."

"So, Timmy, I can carry your bag if you want?" Amy reached for it, but the boy hiked it up to his shoulder. He kept his eye on his drawing. "Bring your artwork too."

Timmy grabbed the paper.

"Hey, that turned out well," Paul said as he bent down to have a closer look.

"So, Timmy, do you want to go in my car, or in the police cruiser?" Amy asked.

"Your car." Timmy didn't look up from his picture.

"Mine it is, then. We'll see you there, then, Constable Shields?"

"You bet." He nodded at Amy over the sullen boy's head.

"You have an identification kit?"

"Yep. That's one reason they sent me."

"Okay, good. See you there."

At the CAS office, Amy and Paul interviewed Timmy. Paul took pictures of the bruise on Timmy's face, holding a ruler up beside the mark to show the width, and then again to show the length of the marks. He put the camera down on the table beside them to write the measurements in his notes. Amy sat across the table, turning to a fresh page in her own notebook.

"Do you want to take pictures of the bruise on my back too?" Timmy shook his head to flick his hair out of his eyes and looked up at Amy.

"What happened to your back?" The police officer set the camera down.

"I have a bruise there from when I drank the last of the orange juice. Dad woke up and was thirsty, but I had just finished the juice, so I had to get punished."

Amy looked at Paul. She was glad she had left the audio and video equipment running while they did the pictures in the interview room.

"Well, you're right, we should probably take a look at that, Timmy," Amy agreed.

Timmy lifted his shirt over his head. Amy watched closely and raised her eyebrows as the child lifted his shirt in front of his face. There were round bruises on his abdomen and bruises on his rib cage extending from under his nipples and under his arms around each side. He pulled the shirt over his head and there were bruises on his back. Amy saw rows of straight lines across the child's back. In a few places the skin had been broken in straight lines and the open wounds were crusty with pus. The skin around these wounds was red and angry looking.

"What happened to your back, Timmy?" Amy kept her voice calm and even.

"Dad hit me with the belt."

"Was that your punishment for drinking the last of the orange juice?"

"Yes."

"How many times did your dad hit you with the belt?"

"I don't remember. It hurt too much to count."

"Timmy, what are the bruises on your stomach from?" Constable Shields asked.

"Oh, that is from when Dad and I were playing. I tried to dodge him, and he punched me. It's our boxing game."

"I see. And what about these bruises here?" the officer pointed to the marks on the child's sides.

Timmy paused before answering, putting a finger to his chin. His eyes lit up as he remembered.

"Oh, Dad was angry that I was in his way. He picked me up and moved me. He grabbed me kinda hard."

"Where was your mom when your dad did that?"

"Oh, she was in the kitchen. She likes to bake and bake and bake. Dad likes cookies and cakes, so Mom bakes to make him happy."

"Timmy. Would you be willing to show us your legs? You would need to take your pants off, but you can leave your underwear on." Constable Shields was picking up his camera again.

"Sure." Timmy dropped his pants with the unembarrassed ease of an eight-year-old. His underwear was pulled down a bit as he lowered his pants, and Amy and the police officer could see the end of the belt marks just beneath the waistband.

The back of Timmy's legs were clear of bruising or suspicious marks. His shins had only a few bruises between the knee and ankle, where you would expect an active eight-year-old boy to be banged up.

"Thanks Timmy. Do you have any marks or bruises anywhere else, besides on your cheek, your tummy, your sides, your back, and these ones on your shins?"

"I don't think so."

"Okay. Can you tell us again where these marks came from? I'm going to take a few pictures as you talk, and I'm going to use the ruler again to show the size of the bruises in the picture, okay?"

"Sure." Timmy recited the story of each bruise, except the ones on his shins. He wasn't sure where he had collected those ones. When the interview and photography was complete, Timmy got dressed and Amy turned off the recording equipment. Paul said that he was going to go to the police station to have a conversation with Timmy's father.

"Okay. He'll probably get mad." Timmy was matter of fact as he gazed up at the officer.

"That's why you're going to stay somewhere else for a little while, Timmy." Paul said. "We need to see what your dad has to say about what happened, but we also need to know that he is not going to get angry with you and leave bruises on you anymore. And we need to talk to your mom about how you got hurt as well."

"Okay. Mom will take his side. When he says I'm too much trouble, she always agrees with him."

"Okay Timmy, well I'm going to go talk to them later today about this. For right now, you are going to stay with Amy, and she will set you up with a safe place while we sort this out."

"Will they have a puppy? We had a puppy, but it died when it woke Dad up. He kicked it in the head instead of the ass. Mom said he meant to kick it in the ass. We didn't get another one."

"When did you have the puppy, Timmy?"

"Oh, a long time ago. I was only little. I named him Happy."

"Okay, Timmy, let's let Constable Shields get on his way. You come with me. We have some backpacks for kids who need to stay with us in a safe place for a few days. They have pajamas and toothbrushes and combs and things like that in them. I'll get you one and you can look and see what's in it while I see where you can stay tonight."

"I'm not staying here with you?" For the first time Timmy looked nervous.

"No, we don't have any beds in this building. Nobody stays here overnight. Sometimes we work late at night like this, but we don't sleep here."

"Oh. I thought you kept kids here."

"Yes, sometimes people think that. Maybe because it's such a big building."

"Maybe." Timmy followed Amy through the security door into the inner offices.

They stopped at a large wooden cabinet in the hallway. Amy opened it and found a backpack labeled 'Boy 6-8'. She handed it to Timmy and led him into her team room.

"Would you like a granola bar, Timmy?"

"Yes, please."

Amy offered the boy a choice of two flavours from the supply in her desk drawer. When he couldn't decide, she gave him one of each. She set him up in a chair and began the process of finding a foster home. Everyone else had gone home for the night, including Rhonda, who had undoubtedly left at four thirty on the dot. It was Friday night, after all, and as the supervisor often exclaimed, "just because I don't have kids doesn't mean I don't have a life outside of work. I leave when the day's done."

So, although Amy would usually have someone else keep an eye on the child while she made the calls, there was no choice tonight.

Maureen Pollard

Chapter 12

Amy called three families and left messages on their voice mail to please call her cell phone. She was relieved when her first call was returned. Donna and Jim Lamont would be her first choice for this battered child.

"Hi, Donna. I have an eight-year-old boy with me. He needs a placement tonight. I would imagine that this one will be a while getting sorted out. He's got some bruises on his face, his back, his sides, and his tummy. He'll need to see a doctor at the clinic tomorrow morning to check him over. The marks on his back look like they might need some attention. Are you able to take him on for the next while?"

Donna knew the code: the child was right there with Amy, so she was not free to talk about any more details. There were multiple injuries and that always meant a court process, so the placement would be at least a week and possibly a month or more.

"We can do that, Amy. What time will you be here?"

"Well, if he and I leave now, I can get him some dinner and bring him up. Maybe six thirty?"

"Don't bother with getting dinner. We just had a ham tonight and there's lots leftover. Does he like ham and mashed potatoes?"

"I don't know. I'll ask." Amy moved the phone away from her face.

"Timmy, do you like ham and mashed potatoes?"

"Yes!" Timmy grinned. "Ham's my favourite!"

"Okay, Donna. Ham is his favourite. I think it's a match," Amy said with a smile as she heard the foster mother laugh.

"Does he have anything?"

"Just a backpack from school and an agency backpack."

Amy motioned to Timmy to come close to her. She checked the tag on his T-shirt. Unlike the oversize sweatshirt, the undershirt fit him well.

"He's about a boy's medium. He's got one outfit on, shoes and a jacket."

"Okay, we've got lots of stuff that size, so he'll be just fine. He can choose some things from my kids' closet to start him off."

This was one reason Donna had been her first choice. This foster mother had been caring for kids for several years. Her own five children were grown and gone. She'd had more than two hundred children through her home in the fifteen years since she'd started fostering. Many stayed just one or two nights. Several stayed for a week or so. A handful stayed more than a year. In fact, Donna had one foster child who had now been with her for five years. Logan was a bright boy and he'd given Donna a run for her money, but she had never given up on him, and they were settled into a good rhythm now. Logan would finish high school the following Spring. Donna had talked about adopting him, but Logan resisted, so they carried on in their fostering relationship and an agency worker visited once a month to check in.

Best Interests

Donna had taken the mudroom of her farmhouse and created a kids' haven. On one wall there were cupboards full of art supplies, board games, musical toys, puzzles, blocks and almost anything else you could imagine.

The opposite wall was one long closet, with organizers inserted so that as you opened each door, shelves or racks greeted you, stacked or lined with children's clothing in all colours and sizes. Arranged by size, the shelves were always full. Donna was given hand-me-downs by many friends in the community, but she also never passed a second-hand store without looking for a bargain. Every item was cleaned and folded and prepared for the closet with the utmost care, so that a child arriving in her home could choose several items in their size, often in their favourite colour. Whatever they chose was theirs to keep.

At the end of the room, there was a floor to ceiling shelf on either side of the door to the backyard. On one side the shelves were filled with books. There were board books on the lowest shelf, picture books and easy readers above that and chapter books that increased in difficulty and maturity as you reached the higher shelves. On the other side, each shelf was filled with stuffed animals and dolls. Every child who stayed with Donna was able to choose books to add to their agency backpack. And every child who stayed with Donna also received a new stuffed friend.

Donna strictly limited children in their choices. She never wanted them to be overwhelmed with material goods and she didn't want to try to show up their parents. But she firmly believed every child should have a few clothes they chose, a book to read and a soft toy friend to hug and love when they were feeling lonely.

Amy told Donna they'd be up to her farm soon. She hung up and helped Timmy gather the items back into his agency backpack. A pair of boy's pajamas. A toothbrush and toothpaste. A brush and a comb. A pair of pants, underwear, socks, and a T-shirt. A colouring book and a box of eight crayons.

When they arrived at the farm it was already dark. A bright light sat atop a pole in the barnyard, throwing a circle of light on the part of the driveway that ran between the house and the barn.

Amy looked at Timmy, who was looking nervous again. Just as Amy was about to speak, Donna came out of the house toward the car. Amy opened her car door.

"You two are just in time! Come on into the barn, there's a calf about to be born!"

Donna opened Timmy's door just before Amy reached it.

Timmy sat in the seat, his back rigid as he looked around him.

"Well, hello there. I'm Donna. This is my farm. My husband, Jim, is in the barn right now helping one of our cows have a baby. My foster son, Logan, is with him too. Logan has lived here for almost six years now. He's in high school."

"Am I going to live here for six years?" Timmy looked up at Amy, who stood beside Donna.

"Oh, I don't think so, Timmy. We're going to try to help your parents sort out their problems first, so that they can look after you without you getting hurt. Donna has lots of children come who just stay here a little while until their parents are ready for them to come home again."

"Okay." Timmy paused. "I've never seen a cow being born before."

"It's pretty cool, Timmy, as long as you don't mind blood. Do you think blood will bother you?"

"Nah. I bled a lot when I fell and cut my forehead and it didn't bother me at all."

"Okay, well let's go see how that cow's doing."

They arrived in the barn just in time to watch a baby calf starting to emerge from the mother cow as she lay on the floor of her stall. A tall man knelt beside the cow. He wore long rubber gloves that went up almost to his armpits. He murmured softly to the cow and watched closely as first the hooves, then the head of the calf slipped out. A teenager stood beside him, also wearing the long rubber gloves. The two waited as the cow heaved and pushed again. A second later the calf slipped out of her, followed by the fluids of birth. The cow stood and began to nuzzle and clean her newborns as they lay in the hay on the barn floor.

"Wow. She licks them clean? That's grosser than when my mom spits on her finger to clean my cheek."

"Well, now, I guess it seems that way to us, but to the mama cow it's just how she takes care of her baby." Donna smiled. "Timmy, shall we take your things inside now and get you a plate of that ham?"

"Yes, please!"

Amy and Donna led Timmy to the farmhouse, leaving Jim and Logan to look after the chores in the barn now that the calf had safely arrived.

Donna pulled two foil-covered plates out of the oven. She set them at the table, one in front of Timmy and one in front of Amy.

"Thank you, Donna." Amy lifted the foil off her plate and inhaled the scent of ham, mashed potatoes, and corn niblets. It had been months since Amy had eaten a home-cooked meal she hadn't prepared herself. The feeling of being cared for warmed her, and suddenly she realized how tired and hungry she was.

"Thank you." Timmy copied Amy's motions removing his own foil and picking up his fork.

Amy and Timmy both made short work of the delicious hot meal. Amy provided Donna with a copy of the paperwork, a few forms she had completed and printed while she waited to confirm Timmy's placement in a foster home. After a short chat, Amy left so Donna could take Timmy on a quick tour of his temporary home. His eyes were starting to droop now that the food was settling in his belly. Amy's were too for that matter, and she was happy to head home knowing the bruised boy would be well cared for.

Maureen Pollard

Chapter 13

Weekends always passed quickly. Amy filled them with painting, quilting, and writing. She usually planned to stay in both days, wrapping herself in the solitude of her comfortable house in the woods. She ran her errands during the week so she could soak in the quiet. Any three-day weekend made her feel grateful for the extra down time, rather than a chance to get involved in community activities.

Right now, she was working on a baby quilt for one of the girls on Phil's team. Her sewing machine hummed away as she fed the fabric through it, guiding the material with one hand on either side of the needle. The tension in her forehead faded as her hands followed the familiar motions and she concentrated on the line of stitches. When her cell phone began to buzz, she ignored it. When the buzzing stopped, her shoulders relaxed. Only for a moment though because the buzzing began again.

"What now? What could it possibly be on a Saturday?" Amy asked herself. When the buzzing began again, she gave up on the quilt and picked up her phone.

"Amy Malloy speaking," she snapped without looking at the number.

"Hello, Amy Malloy. Am I interrupting something?" The voice on the other end of the line was familiar.

"Evan." Amy sighed with relief. "I wasn't going to answer. I thought it was work."

"Nope. It's play calling this time," Evan said.

Amy could almost see the twinkle in his eye shining through the tone of his voice.

"Listen, I have two tickets to go see that band you like."

"Which band is that?"

"The trio from Newfoundland you love. They're playing at the Grand Theatre tonight at seven. Would you like to go with me?"

"Evan Grant, are you asking me on a date?"

"Yes. Unless that makes you uncomfortable. Then it's just a friendly outing."

"Somehow I knew you wouldn't give up that easily. Evan, it's been a long week…"

"I know. That's why I thought this might be just the thing."

"Maybe you could ask Paul?" Amy tried.

"Nope, he's at his kid's piano recital. Anyway, this is your kind of music, and we all know that music soothes the soul. Unless your tastes have changed since the last time we talked. Besides, I know you're not that tired. I've seen you too many times on the court at night to believe you're out of energy."

"Fine. A friendly outing. Because I love that band."

"Music to my ears," Evan said. "I'll pick you up for supper at five thirty. And don't tell me you can drive yourself. This whole evening is on me. After all, I missed your last birthday."

"Evan!"

"Seriously. I'll see you at five thirty," Evan said, hanging up before Amy could argue.

Staring at the phone in her hand, Amy grinned. Evan was relentless. Thoughtful, but relentless.

Still grinning, Amy went back to work on the baby quilt, finishing it up before the afternoon was out. She tidied her workspace, and then took a shower.

At five thirty on the nose, she watched Evan's pickup truck come up her driveway. She smiled. He was much better at being on time than she was. She was ready though. She tossed Wiley a bone and told him she would be out late tonight, then stepped out on her porch and locked her door.

Evan met her at the stairs and offered her his arm.

"I'm not taking your arm to walk across my driveway, Grant." Amy stared at him before she strode over to the vehicle.

"Suit yourself. It will be good to get out and have a little fun, don't you think? I mean, I like our squash games, but they sometimes feel more like a kind of debrief than actual downtime."

"I know what you mean. Like a physical escape valve for the tension of the week," Amy agreed. "So that kind of makes it a part of work, in a way."

The ride to the theatre in the next town was comfortable. Evan stopped teasing her, and they both relaxed. At one point he turned the radio on, and as a song ended, the announcer began reporting the news. "Local police conducted a pre-dawn raid this morning, seizing…" Evan quickly changed the channel and a rhythmic bass line vibrated in the cab before he turned the volume down. Amy looked over at Evan. She'd always found him interesting. He was a good cop, but he was also more than who he was on the job. She was curious about him, and although she rarely asked her friends personal questions because she didn't want them to think she was "social working" them, her curiosity got the better of her.

"So, Evan, what made you choose police work? I don't think we've ever talked about it."

Evan smiled at her, then returned his eyes to the road as he began to talk.

145

"The truth is, I was headed for some trouble when I started high school. It was just after my parents' divorce, and I was angry. There was a police officer attached to our school, there once or twice a week. He got me to join an after-school basketball league and ran me hard at practices. Then, he'd give me a ride home. I don't remember how long it took, but I do remember the first day I just started talking. I told him everything. My parents and their fights, how much I hated going back and forth between their houses, never knowing what I would find. He just listened and kept driving until I started to wind down. That was when he told me it was up to me what I did with my life. I could stay angry and get into trouble, or I could choose to deal with it by making something better for my own future."

"Wow," Amy said. "He sounds like a really great guy."

"He is. We keep in touch. He's been retired a few years now, and he's got a place out east where he spends his summers, so I don't see him as often now. We do get together when he's back in Ontario for the winter."

As they pulled into the parking lot near the theatre, Amy thought about that school cop and how his compassion for one angry teen had made such a difference in the world. And the angry teen became a cop with compassion who was also making a difference in the world.

The tickets were great. Somehow, Evan had managed to get front row seats. Amy sang along with every song and when the strains of one of her favourite ballads began, she grabbed Evan's hand and whispered that she loved this song. He kept her hand fitted warmly in his and watched her as she closed her eyes and listened as the sweet harmonies of the trio filled the auditorium with the words Amy found so powerful.

When the concert was over, Evan drove her home. Amy sang the whole way, regaling him with her own version of the songs the band had played. He just smiled, enjoying her happiness.

Evan parked his truck. Amy turned to face him.

"I had a really good time at the concert. Thanks." She smiled, suddenly feeling shy with her friend.

"I'm glad you liked it. I had a really good time, too." He leaned toward her, but she moved swiftly to open the truck door and jump out.

"Okay, then. See you Wednesday for squash?" Amy asked, safely on the driveway.

"Yes. See you Wednesday for squash." Evan smiled ruefully. "Sleep well, Amy."

"Goodnight, Evan. Thanks again!" She called as she ran up her steps to open her door. He waited and watched until she was safely inside with Wiley, who greeted her enthusiastically. As she patted the dog's big head with the hand that had grabbed Evan's hand earlier, she smiled. She was starting to get used to feeling her heart flutter a little at the thought of him. She'd have to give some thought to what that might mean.

Amy drove into work Monday morning, listening to music to distract herself from mentally reviewing the tasks that would consume her as soon as she pulled into the agency parking lot. She would be immersed in her to-do list soon enough, so on the drive she sang along to her music.

"Morning, Maeve," Amy greeted the receptionist, who was almost always the first one in the building.

"Morning, Amy. Have a good weekend?"

"Glorious. You?"

"Excellent. The grandkids were a blast. Of course."

"Of course! Have a muffin." Amy opened the container of still-warm baked goods she was carrying and tilted it toward the receptionist.

"Ah, I do love Muffin Mondays!" Maeve said.

Amy walked through the building, and into her team room. She put the muffins on the counter by Janet's workstation, then stopped at her desk long enough to turn on her computer so it would be up and running when she came back from the break room with her coffee. She nodded at Rhonda, who didn't like anyone to talk to her before nine in the morning. She got to the office a few minutes after eight, went into her office and closed the door, only opening it again after nine. Amy rolled her eyes as Rhonda's door banged shut.

"Every day. Every. Single. Day," Amy said to Tanya as she walked into the team room from the corridor.

"She's started to keep it closed until nine fifteen on Mondays and Fridays now," Tanya replied, tilting her head in the direction of Rhonda's closed door as she took a muffin for herself.

"Wow," Amy said. She wasn't surprised, really. But she couldn't think of anything else to say. She sometimes wondered if Rhonda's attitude was a front, but then she would remember their conversations. On reflection, she realized that Rhonda showed people just who she was: someone who didn't care much for people.

"Do you have any visits that you need to schedule this week? I heard you had an apprehension Friday afternoon." Tanya followed Amy as she carried her coffee back to her desk.

"I will. Do you happen to know if there's a room available?"

"I checked for you," Tanya said. "Room three is open Wednesday and Thursday after two. I can book it for you."

"That would be great. The family name is Rankin. Timothy and Lynn are the parents. Timmy is their eight-year-old. Please make it Wednesday. Court's Thursday, and who knows if it'll be heard and over by two."

"Got it," Tanya replied as she headed back to the reception desk to book the room.

The computer screen was on, and Amy logged in. She checked her email. Nothing urgent this morning, just a few updates from the afterhours workers about inquiries from some of the people on her caseload. She checked her voice mail. Lila had called with a message that Amanda seemed off over the weekend. Nothing Lila could put her finger on, just not quite right. Amy copied the message into a case note form.

Amy sipped her coffee as she scanned her calendar entries for the day. It would be a fairly routine day. She would start with her unannounced visit to Phil's seven-year-old. See how they made out over the weekend, knowing Phil would be away. Then, she supposed she might as well do the home visit to check on that infant. There was the Somani family over on the edge of town that she'd scheduled a final visit with before closing the file. Conflict between worried parents and their defiant teenager was mostly resolved after a few sessions with Amy. Resolved for now, anyway. She would drop by to check on Faye and Justin on the way to her last stop this afternoon.

Amy looked at the rest of her week. She looked ahead and decided she could have her seven-day visit with Timmy at Donna and Jim's on Thursday. She could drive him to the foster home after the supervised visit with his parents. The interviews with the parents had not gone well Friday night at the police station. Timmy's father was charged with assault. Two counts of assault causing bodily harm and one count of aggravated assault. Timmy's mother had been charged with failure to provide the necessities of life. She had clearly known about the assaults and hadn't done anything to protect her young son. On top of that, she had not taken Timmy for medical care when the wounds on his back got infected.

Amy shook her head. She knew it was complicated. People lived with abuse and violence for many reasons. Sometimes, they had grown up with violence and didn't know any different. Sometimes they had other problems, like addiction and mental health issues that interfered with their ability to protect their children. Still, she was not sure she would ever really understand how a parent could choose to shield an abuser rather than protect the child.

Amy shut her computer down and gathered up her notepad and briefcase. She threw her standard granola bar in her bag. If she didn't get a chance to stop for lunch, at least she would have something. She signed out of the office for the day, with her planned home visits noted.

The first visit was easy. The seven-year-old was dressed and eating a piece of toast. He would be on time for school this morning. Mom looked tired, but not hungover. There was no smell of stale booze on her, and no empty bottles in the kitchen or on the porch beside the garbage. Good enough, for today.

Amy drove over to Faye's house. Justin met her on the porch. His eyes were sad.

"Hey, Justin. How is she today?"

"Not very good, Amy. It hurt a lot today, she said."

Amy set the box of food down on the top step and held her arms out. Justin hesitated, then stepped forward. She wrapped him in a hug, holding him as he shook with sobs. She didn't say anything, though her own tears flowed. They stayed this way for several minutes, as gradually, Justin's crying subsided.

"I'm sorry, Amy." Justin pulled away and looked at the ground as he wiped at his eyes with the back of his hands.

"Never be sorry for how you feel, Justin. This matters. Your love for your mom matters. Her being so sick matters. It's okay to cry when you feel so sad." Amy put her hands on his shoulders. The boy looked up and saw that her cheeks were wet with tears, too. The corner of his mouth turned up as he tried to smile, but he wasn't successful, so he bent down and picked up the box of food.

"She's still eating the soup, at least. I think it's just because she feels like she has to if I cook it, though."

"You're doing a good job, Justin. Better than some grown-ups I know could do. She's proud of you, and she loves you very much."

"I know. She tells me every day. She said she isn't up to a visit today, but if you come back Friday, she might be up for a cup of tea."

"Okay, Justin. You know how to get a hold of me if you need me." Amy paused. "You're missing more school. Like today."

"Yeah. Some days she needs me to help her get to the bathroom. I can't leave her alone when it's that bad."

"I know." Amy touched his shoulder. "I know, kiddo."

Amy thought about the lack of home care assistance. Amy tried to fill the gap a little bit, but she really wasn't equipped to do more than show up for a visit with some food. She really hoped Rich Mahood would be able to connect a friendly visitor with the family soon.

She gave Justin a hug before getting in her car. She waved to him as she pulled away from the curb.

At the next house, Amy knocked firmly on the door. Her usual routine, with four firm raps. She heard shuffling sounds behind the door, but no one answered it. She knocked again. The door opened just enough to reveal a pale face partially covered by stringy black bangs that hung down, shielding the eyes.

"Sonya? I'm Amy Malloy. Here from CAS. I'm here to see you and Felix while Phil's on vacation."

The young woman shuffled backward and opened the door a little wider, though not wide enough for Amy to step into the apartment.

"He's asleep."

"That's okay. I still need to come in and see him, Sonya. I think Phil probably told you we need to come in every three days?"

"Yeah. Whatever." Sonya flicked her greasy bangs to the side, but they fell right back over her eyes. She shrugged bony shoulders and walked over to sit on the couch.

She left the door opened when she turned and retreated into the apartment. Amy pushed it open further, stepped in, and then closed the door softly behind her. The apartment was dark, with blinds drawn and no lights on. It was a two-bedroom apartment. Both bedroom doors were closed.

Amy looked around. As her eyes adjusted to the dimness, she noticed that the place was relatively tidy. A few pop cans and beer bottles on the table. A chip bag on the wide arm of the couch. Two socks pulled off and left lying inside out on the floor in front of the big screen television.

"Sonya, how are you feeling since the baby's been born?" Amy peered at the young woman sitting in this dark space.

"I'm tired. I can't seem to get enough sleep. I just slept for twelve hours, and I still feel tired." Sonya yawned, as if to prove her point.

"Have you mentioned it to the doctor?" Amy asked, wondering if the woman's iron levels had been checked lately. Low iron could cause fatigue like this.

"The doctor only really cares about the baby."

"Ah. I think you should mention the fatigue next time and ask the doctor to do some blood work."

"Yeah, I guess maybe that's a good idea."

"Which room is the baby's?"

"Second door. Go ahead in if you want." Sonya sat on the couch, used the remote to turn the television on. She stared at the talk show that filled the screen. It was one of those over-the-top reality dramas.

"Okay. Is Brian home?"

"No. He left early this morning. He had a job lined up and we need the money."

"Ah. Okay. Do you have anyone else to help you, since you're feeling so ill and sleeping so much?"

"No, there's no one. Brian tries to help when he's home, but he's tired too. He works as much as he can."

Amy thought about calling the health unit to connect the family with the well-baby program. Their volunteers might be able to offer some support here. She made her way down the short hall to the second door. She opened it and peered into the room. This room was bright with sunlight. There was no blind on the window. There were no decorations at all, in fact. The crib was against the far wall. Aside from that, there was a box on the floor that held baby clothes. A bag of diapers and a container of wet wipes lay beside the box. There was not a toy, nor any speck of cheer in the room at all. No suggestion that this baby was welcome and loved.

Amy approached the crib. She peered in. The baby was swaddled in a receiving blanket. His head was covered with a knitted hat. Almost none of his face was showing, but as Amy took the last step up to the crib, she could see that his lips were a dusky blue colour. She felt her heart leap into her throat and her rapid pulse throbbed as the blood rushed through her system with the adrenaline.

Amy laid her fingertips gently on the baby's cheek. He was cold. Too cold. Too blue. Took off the hat. The baby's fontanel was sunken. His eyes, now that she could see them, were sunken too. This baby had starved to death.

Amy looked out the window at the grey fall sky and tried to slow her heartbeat as she reminded herself to breathe. She took her cell phone out.

"911. What's your emergency?"

"I have a baby. Felix. Four months old. Vital signs absent. I'm at three twenty-two Cherry Lane, apartment two oh one."

"Do you need an ambulance?"

"I'm not sure. He looks as if he's been gone a while."

"What's your name?"

"Amy Malloy. I'm a CAS worker."

"Okay, Amy. Is anyone else there?"

"Yes, the mother is here. Sonya Wells. Her boyfriend is out. Brian Keeler."

"Are there any other children?"

"No, he was the only child."

"I'm sending an ambulance. Can you tell if he has a pulse?"

"He has no pulse. His fontanel is sunken and so are his eyes. His lips are blue. His skin is cold to the touch. I've never seen a baby with such dry skin."

"Okay, Amy. Help is on the way."

"Sure."

Amy stood beside the crib, stroking the small, cold cheek with her fingers. She stayed this way when she heard banging on the apartment door, heard the paramedics asking Sonya where the baby was.

"What do you mean you got a call about a baby? Who the fuck called you?" Sonya's voice rose in the hallway.

"Are you Amy?" The paramedic was pulling on blue nitrile gloves. She looked at Amy, then glanced into the crib.

"Yes. I'm the CAS worker. I came to check the baby." Amy didn't look away from the window, her hand still resting on the baby's cool cheek.

"Okay, Amy. My partner's going to take you to the living room and ask some questions." The paramedic touched Amy's arm. "I'll take care of him now."

Amy turned finally to look at the paramedic. She glanced down at Felix one more time, then lifted her fingers from his face. She allowed herself to be led out to the living room.

Sonya was back sitting on the couch and staring at the television. As Amy and the second paramedic reached the living room, Evan Grant walked through the door into the apartment.

"Amy? Are you all right?" He peered into her face in the dim light.

"Fine. I'm fine. The baby is not fine, though. Not fine at all. Three days was too many days."

"What are you talking about?" Evan stepped close to her, his hand coming up to grasp her elbow.

"Every three days. The judge said to give them a chance. The supervisor said visiting more than every three days would be too intrusive." Amy's brow furrowed. "Three days was too many days."

Amy gave her head a shake. "I should call Rhonda." She was going to have to pull herself together. There was going to be a lot to do.

Evan watched Amy. She looked away from him as she pulled out her notebook and cell phone, preparing to call into the office to report the news and to get directions about what to do next.

"You okay?" He asked, squeezing the elbow she hadn't realized he still lightly held.

"I'm okay. I'll be okay." Amy dialed her cell phone.

"Hey, somebody's going to need to call the coroner," the first paramedic called from the bedroom. The second paramedic stepped into the living room to make the call to Dr. Thayer on his cell phone.

Constable Paul Shields entered from the hallway.

"Hey, Grant. What do you need me to do?"

"Thayer's just been called. We're going to need forensics here to go over the place. That's the baby's mother on the couch. Hasn't moved or spoken since I've been here."

"Okay. There a dad around?"

"She said her boyfriend left early this morning for work," Amy reported as she waited for her supervisor to answer the phone. She checked her watch. It was after nine fifteen now, so surely Rhonda would pick up.

Paul moved to stand beside the couch. He started to ask Sonya questions about what had been happening in the apartment over the last twenty-four hours. Evan moved into the baby's bedroom to see what was happening in there.

"Rhonda Selleck speaking."

"Rhonda, it's Amy."

"What the hell is wrong with you? You sound like you've got a frog in your throat."

Amy cleared her throat.

"Rhonda, I'm at the apartment of Sonya Wells and Brian Keeler. The failure to thrive baby I'm covering for Phil."

"Yes." Amy could hear Rhonda's fingers drumming on the desktop.

"Rhonda, the baby's dead. Paramedics are here, and they've called the coroner."

"Shit." The drumming sound stopped. "Shit. Shit. Shit."

"Police are here too. Mom's in the apartment and they're talking to her now. The boyfriend was out. At work, she said."

"Fine. The coroner is going to do his thing. The police are going to do theirs. See if you can sit in on the interviews."

"They are not going to let me sit in. Not on a death investigation. I might be able to watch in the video room."

"Do that, then. Call me when both of them have been interviewed."

"Okay. Can you have someone call the Somani family, that parent-teen conflict file I'm ready to close, and let them know I'll have to reschedule our appointment this afternoon?"

"Look. I'm going to have to go talk to Kent about this. We'll need to make a serious occurrence report, and he has to sign it." Kent Nakahara was the Executive Director of Green Valley Children's Aid Society. He needed to be notified if there was any serious occurrence, and a dead child was right at the top of the list of serious occurrences. "You just call back and talk to Rosa. Ask her to call that family." Rhonda had never bothered to learn how to transfer a call, so she couldn't transfer Amy directly to her teammate. Amy heard the click as Rhonda ended the call.

"What the hell is going on in here?" Amy guessed Brian was home.

"Are you Brian Keeler?" Paul Shields asked the young man who stormed into the apartment.

"Who wants to know?" Amy registered the belligerent tone. She recognized Brian's kind of fear-based hostility. It was a pretty common stress response for vulnerable parents who faced the powerful and sometimes unpredictable authority of police and the child welfare system.

"Constable Paul Shields, Green Valley Police. Are you Brian Keeler?" The officer brought himself to his full height as he moved to stand before the angry young man.

"Yeah. So, what if I am? What the fuck is going on here?"

"We had a call about Felix."

"Somebody call because he was crying again? Babies cry, for chrissakes."

"No. The baby wasn't crying," Constable Shields said.

"What then?" some of the bluster left the young man's voice.

"Felix isn't breathing. The paramedics are in there now."

"Well, hell." Brian looked at Sonya, who was still sitting on the couch staring at the television, although she had turned the volume down.

"He's gone, babe," Sonya said in a quiet voice. A tear rolled down her cheek as she covered her eyes with one hand.

"Well, hell." Still surly, but with less fire in his voice, Brian looked at the cop.

"We're going to have some questions for you. Both of you." Constable Shields looked from Brian to Sonya. "Let me check with my partner first. Then we'll leave for the police station for questioning."

Paul and Evan spoke quietly in the baby's bedroom. After a moment, Paul came back to the living room.

"Constable Grant is going to wait for Dr. Thayer to arrive," Paul told Sonya and Brian. You both need to come to the police station with me."

"Amy, you should come to the station now, too."

Amy knew the coroner would examine the scene, then take the baby to the morgue for examination. Knowing this was going to be the case, the paramedics had not moved Felix from where he lay when they found Amy stroking his cheek.

Amy did as directed. As she drove to the police station following the cruiser, she called the office and asked Rosa to call the Somani family. Once at the station, she was settled in the small room that held the video monitors and there she watched Paul Shields interview first Sonya, then Brian. Amy took notes as she sat in a hard chair at the small desk in the video viewing room where the officers made copies of the recordings they took of interviews. Sometimes she glanced at the images on the screen, but mostly she listened and kept her eyes on her page as she wrote.

The interviews weren't terribly long. Sonya walked them through the last three days, and then Brian did. Sonya repeated what she had already told Amy about feeling tired and sleeping a lot. Brian asked them what he was supposed to do, since someone had to work to pay the bills and he did check on the baby sometimes, but he was tired, too. When asked directly about what care Felix received, Sonya said he had cried all morning Saturday, then finally fell back asleep and slept through the rest of the weekend. She'd been so tired herself she had hardly moved off the couch.

Amy closed her eyes and lowered her head as tears slid down her cheeks, though she was silent. She moved her notes so the tears wouldn't land on her paperwork and blur her writing.

When the interviews were done, Amy went back to her office. She spent the rest of the afternoon entering her notes into the system. Waves of anger and despair rolled through her as she checked that all of her t's were crossed and i's were dotted. They did not have any other children now, but they were very young. She wanted to ensure nothing prevented Sonya and Brian from being registered on the Child Abuse Registry. They were both being charged with failure to provide the necessities of life. For the moment, Amy focused her attention on blaming the parents, ignoring the ways the system had failed them, too.

When she shut her computer down, Amy took her headphones off. The office was quiet. She looked and sure enough, it was after four thirty. She packed up her bag and headed out, past Rhonda's door. Her supervisor was gone, too. No early mornings for Rhonda Selleck, and no late nights, either. Amy didn't bother to hold back the tears.

Amy left town, headed home on the lonely country roads. At her house, she pulled into her driveway. She could barely wait to get into the house and take Wiley into her arms so she could sob freely as Justin had cried while she held him. Wiley was waiting, and he sat patiently as she dropped to the top step of the porch and clung to him, occasionally licking Amy's cheek to catch the tears.

Full moon time was always busy. Amy knew a lot of people thought it was nonsense, but she had worked with people long enough to know that in fact there is a rhythm to crisis work that regularly involved a spike in incidents in the days surrounding the arrival of the full moon in the sky. She was staring at the moon through her living room window as she lay on her couch with Wiley beside her when the knock on the door startled her. She had not bothered to undress, eat, or bathe.

She had sobbed until she had nothing left, then she had pulled herself from the porch to her couch and stared up and out at the night sky, wondering what else this week might bring. It was only Monday, after all. Who could be at her door?

Wiley stood on alert but didn't bark. Amy walked over to the door and peered through the window as she turned on her porch light. It was Evan. She opened the door.

"You scared the hell out of me. Come in," Amy said. Evan walked into the house, and she closed and locked the door behind him.

"Amy. I'm so sorry," Evan said. He opened his arms up, and Amy stepped into them. As he wrapped her in a powerful hug, she felt more sobs welling up in her, tearing out of the space in her heart she had thought was empty. He didn't say anything, just held her as she cried. Wiley went back to his spot by the window and lay down again.

"I'm sorry," Amy said when she could speak again. She pulled back from his chest to look up at him. "I seem to have gotten your sweater wet."

"You did. It's okay," Evan said. She leaned into his chest, as if she were trying to absorb his strength. He raised a hand to wipe away her tears, and then handed her a tissue and waited while she blew her nose. They went to the couch and sat down, side by side.

"That was awful," Amy said.

"Yes. It was." Evan waited.

"I should have gone on Friday."

"Phil went on Friday, remember? This was not your fault."

"It feels like my fault."

"That's because you found him. That's going to take a while to process. It was not your fault, and it wasn't Phil's fault, either."

"He was so tiny. So beautiful." Amy's chin quivered again, and Evan pulled her to him.

"Yes. He was."

"I don't understand."

"I don't think anyone ever does," Evan said.

Amy looked up at him. He was looking back at her. She felt that flutter again. The one that she'd felt thinking about holding his hand at the concert. He lowered his head and met his lips gently with hers. She didn't withdraw this time. She leaned into him, and he deepened the kiss. He laced his fingers together with hers, and she pulled him up from the couch, moving toward her bedroom door.

"Amy, are you sure?"

"Yes. Please." She tugged his hand gently.

He followed her into her room.

Amy let go of his hands long enough to pull her shirt off and undo her jeans. She pressed back up against his chest, pushing his shirt up so that she could feel his warm skin against hers. He raised his arms so she could pull his shirt off too, then brought his hands back down to rest on her hips.

"Amy, are you sure? We can stop. I'll still be here tomorrow, and the next day. We can pick this up anytime. It shouldn't be now if you're not sure."

"I don't want to stop. I'm sure." Amy worked the buckle on his belt, then the button and zipper. They slid easily to the floor and Amy rubbed her cheek against his skin as she stood back up to embrace him once more. Evan lifted her onto her bed, and slid her jeans down over her hips, dropping them to the floor beside his own. They came together tenderly. Afterward, Amy pulled herself up so she could kiss him again. Finally, she settled, resting her head on his chest.

"I didn't come here for this. I came here to make sure you were okay," Evan said.

"I know. I'm glad you came. And that was amazing."

"For me, too," Evan said, shifting her in his left arm so that her head rested on his shoulder as he pulled the blankets up with his right hand. "I think I love you, Amy."

"Nah. That was just a reaction to our brush with death." Amy snuggled into him even as she dismissed their intimacy with her comments. "People think there are only three responses to trauma—fight, flight, or freeze. There are really five. Those three, plus feed and fornicate."

"Maybe. I still think I love you," Evan said, a mischievous smile playing at the sides of his mouth. But we can agree to disagree if we can do that again sometime."

"Maybe." Amy smiled sleepily. She knew better than to make any promises. But she would hang onto him tonight and worry about what would happen next later. Much later, she thought as she yawned and closed her eyes.

Maureen Pollard

Chapter 14

Amy started awake, her heart racing. She sat up and took a deep breath as she got her bearings. Home. She was in her bedroom. She stretched her hand out, expecting to feel Wiley's coarse hair and warm breath. Her heart jumped a little when she felt an arm instead, and then she remembered Evan. Last night.

"Amy?" Evan mumbled as he rolled to face her.

"I just had a dream." Amy focused on slowing her breath, staring at the ceiling although she left her hand where it had landed on his arm.

"Bad one?"

Just the usual. It happens once a week or so. I usually just hug Wiley until I calm down. I'm holding a baby, running up a stairwell. Footsteps pounding behind me. Gaining on me. Then I wake up."

"That's the usual?" Evan asked.

"Well, sometimes it's a toddler I'm carrying, or a bigger kid and I'm holding their hand, pulling them with me. But the stupid stairwell is always the same. And the footsteps. And the feeling that I'm not going to be able to escape. After yesterday, that dream feels too real."

"Ah." Evan pulled her into his arms. "Yesterday, one of the things you fear most came to life."

Amy didn't say anything else. She listened to his slowing breath as he drifted back to sleep. She stared at the ceiling and tried to think about anything but work. Every time she closed her eyes, she saw Felix's blue lips and sunken features. She knew she was done with sleep, but by the look of the light under the curtains it was almost time to get up anyway.

When Evan was snoring, she slipped out of his arms. Pulling on her robe she headed to her writing desk in the spare room down the hall. She sat there, looking at the paper. Her mind skittered around from image to image. She didn't think she could write about it yet.

She pulled a writing prompt book from the shelf beside her desk and flipped through the pages until she found a prompt she could work with.

Write a scene about sound and fury.

Amy wrote about the rattle of windows as furious winds blew, flashes of lightning illuminating a dark room, thunder cracking and rolling nearby as rain pounded a steady rhythm on a tin roof. She set her pen down several pages later. It wasn't what she needed to express, but it would do for now.

She headed to the kitchen to make coffee, surprised to see how much time had passed. Evan was already there and handed her a mug.

"Here you go. Scrambled or over easy?"

"Over easy, if you can do it without breaking the yolk," Amy said.

"You've got it."

Amy sat at the table, watching his back as he deftly flipped eggs, timing them perfectly and finishing just as the toast popped up. He hummed to himself, and she thought she recognized the tune, but she couldn't quite put her finger on it.

"Listen, about last night," Amy began as he turned toward the table with their plates.

"It's okay. I know. You're not looking for more from our relationship. I get it."

"Evan."

"Amy. We'll just carry on with our plans for squash, and it will be fine. I'll behave. I promise."

Amy just sighed as he set her plate down at the table.

"Now, eat. You'll need your strength today."

He was right about that. There was more paperwork to process and an affidavit to be written. She ate, even though she wasn't hungry, because she knew he was right.

At her desk, after a few hours of intense focus, Amy stopped typing and stretched her neck, rolling her chin down and across her chest before rolling it up again on the other side. It didn't really help the knot in her neck, so she stood up and stretched her shoulders, too. Maybe it was time for a break.

Kiyana and Tanya were in the break room when Amy walked over to the coffee.

"I don't think Kent has any idea what hours the supervisors keep," Kiyana said.

"It's true," Tanya said. "If he's not in Toronto at meetings, he's holed up in the board room with committees or community partners."

"You think he'd take a walk around the place at four thirty sometime, and maybe notice that it's the people making the least money who are still here working late most of the time."

"Yeah. Rhonda's one of the worst for that, right Amy?" Tanya asked. "And even when she's here she shuts her door so no one will bother her with the messy little details of the work."

"Amy?" Kiyana prompted.

165

"What?" Amy looked up from her coffee cup as she continued to stir in the milk and sugar.

"You haven't heard a word we've said, have you?" Kiyana shook her head. "You're in a bad way. You should have taken the day off."

"Too much paperwork left. Besides, if I were home, I would just sit there reliving yesterday, so I might as well be here getting my affidavit done."

"Well, that's true. We all know it. The forms must go on!" Tanya said.

Tanya raised her mug in a mock salute as Amy carried her coffee out of the break room. On another day, this flippant gesture might have amused Amy, or irritated her, depending on the context. Today, Amy didn't acknowledge it. She hardly even saw it. She didn't care what schedule the supervisors were keeping, or whether Kent noticed that most of them arrived just in time and left at four thirty on the nose. She would have joined in with her own gripes about Rhonda just thirty-six hours ago, but now a baby was dead, and Amy didn't care about any of the office politics at all.

At her desk she raised her mug in both hands, feeling the warmth. She inhaled deeply; eyes closed. She listened to the conversations of her co-workers.

Matt and Ella were planning a playdate with Leigh Ann for Saturday morning. The three families hung out together often on Saturday mornings. The dads hung out with the toddlers in the yard or the basement, depending on the weather. The moms sat in the kitchen or living room bouncing babies on their laps while exchanging tips and horror stories about breastfeeding and sleep training.

"There's an end-of-season sale at Shaw's Greenhouse," Rosa said.

"Oh, let's go after work. I want to get some burlap to wrap the hedge for winter," Jyoti replied.

"Amy, do you want to come with us to Shaw's today?" Rosa asked, peaking around the cubicle wall into Amy's workspace.

"No, thanks."

"Aw, come on," Rosa coaxed.

"I'm not feeling like gardening and anything that's on sale is going to need to be planted soon," Amy said.

"Amy, you shouldn't be alone so much this week."

"I'm fine," Amy said.

"Amy…"

"I'm fine. Really."

"Suit yourself. If you change your mind, we'll leave here just after four thirty."

"Thank you." Amy closed her eyes and took a sip of her cooling coffee. She'd need to stay late anyway to double-check her paperwork and look over her files. She was going to step up the schedule of home visits with some of the families with young children, and she needed some uninterrupted time at her desk to rework her calendar.

Maureen Pollard

Chapter 15

Amy started coming into the office at seven. She was up by five every morning, and after writing, working out, and showering, she ran out of things to occupy her at home. So, she came to work.

Most nights she was falling asleep on the couch after dinner. She'd jolt awake from a bad dream about Felix and pace for a while. She tried reading but couldn't find a book that would hold her attention. She tried music, but her usual favourites just weren't soothing her the way they used to.

So, she would lay in bed, staring at her ceiling, with images of the baby's blue lips playing in her mind.

Phil came back from vacation. When she saw him come around the corner into her cubicle, she hung her head in shame.

"Amy." Phill had gripped her shoulders and brought her to her feet. He hugged her, until she stopped standing so rigidly and finally hugged him back.

"Amy, I'm so sorry."

"No, Phil, I'm the one who's sorry. I didn't do a very good job of covering for you."

"Amy. It wasn't your fault."

"Three days was too long, Phil."

"Look at me," he said, then waited.

Finally, she looked up at him. There was no revulsion or anger in his eyes as she'd imagined there would be. Just pain and compassion.

"Amy, three days was too long, but that was never your decision. You did exactly as you were asked. This was not your fault. It was just dumb luck that you were the one there that morning instead of me."

"Oh Phil, it was awful."

"I can only imagine. Listen, let's go for a walk." Phil led Amy outside, and they walked around the block as she filled him in on the details. He just listened, occasionally nodding.

"I can't tell you how much of a relief it is to tell someone everything," Amy said as she finished the story.

"You haven't told anyone?"

"No. Rhonda would rather not know more than she needs to. And I didn't want to lay this on anyone else."

"Amy, you can't keep this shit in. You've got to get it off your chest."

"Well, it definitely feels better for the moment, anyway," Amy agreed. "We'll see if it helps me sleep tonight."

"Well, if it doesn't, try getting up and writing everything that's running through your mind. Don't worry if it doesn't make sense, and don't worry if it's not spelled right. Just write it all out on the page. It can help. There was a guy who did a study on it. Pennebaker. They found that writing about trauma can help people recover."

"I do write. I write all the time."

"I know. But when you're upset, write about the trauma, Amy. Not just for the sake of writing, and not your usual short stories. Those are great, but save them for another time," Phil said.

"Maybe. I haven't got anything to lose by trying."

They headed back to the office, and made plans for lunch the next week, when Phil had a chance to get caught up on his other cases.

Amy went into the lunchroom and put the kettle on to boil. As she stared out the window, she listened to the conversation around the table. Rosa and Jyoti were talking, and their raised voices caught her attention.

"Well, I couldn't believe it when he just stood there lying to my face. The evidence was right in front of me, and he could see that. Still, he tried to lie," Jyoti exclaimed.

"You know, maybe there's something to what Rhonda says about how you can't cure stupid, but stupid is what keeps us in business."

"Well, when someone tries to pull something like that, I have to wonder," Jyoti agreed.

Amy turned to face her teammates. She saw them laughing, and she thought about Sonya, who probably had a mental health problem like post-partum depression. She thought about Amanda, who seemed to have everything going for her as a youth—loving parents, a good, safe home—and who still ended up with a mental health problem that interfered with her ability to simply function like others do.

"I don't agree," Amy found herself interjecting. "I don't think people are stupid. I think they have problems, and I think they have needs they can't meet sometimes. I think they feel isolated and like no one is on their side. And I think we use our power too often to stay in business, when we could teach people, or help them get the resources they need and give them a fighting chance to do their best parenting instead of judging them and punishing them for their circumstances."

When she finished, she looked at her colleagues. Rosa's cheeks were red, and her lips were pursed.

"Hey, Amy. We know all that. We're just making conversation," Jyoti said.

"Yeah, and anyway, it was Rhonda's opinion, not ours," Rosa added.

Amy's shoulder's slumped and the fire went out of her.

"I'm sorry, I'm probably just tired." She turned to the kettle and poured water over the tea bag in her mug.

"Maybe you should take a day," Jyoti said. As Amy left the room, she continued in a quieter voice. "Or a month, if you're going to lose it like that." Amy heard but didn't show it as she went back to her desk where she didn't bother to turn on her computer. She put her earbuds in and started the music on her phone, and she sat holding her warm mug in both hands, taking in the scent of peppermint with every deep inhalation.

When her tea was done, and her breathing was back to normal, she started up the machine on her desk and finished up some paperwork.

Chapter 16

On Thursday morning, Rhonda's door was open when Amy walked into the team room at ten in the morning. Amy had been waylaid at the front desk with a message from the school. Rich Mahood was worried about Rex and Angel. There was a message from Lila, too. She'd called the afterhours worker, worried about Amanda. Before Amy had even hung her bag on its hook at her cubicle, Rhonda summoned her into her office.

"I heard it was a busy night on one of your files. What's going on with Amanda and the kids?"

"I haven't heard from Amanda. I've called her every few days to try to schedule an appointment since we decided I shouldn't make unannounced visits anymore. She hasn't answered, and she hasn't gotten back to me."

"When was the last visit? Has it been three weeks? Have you called the school?"

"It was the week Felix died. Three weeks and four days. No, I didn't call the school. You told me to back off."

"I didn't tell you to ignore them," Rhonda snapped.

"The school called this morning though," Amy continued without acknowledging Rhonda's interruption. "Apparently Rex and Angel have not been there in a week. The first three days Amanda called in to report they would be absent. Secretary said she didn't sound well on the phone herself. This morning, the kids didn't arrive, Amanda didn't call in, and they can't reach her."

"Okay. I guess you'll need to do an unannounced visit today, then. The kids should be seen if they haven't been at school."

Amy went to her cubicle, grabbed her bag off the hook and headed back out of the office. She was worried. She couldn't provide the kind of proof the court wanted to justify taking any action, but she was worried, nonetheless. Something was changing with Amanda, and Amy didn't know how to help. Psychosis didn't respond to mindfulness or strategies like cognitive behaviour therapy, and Amy just wasn't equipped. She wished she felt more confident about the psychiatrist's involvement, but he was so evasive that talking with him left her with more concerns than it resolved.

She drove to the old house where Amanda lived. She pulled into the driveway and looked up at the windows on the second floor. She saw the curtain swish in the window that she knew looked out from the living room. As she watched, a face appeared briefly. She couldn't tell if it was Amanda.

Amy went to the door at the base of the stairs that led to the second floor. She knocked on the door. Five firm knocks.

There was no answer. Amy heard a bang from inside the apartment and thought that someone must be coming to get the door. No more sounds followed from above, and she did not hear anyone on the stairs.

Amy knocked again. Seven knocks this time. Very hard. She waited, but once again there were no footsteps.

As she stepped back and looked up, she saw the face appear in the window again, then withdraw just as quickly. That curtain was pulled shut and Amy watched as all the other living room curtains were pulled shut.

Amy stepped up and tried the door to the stairway. Locked.

She went around the house, following the cobblestone pathway to the back door. She knocked there. Five times, hard. No one came.

As Amy looked up again from the side yard, she could see that the bedroom windows on this side were painted black.

Her heart started to race. She could feel the blood pound in her head. She took out her cell phone to call Rhonda.

"There's someone home. I saw a face in the window, twice, but whoever it was pulled back. No one is answering the front or back door. The bedroom windows are all painted black from the inside. Both doors are locked."

"Amy, you're going to have to call the police. They're going to need to get you into the house so you can see what's happening with the children. Call me again once you get inside and see what's going on."

"Right. I'll let you know." Amy hung up. As she dialed the police, she felt her senses sharpen in an unfamiliar way. She was used to the adrenaline rush of crisis situations, but this felt different. Everything was crystal clear around her, like the sun's brightness was turned up. Her pounding heart seemed to threaten to break free of her ribcage, and even her well-practiced breathing exercises couldn't seem to slow it down. She pushed away thoughts of the baby who had just died. She didn't have time and couldn't let her thoughts return to that apartment. And yet her gut clenched as the panic of the moment she found him washed over her again.

The non-emergency number for the police was as familiar to her as the number for the Children's Aid Society was. She had called many, many times over the years to ask for support in an investigation, but she had never been as worried as she was today. While she waited, she stared up at the painted windows, something shifting in the back of her mind as the sun glinted off the surface.

It was several long moments before the first cruiser arrived, followed quickly by a second cruiser. The first officer on the scene, Constable Will Granger, was just getting out of his car when the Sergeant pulled up as well. A third cruiser parked on the street and Constable Jacques Menard came up the walk where Amy and Will were standing, waiting for the Sergeant to join them. Amy was relieved at the response.

"So, you think someone's in there?" Will looked at the upper windows. The curtains were still.

"I saw a face in the front window and the curtains moving when I arrived," Amy said.

"Could you see who it was?"

"I couldn't tell for sure if it was Mom. The face had sort of a weird colour, very pale. The hair was dark and wild."

"Okay, the kids have been out of school all week?" Will pulled his notebook out.

"Yes. Mom called every morning but today to report their absence. She didn't answer when the school called today."

"We had a call here the other day," Menard chimed in. "The building owner complained about noise from the upstairs apartment. Thought the mother was letting the kids kick a soccer ball in the house or something because she kept hearing thuds and running feet. When we checked in, Amanda said she would keep the kids quiet and tell them not to throw the ball in the house."

Sergeant Watson walked up to join their group. "Did anybody lay eyes on the kids when you were here?" Watson asked as he approached.

"It was me who was here," Menard said. "I didn't see the kids, no. I heard cartoons on the television in the next room. Amanda said she was trying to get them to settle down with some TV."

"Well, when I went around to the back door just now, the bedroom windows all look like they're covered with black paint," Amy said.

"How well do you know the layout of the apartment?" Sergeant Watson asked Amy.

"Pretty well. I've been in there most weeks since the children returned to Amanda's care." Amy got out her notebook and sketched the floor plan.

"The stairs go up here. There's a door at the top. I'm pretty sure I heard it slam while I was knocking today. Then it opens into the living room and eat-in kitchen area that is across the front of the house. That's what's behind these windows above us."

They all paused and looked up. The curtains twitched in the middle window.

"The bathroom and the small bedroom are off the kitchen on the north side of the house. There are two bedrooms across the back of the house." Amy finished the sketch.

"This is Rex's room, and this is Angel's room, here, beside the bathroom."

The three officers looked over the drawing.

"There are back stairs as well. The door is here, at the south end of the living room and the stairs go down through the back porch."

"Let's see if she will open the door for us. If she won't open, we'll knock down the front door here and make our way in," Menard said.

Sergeant Watson went around the back of the building with Granger.

Amy stepped aside. Menard stepped up to the front door and banged. Seven loud bangs. There was no answer. He banged out another seven and shouted.

"Open up! Amanda? It's the police! Open up!"

Still no answer. Amy watched the window upstairs. There was no movement in the curtains as the police officer banged one more time.

Sergeant Watson came around the front of the building.

"Granger is going to keep watch on the back door. I'm going to watch the downstairs entrance. Menard, you take this door."

In a moment, Constable Menard put his shoulder up against the door, banging his billy club on the cheap hardware of the lock and doorknob. The wooden door splintered and fell open into the dark stairwell.

Amy reached around and flicked on the light switch. The stairwell lit up. She saw the door at the top close just as the light came on.

"Someone's behind the door," she said. She grabbed the officer's elbow as she gave warning.

"Police! Open the door now and come out with your hands in front of you!"

Amy stood behind the officer, looking up the stairs. The door did not open.

The officer started up the stairs, his billy club in his left hand and his right-hand hovering over the gun on his belt.

"Police! I'm here with the Children's Aid Society! Open this door now, or I will open it for you."

Menard waited a moment on the landing, then tried the knob on the door at the top of the stairs. The knob turned easily, and he pushed the door open.

"Amanda, come out where I can see you. It's Constable Menard with the Green Valley Police. I'm here with Amy Malloy from CAS, and she needs to see the children. Come on out now."

There was a scuffling noise from the direction of the kitchen. Amy turned to look and took a slow deep breath.

Amanda was standing in the centre of the room. She had on black jeans and a baggy grey sweatshirt. Her hair was loose and messy, as if she'd been running her hands through it. Her eyes darted from face to face as Amy and the police officer moved into the room.

"Amanda, where are the children," Amy said in a low, calm voice.

There was no response from the confused looking woman. She was wringing her hands as she stared at them.

"Amanda, where are the children?"

"Sergeant, we're in the main room of the apartment," Menard spoke into the radio on his shoulder. "Suspect is present, not responding to our questions. You want to come up here?"

"Be right up." The Sergeant's response crackled in the still apartment.

Amy looked around the room. Things had changed drastically in three weeks' time. What had been a warm, cheery room with Amanda's brightly coloured art on the walls now looked dark and forlorn with the curtains closed and the lights off. There were sheets draped over the television set.

"Amanda, if you don't tell us where the children are, we are going to start searching the apartment."

"They're in their rooms." Amanda's hands kept working as she spoke in an unsteady voice. "I did everything I could to try to keep them safe."

"Where is Rex? Where is Angel?"

"Rex is in his room. Angel…" Amanda's voice broke. "Something bad…"

Amy moved toward Rex's bedroom door. Menard walked across the room with her as the Sergeant appeared in the door frame.

"Where is Angel?"

"The crone was going to steal her life force. I tried to save her."

Amy heard her speaking about Angel in the past tense, and it was as if everything in the room was frozen in time. It felt like she was on the edge of a nightmare deeper than those she'd been having since finding Felix dead in his crib.

"Amanda, where is Angel?" Amy looked at the woman.

"She's in her room. She was supposed to be safe there!"

Amy opened the door to Rex's bedroom. She looked in and saw that he sat on the edge of his bed reading a book. Rex looked up with a blank stare.

His windows were painted black. Amy stared at them for a few seconds before turning toward Rex again.

As he recognized Amy, his eyes lit up and his features contorted before he quickly pulled the blank mask back on his face.

"Hi, Rex. You okay?" Amy greeted him casually as she approached.

"Yes, I'm fine," he answered in a flat tone. He looked at the floor. Amy suspected he was in shock.

"Good. We're here to see what's been happening. Mrs. Hopkins is missing you in class."

"I'm fine. It's fine," Rex repeated the words and looked down at his book.

"Great. You keep reading in here, Rex. I need to find Angel."

When Amy said his little sister's name, Rex flinched. His face remained expressionless, and he didn't raise his eyes from his book.

"Constable Menard is going to come with me. We'll be back soon, Rex."

"Fine." He still didn't look up.

Amy and Menard went back into the living room, closing the door to Rex's bedroom behind them. Amanda remained exactly as they had left her, wringing her hands and repeating that she was only trying to keep her children safe.

"I tried to protect them," She repeated. "I tried to stop it."

Granger had come upstairs as well, called in by the Sergeant. He walked toward the largest bedroom, so Amy headed toward Angel's room.

Amy swallowed hard as she walked. Her mouth was dry, and her hands were shaking. She glanced over at Amanda, taking in the woman's pale face and noticing that the young mother had lost weight, though she hadn't had much to spare.

Amy looked at Menard. He nodded and Amy opened the bedroom door. The smell made Amy cough and the police officer beside her covered his mouth with the back of his wrist. This window was painted black, too, and the room was dark. Amy felt beside the door for the light switch before stepping in. She resigned herself to the fact that she was likely to see the worst sight yet of her long career.

As the light from a bare bulb in the ceiling flooded the small room, Amy and Constable Menard stood at the threshold and their gazes swept the scene.

The room held a bed, a bookshelf, and a rocking chair. There was a child's drawing tacked to the wall over the bookshelf and Amy stared at it, taking in the bright colours and crooked lines. Amy finally forced herself to look at the bed.

Angel lay in the centre of the mattress her small, body sprawled across the soft pastels. The bedding around the child's head was stained with something dark. A stone sculpture of a cherub, about six inches long, lay on the floor at the foot of the bed. Amy stared at the little girl as her mind slowly registered the fact that the dark substance was blood. Angel's blood.

"Blunt force trauma to the head." Menard stared at the body as well, his face pale as his eyes traced the same damage that Amy saw. "Looks like maybe she was hit in the head with that statue."

"Oh," Amy said, staring at Angel. She registered that her hands were shaking.

"Uh, Sergeant. We're going to need Dr. Thayer," Jacques called to his superior without turning away from the small, lifeless body.

Amy stepped toward the bed. She reached out a hand toward the body, but the police officer grasped it and pulled her back.

"Don't touch anything. We're not even going to go any further inside the room. The forensic team is going to be on their way soon, and they'll need to have the room the way we found it."

"Right." Amy stopped moving and simply stared.

A hand fell on her shoulder. Amy didn't turn.

"Rex is in the next room. He's going to need some help."

"Right." Amy still didn't turn away from the sight of the dead girl on the bed. Little Angel, whose mother had tried to protect her. Amy wondered just what it was that Amanda saw, and how it led to this terrible, violent death.

The hand on her shoulder tugged gently and turned Amy away from the child's room.

Amy looked at Jacques, and for a moment she saw the same horror reflected in his eyes as he looked past her. Then he shuttered those eyes and focused on Amy instead.

"Come on, you can call your supervisor over here." He gestured toward Rex's room.

Amy blinked several times and took another deep breath. The smell of death was less noticeable out here, and she continued to breathe deeply as she reached within herself to find the strength to face the boy sitting on his bed, reading a book.

Amy paused just outside of Rex's room. Jacques nodded at her, then headed into Rex's room. She heard the officer making conversation with the boy. He talked about the superhero posters on the boy's walls as Amy dialed the office.

As she waited for Rhonda to pick up, Amy's eyes suddenly widened as they landed on the hook holding two silver capes. Black windows. Like the Silver Surfer's clothes.

Oh no. She should have looked in the children's room weeks ago. She should have insisted on it. She thought he meant new curtains.

"Rhonda Selleck speaking."

"Rhonda. We're, uh, we're…" Amy started coughing. She held the phone away from her mouth until the coughing fit subsided, then tried again.

"We're going to need a plan for Rex. Amanda is being arrested." Amy watched as Granger interrupted Amanda's handwringing long enough to put handcuffs on her wrists. Once they were secured, her hands tried to resume their motions, despite being impeded by the hardware.

"Angel, uh, we're waiting for the coroner to arrive to pronounce her."

"What? Amy? Is that you? What are you talking about?"

Amy shook her head and concentrated.

"I'm at Amanda's with the police. We had to break in. Angel's dead, and we're just waiting for the coroner to pronounce her. Rex is physically fine. He is going to need a plan. Do you want me to call his grandparents and have them meet us at the hospital? He should be examined. I think he might be in shock at the very least."

"Oh, for fuck's sake," Rhonda said. "This is very bad. I'll have to notify Kent again. Two child deaths in the space of a month. They're going to want an inquest. Fuck." Rhonda paused and Amy could hear her long fingernails tapping on the desk at the other end of the phone.

"Do you think the grandparents can care for Rex? You'll need to update the place-of-safety assessment with them, but their kinship placement approvals should still be valid unless something has changed."

"I don't know if they'll be able to take him. I guess it depends on how they take this news. I suppose they might be in as much shock as Rex is when they find out. I think we need to get Rex to the hospital to be assessed. I can ask them to meet me there and see how they handle it."

Amy felt her head clear a little bit as she focused on the next steps she would need to take.

"Okay. That's a good idea. I'll have Rosa line up a tentative foster home just in case they're not in good shape. Call me once you've talked to them, and to the doctor. I'll get the serious occurrence forms ready for you to fill out later this afternoon."

"All right. I'll call you from the hospital."

Amy hung up her cell phone and looked into the bedroom. Amanda had been taken down the stairs.

She could see Rex was talking with Jacques and listened for a few moments from the hall. The police officer was kneeling beside the boy's bed as Rex pointed at a picture in his comic book.

"That's his stun gun. He uses it to get the bad guys." Rex turned the page. "This here is his shield. He can stop any weapon with it. Even lasers. Lasers are scary. They can get through anything that isn't metal. That's why his cape and shield can stop them."

"I see. That's a cool cape and shield combo."

"He wears black because it attracts warmth. That's why our bedroom windows are black. To attract warmth and keep out the cold evil."

Amy walked into the room. She knelt down beside Jacques. Rex looked up at her.

"My baby sister is dead, Amy."

"I know she is, Rex. A special doctor is going to come and take care of her now."

"My mom said the crone tricked her. The crone was always trying to get Angel and she tricked Mom."

"Your mom is sick again, like when you were little. You might not remember all of the things that happened when she was sick before."

"She talked about the crone when I was little, too."

"Yes, she did. Your mom has always tried to keep you and Angel safe. Rex, we're going to go to the hospital together."

"Is that where my mom is?"

"Well, she might go to the hospital later, but right now she is going to talk with the police at the police station."

"Mom wouldn't let me leave my room all weekend. She brought me in my favourite, bologna and cheese sandwiches, every day. With chocolate milk. I heard her yell in Angel's room. She yelled 'Leave my baby alone!' and then I heard her crying."

"Did she say anything else?"

"No." He shook his head, then paused. "Well, just that she tried to protect Angel. She kept saying that."

"Okay, Rex, let's go to the hospital so we can get you checked out. We can talk some more about what's happened this weekend when we get there."

Amy helped Rex pack a bag with his favourite items. He packed his superhero costumes, including the two silver capes. He added his teddy bear, his superhero comics, and some underwear and socks. He looked toward his bedroom door, then dashed back toward his bed.

Rex reached under his mattress and pulled out a doll and a pink blanket. He turned to face Amy and Constable Menard, gripping them tightly.

"These were Angel's. I snuck them in here while Mom was in the shower."

"I'm glad you have something of Angel's, Rex." Amy wondered if he got them from his sister's room, and if so, what he had seen. Did he turn on the light? "Where did you get them?"

"Angel left them on the couch when Mom made her go to bed early one night."

Amy sighed inwardly with relief. Maybe the little boy hadn't seen his sister, and all of that blood, after all.

"Okay, we need to go now. Are you ready?"

Rex nodded. Jacques carried the small suitcase. Amy took Rex's hand in hers and together they walked across the living room. Rex stumbled when he passed his sister's bedroom door, then righted himself and kept walking. Amy's heart plummeted and her gut clenched as she watched his lower lip tremble.

Maureen Pollard

Chapter 17

At the hospital, the doctor declared Rex to be in perfect health. He was well hydrated, he was a healthy height and weight for his age, and his eyes, ears and lungs were all clear.

Lila and Rick arrived and joined them in the examining room while they were waiting for the doctor to sign the release forms. Amy and Constable Menard broke the news about Angel's death to them together. Lila broke down sobbing into Rick's shoulder. Rick stood still, biting his lower lip and breathing hard as he fought against his own tears.

"I should have gone over. I should have gone over and broken the door down myself," Rick sputtered.

"Now Rick, that wouldn't have worked. You can't blame yourself." Constable Menard's voice was calm.

"You have both done the best you could do for the children," Amy said. "Amanda didn't appear to be a threat. She seemed to be taking her medication, and she wasn't talking about any hallucinations. Even the school was not really concerned until today when Amanda didn't call and wouldn't answer the phone. When she was calling in, they thought she sounded like her normal self, maybe just a little under the weather."

"She wasn't answering our calls all week," Lila said.

"Even when we attended yesterday, she seemed fine when she answered the door. We saw no signs for any concern," Jacques said.

"You saw Angel yesterday?" Lila gripped the officer's arm.

"Well, I didn't actually see the children." He looked away while he spoke. "We had a noise complaint from the woman downstairs. She said she heard yelling and a thump. Amanda answered the door, and she was reasonable when I asked her about it. I could hear cartoons on in the background, and she said she was letting the children watch TV to settle down."

"Oh. Well. I thought maybe you had seen Angel." Lila seemed at a loss.

"I'm sorry I didn't," Jacques said, his voice low and sincere.

Amy's stomach clenched. She realized now that the noise the downstairs neighbour heard was probably the sound of the sculpture hitting the floor. The dark spot on the pastel bedding didn't bear thinking about, but for a moment it was all Amy could remember.

"Can Rex stay with us?" Rick looked at Amy and his question drew her out of her horror.

"I think so. We need the doctor to release him. I'm concerned that he might have been in shock when we got into the apartment."

"Of course. But CAS is okay if he comes with us?"

"As long as you both feel capable of caring for him, of helping him deal with this horrible tragedy even while you deal with it yourself. It's the best place for him. We just need to complete the place-of-safety paperwork again, so I need to come to the house, and you'll need to walk me through."

"We can do this. We failed Amanda, and we failed Angel, but we will not fail Rex. We can do this." Rick stood with his arm around his wife, who was drying her eyes.

"Yes, of course. We can take care of him and put him first, Amy. Poor Rex. I can only imagine what he experienced," Lila agreed. She bit back a sob before continuing. "Poor Amanda. She just wanted to protect her children. I don't know how she'll live with this. With the knowledge of what she did, on top of living with the pain and confusion her illness causes."

"Let's hope Amanda has access to good psychiatric support to help her through this. That will be important," Amy said. "As far as Rex is concerned, it seems like he was kept in his room and protected from witnessing what happened. He heard Amanda yell, and he heard a thump, but didn't see much, if anything."

"We'll need him to give a statement on video recording at the CAS or police station. We can do that tonight if he would rather get it over with, or we can do it tomorrow, but we will need to do it, for the record." Constable Menard's voice was low and calming, even as he pressed.

Lila began coughing, and Amy said she'd find her some water. In the hall, Amy took a moment to call Rhonda again, giving her a brief update. She retrieved a water pitcher from the nurse's station and filled it at the tap in the washroom, taking it back to Lila, along with a paper cup.

"Yes, of course," Rick was saying to the police officer when she returned. "He's the only witness to any of it, even if he only heard things. We can ask him if he feels up to doing it tonight." Rick stepped toward the examining room that Rex was in. Amy followed him.

"Rex, Constable Menard and I need to ask you a bunch of questions about what happened at your house this weekend. We need to make a video of it, so we have to do it at the police station or the Children's Aid Society. Do you think you can do that tonight if Grandma and Grandpa bring you?" Amy was kneeling in front of Rex, who had jumped from the gurney and was now sitting in the chair.

"Yeah, I can tell you what happened. I stayed in my room yesterday and today. But Mom started acting afraid before that."

"Would you rather go to the police station, or to the Children's Aid Society?"

"If we go to the police station, can I see a cruiser?"

"If you want, you can ride over in one," Menard offered.

"Okay, let's go to the police station then."

"We just have to make sure the doctor says it's fine for you to leave the hospital."

"I'm sure it's fine. This is one healthy young man." The doctor spoke from the doorway. He held Rex's chart in his hand.

"Everything looks fine with his tests, and I would say his interest in a police cruiser suggests that any shock seems to have passed for now. Who am I discharging him to?" the doctor asked.

"To me, Amy Malloy, representing the Green Valley Children's Aid Society. We're going to be placing Rex with his grandparents tonight," Amy confirmed as Rick and Lila stepped forward. Rhonda had texted Amy to give the approval to place Rex with them a few minutes after Amy's call.

Once the paperwork was complete, the small group stood together in the Emergency Room waiting area.

"Now, Rex, it's time for your ride with me in the cruiser. Would one of you like to come?" Constable Menard looked at Rick and Lila.

"I'll drive our car over. Rick, you go in the cruiser with Rex." Lila was pulling her keys out of her purse.

Rick nodded.

"I'll meet you over there," Amy said.

In the parking lot of the hospital, Amy sat with her head resting on her steering wheel. She closed her eyes, and the image of Angel's small body in a pool of drying blood and the image of little Felix with his sunken fontanel and pale, dry skin vied for her attention. Both of them babies, really. Helpless. Both babies, her responsibility to keep safe. Both babies, dead.

Amy opened her eyes and looked around her. She tried to replace the grim images that filled her head with the more benign images of cars in the parking lot, the hospital sign, and the windows of patient rooms, but the other ones kept rising to the front of her mind. It was going to take some time, and maybe some therapy, to get over this combination. She shook her head and turned the key in the ignition. She switched the radio off and drove to the police station in silence.

Maureen Pollard

Chapter 18

At the police station, Amy entered the lobby. Constable Menard was there talking with Lila and Rick and Rex coloured as they waited for her. When she arrived, Constable Menard led her into the interview room they would use this afternoon.

"If you sit here, and Rex sits there, I'll sit here. I'll lead the interview if that's fine with you. If you have any questions, use the usual sign, and I will work them in. Is that all right?"

"Sure, that's fine with me."

Amy never minded that the police preferred to lead the interviews in a criminal investigation. Some of the officers she'd worked with in Green Valley were extremely skilled at interrogation, and Amy had learned a lot by listening to them. Rarely, when the child was very young, or if the officer were inexperienced, the police would ask Amy to lead, relying on her greater experience interviewing young children about very sensitive topics such as sexual abuse.

The interview unfolded as expected, revealing a tragic story. Rex said they went to the park on the weekend. A woman approached Angel and told her to stop picking the wildflowers growing along the edge of the path since they were there for everyone to enjoy. Amanda had grabbed Angel, pulling her away from the woman, and they had hurried home.

"I still wanted to play on the swings, but she said we had to go home. Then, she kept following Angel around the house, asking her weird questions."

"What kind of questions did she ask?" Menard wanted to know.

"Well, on the day we went to the park, after we had supper, Mom asked Angel if she felt cold, or if she saw any shadows in the room. I couldn't hear everything when they were in Angel's room, but I did hear her ask Angel if she saw the shadows a few times when her voice got really loud, like she was scared. Every day she did this, and Mom was getting louder."

"What happened then?"

"I heard someone at the door, but Mom turned the cartoons on, and I couldn't hear what they said. Mom came back to my room and told me to stay put, no matter what."

"When was that?"

"Two days ago, I think." Rex said. "Then, this morning, I heard a lot of knocking on the doors, and then I heard the door slam at the top of the stairs. Then I heard Amy talking, and I thought it would be all right."

Constable Menard asked him open ended questions, encouraging the child to expand his answers in his own words. He skillfully repeated some of the child's key phrases in the form of a question to encourage the child to continue. Amy occasionally rephrased a question if Rex seemed confused by the police officer.

The interview took almost two hours. Rex did not show signs of flagging. He seemed as if he could talk for another two hours when he had answered all of their questions. He twisted

Angel's blanket around his hands as he spoke, and her doll sat on the chair beside him.

Amy sent Rex home with Lila and Rick. Then she and Jacques went to the video monitoring room to look in on the interview that Constable Granger was attempting with Amanda. Sergeant Watson was watching, and they joined him in the small space.

"She isn't making any sense at all. She says an evil crone was after her baby. She recognized the crone at the park and thinks they must have been followed home. The crone wanted her baby, and it was hovering over Angel. She tried to kill the crone, but it tricked her."

Amy closed her eyes, cringing. It made her queasy to listen to the tragic details of Amanda's statement. She opened her eyes and saw Jacques cringing, too.

"You two go sit down. You look terrible. I'll watch this." Sergeant Watson waved them to the administration room, where three pairs of desks sat in formation, waiting for police officers who needed to complete paperwork.

"Shirley! Get these two something hot to drink, please."

Shirley came through the administration room from the reception area, then went back into the kitchen and came out again, setting two cups of black coffee on the desk between them. Beside the paper cups she dropped a handful of sugar packets and creamers.

When Shirley went back to the reception desk, the Sergeant came into the administration room. He had a small bottle of amber liquid in his hand. Fireball, the label read. He placed two shot glasses on the desk, took the lid off the small bottle and poured.

"Emergency measures. You two drink these and sit here for a few minutes. Give your heads a shake and let this thing go. You've got jobs to do, and you are damn good at them, but you can take a few minutes now to shake this off."

He left the administration room, taking the bottle with him.

"I heard he had a bottle around and gave a shot to any officer who had dealt with a gruesome death. Didn't think it was true before. Guess I hadn't dealt with a death gruesome enough before this." Jacques lifted one of the shot glasses and held it out toward Amy.

Amy hoisted the other glass, almost touching it to Menard's glass automatically. She jerked her hand back before the gesture was complete. They both held the glasses to their lips and tipped their heads back. The cinnamon whiskey burned down Amy's throat, and she made a face as she swallowed it all in one gulp. She figured she must be in rough shape, because she had never in her life been able to drink a shot of anything and not throw it right back up.

The social worker and the police officer sat at desks in the administration room, working side by side as they completed their paperwork. Page after page, Amy wrote every detail she could remember of the horrific day. She heard Menard's boot, tapping ceaselessly as his fingers worked on the keyboard in front of him. She stole a glance at him and saw him grimace as he worked.

Her cell phone rang.

"Amy Malloy."

"Amy, where are you?" It was Rhonda.

"At the police station. Working on case notes. They're still interviewing the mother. The coroner and forensics team are at the house."

"Did Rex go with his grandparents? It's almost four thirty, and we need to know if he needs a foster home."

"Yes, sorry. I forgot to call you to confirm," Amy apologized.

"Okay."

"We finished interviewing Rex here at the station about twenty minutes ago. He did a good job answering the questions."

"Good. Will I see you back at the office this afternoon?"

"I'll come in to drop off my notes, but I think that's all I'm good for today."

"Okay. I'll see you in the morning if I'm gone when you get here with the file notes."

"Fine. See you later."

Rhonda didn't ask how Amy was doing. Amy remembered the unwritten rule—don't let it bother you and for fuck's sake, if it does, don't talk about it. Amy took a deep breath and fought back the surge of resentment. She supposed Rhonda had never dealt with two child deaths in such a short time span before either, and she surely had no idea at all what Amy had walked into today.

Amy wasn't sure she knew yet herself.

Amy drove over to the Children's Aid Society. She pulled in the parking lot and looked at the cars there. The three agency cars were lined up in the designated spots. Kent's sports car was in the spot reserved for the Executive Director, near the door. Phil's car was in the parking lot, too. He must be working late again, as he had every night since he returned from vacation. No surprise given the poor job she'd done with the case he'd entrusted her with.

Amy walked up the steps to the front door of the agency. Her swipe card allowed her entrance into the locked building. It was almost two hours after closing.

She went first to the executive offices. Kent handed her the serious occurrence forms.

"You can just sit at the table in the board room and fill them out. I've got to fax them to the Ministry as soon as they're done." He turned back to his computer screen, dismissing Amy to do what he required of her.

Amy sat and completed the forms. She filled in the blanks and summarized the situation. A few measly pages to document the death of a child the agency was involved with. A child the agency was supposed to protect. A child Amy was supposed to protect. She took a deep breath and filled in the blanks. Again.

"We've got to stop meeting like this," Kent joked as Amy returned to his office and handed over the completed forms.

Amy stared at him blankly, taking a moment to register that the Executive Director of the child welfare agency was making a joke. Two children were dead in the space of four weeks, and he was making a joke. She lay the paperwork on his desk, turned on her heel and left his office without a word.

Chapter 19

Amy spent the next week going over the information in her file, talking to the school and community professionals who had been working with Amanda. She and Constable Menard worked together, interviewing people to try to piece together the last weeks and days of Angel's life.

Amy worked late in the evenings, making sure her notes were detailed and clear. She prepared the documents that would support Lila and Rick's application for custody of Rex. Her affidavits would be important in that matter. The agency would consider Rex to be at high risk of imminent harm in his mother's care. Lila and Rick had provided good care for their grandchildren in the past, and they were prepared to make a permanent plan to care for Rex.

No matter what happened with Amanda, it was clear to Amy that Rex needed a stable, safe home environment to heal in. A place where he could grow up and still love his mom but understand why it wasn't safe for him to live with her. His grandparents shared in his predicament. They loved their daughter, but they couldn't allow her to live with them again. The grief was deep, but the risks were too high, and it brought grandson and grandparents together. They would need to complete a more in-depth SAFE home assessment with a worker from the resource team, under the supervision of CAS, but this was the least of their concerns.

Amy met Jacques at the police station to review the video-taped statements and the forensics materials. They were silent as they reviewed the evidence. Amy noticed Menard wasn't grimacing as he had over his notes that first day of the investigation, but she didn't give it much thought. She felt rather numb herself.

Amanda had been charged with manslaughter, but she was being assessed in a locked psychiatric facility to determine if she could stand trial. Amy read the hospital staff reports submitted as evidence. With her medication, she was stabilizing. She was able to hold a conversation, she was keeping up with her personal grooming, and she was no longer talking about evil shadows. In fact, as she became more lucid, she alternated between disbelief and horror over what had happened.

Amy and Jacques listened to the interviews. First to Amanda's and then to Rex's. They reviewed the photographs of the apartment. Every room had been carefully examined and every detail documented.

The pictures from Angel's room were last. Amy felt her stomach clench, as it had that day. The rusty smell of dried blood flooded her nostrils again and when she closed her eyes, the images remained burned into her brain.

Amy had seen this room and this child every night in her dreams. She had seen this room and this child when she was awake. The smallest thing would bring the visions and smells rolling back over her. A small blonde child at the mall. A mattress store, or even a mattress commercial. The deep reddish-brown colour of drying blood.

Amy took deep breaths, trying to steady the hands that shook as she held a photo of the child on the bed.

"You okay?" Menard peered at her over the file notes he was reading.

"Yeah. I will be," Amy said, rubbing her temples with her fingertips. "She was so little." Amy looked at the police officer sitting beside her, seemingly unaffected by the gore and violence spread out in front of them.

"She was," he agreed, turning his attention back to the file notes.

Amy shuddered. She had seen many children injured over the years. Some were accidental injuries, and some were inflicted by a caregiver. Some children had been treated and released from the emergency room, while others had been admitted for care. A few had long-term medical complications related to their injuries.

Suddenly, in the space of one cycle of the moon, Amy had been the worker of record in two terrible child death cases where the caregivers of the children were being charged. Two deaths. Two criminal cases. Within four weeks.

Amy thought of the baby, still and blue and shrunken in his crib. His body delicately wrapped and thoroughly covered in the bare room where he had been kept.

Amy thought about one of her first terrible abuse investigations. A six-year-old girl had been tossed against the wall during her mother's boyfriend's drug induced rage. Her head injury would render her helpless as long as she lived. There were others: children with life-altering injuries, or long-term damage that resulted from enduring patterns of abuse and neglect.

Still, Amy had never seen such a violent scene as Angel's death. So much blood for such a little body. There just weren't that many of them in Green Valley. She supposed she had just been lucky not to see even worse when she worked in Toronto.

"Where did you work before?" Amy asked Jacques.

"I was in Windsor. Busy all the time down there. We had our share of child death scenes every year. Most of them were accidents. Falls from high rises. Car accidents. Sick kids whose parents didn't take them to the hospital. But there were a few murders, too."

"I can't imagine. I worked in the city for a few years, but I didn't have any child deaths while I was there," Amy said.

"Yeah, I didn't deal with any directly, but I knew some of the cops who did. They always said it was just part of the job. We signed up for this." He put the papers he was holding down and looked at her intently.

"It doesn't pay to care so much, you know."

"I guess so," she said.

Amy put the photos down. She was going to have to pull herself together. She needed to see that Rex got placed permanently with his grandparents. The criminal trial, if Amanda was deemed fit to stand, was likely to be a long process. If she pled not guilty, that is. No plea would be entered until the full psychological assessment was done, and that would be another six weeks. It would be more complicated than the criminal matter for Sonya Wells and Brian Keeler, neither of whom had any psychiatric issues to weigh against the question of guilt or innocence.

"Okay, I think we have as much evidence as possible. It's all here and organized. I'm going to head home," Amy said.

Jacques didn't look up as he continued to read the file notes. He lifted a hand in a casual wave.

Evan was standing by the door to the parking lot.

"Hey, Amy." Evan looked tired.

"Hey, Evan." Amy stood before him. She supposed she couldn't avoid him forever. She had been doing a damn good job of it since the night he came to her house to see if she was okay. That felt like a long time ago now. He walked with her toward her car.

"I've been missing our squash dates. If you're not up for a game, how about just dessert? If there's nothing else good right now, there's still chocolate."

"Not tonight," Amy said. "Not after the day I've had."

"I know it was a terrible day. That's why tonight is actually just the right night," Evan said, crossing his arms over his chest. "If you don't feel like squash or dessert, what about a walk? Or we could stream a movie. Or we could do nothing, just be together in the same room, doing our own thing. So you don't have to be alone."

"I don't think I can manage it tonight."

Evan reached out and tipped her face up toward his.

"I think you can. I'm here for you, Amy. Unless you tell me to leave you alone, I'm not going anywhere."

"You've said that before."

"I mean it. I am not going to get tired of waiting for you. I'm not going to stop asking you to play squash and have dessert with me. I'm not going to let you down and leave you behind."

"Fine, Evan. But I'm not going to play squash or have dessert or go for a walk or watch a movie with you tonight. I'm going home." Amy wished she hadn't been so open with him about her past. She wanted some space. She didn't want to feel vulnerable, and if she let him in any further, she would definitely be too vulnerable. They had reached her car, and she just wanted to go home and have this day be done.

"If you change your mind after you feed Wiley, just text me." Evan touched her chin again and bent down to place a gentle kiss on her lips before she could pull away. Amy stared at him as he walked toward his truck, then she got into her own car and drove away.

At home, Wiley was waiting for her. She played with him in the yard for a while, following their usual routine before she took him in and prepared his dinner. Amy wasn't eating much herself these days. She couldn't eat anything red. She could hardly eat anything, no matter what colour it was.

Amy cut a few pieces of cheese and took some crackers from a box. She got some grapes and took her plate to the couch. Wiley came up on the couch beside her. Before Angel's death, Amy had been very strict. She didn't allow Wiley on the furniture. She didn't let him beg at the table. She didn't let him sleep on her bed.

With Angel's death, Amy dismissed all the rules. She had coaxed Wiley up on the couch beside her that first night, and she had wrapped her arms around his massive neck. She buried her face in his fur and sobbed for the beautiful child who had been murdered, and also for the tiny baby who had been starved to death.

Chapter 20

The morning of the court date for custody of Rex, four months after Angel's death, Amy's alarm blared. She was already awake, staring at the ceiling and seeing images of a sunken fontanel and blue lips, alternating with images of Angel and the dark blood under her head that was such a sharp contrast to the pastel sheets. The days had passed in a kind of grey blur, each one like the one before it. To work, doing what needed to be done, then home again, already dreading the prospect of either a sleepless night or the nightmares that came when she did sleep. She willed the days and nights to be over, and although they dragged, suddenly months had passed. She felt like she was on some sort of morose auto-pilot setting.

Sometimes, after a nightmare, she'd lay awake thinking about Evan. She was still turning down his invitations to get together, so she only saw him if they had to work on a joint investigation. She was civil. He was kind and patient. The lonely hours left her filled with a longing she didn't want to acknowledge.

Amy dressed in a business suit and drove to the courthouse where she sat in the waiting area until the case was called. When their names were called over the PA system, she stood with Lila and Rick, and they walked into the courtroom together.

Rex was in school, where he had been doing well. Lila found him a counselor and he saw her once a week to talk about his mom, his grandparents, and whatever else was on his mind. The counselor's notes clearly showed that Rex understood his mom had an illness that affected how her brain worked.

Rex knew the illness made her imagine things that weren't real. It made her feel like she had to do things. That was what happened when she hurt Angel.

Rex knew that because of this it probably wouldn't be safe for him to live with his mom. He loved her, but maybe next time the illness would make her think it was him that being attacked. He wanted to stay with Grandma and Grandpa. They understood what his mom was like and didn't ask him a lot of weird questions about her, like his teachers sometimes did.

Grandma and Grandpa loved his mom too, but they knew that she might get sick again and hurt someone. She was a grown up and no one could make her take the pills that would stop her from getting sick again. She didn't like those pills. She told Rex that lots of times.

Amy shook her head slightly to clear her mind of all she had read in the counselor's report about Rex. She turned her attention to the court proceedings. The justice had Lila and Rick's application for custody of Rex, along with Amy's affidavit in support of their application. Her documents stated that the CAS had no concerns about the child's well-being if he was in the care of his maternal grandparents, and no concerns had arisen during the process of completing the more in-depth SAFE home assessment with the family.

The judge asked Rick and Lila if they were prepared to raise Rex to adulthood. They agreed that they were prepared to do so. She then asked if they were prepared to stand by him if he, too, developed symptoms of mental illness.

Rick and Lila explained that they felt that by seeking education and support they would be prepared to monitor Rex for signs and symptoms in a way they had not been prepared for when Amanda was growing up. They were more aware of services and treatment options as well, so they felt that they would be able to support this child no matter what was in his future.

Lila and Rick committed to maintaining Rex's counselling and acknowledged they were also in counselling to help them manage their own grief, and their guilt over not preventing Angel's death, and over the terrible turn their daughter's life had taken.

The judge was satisfied, and she made the final order placing Rex in the custody of Lila and Rick. Any access to Amanda would be at their discretion and supervised at their discretion as well. They would have the right and responsibility to decide whether Amanda was well enough to have any visits with Rex, and whether someone should be present during the visit in order to keep Rex safe.

Amy met Rick and Lila at their house after school. Lila put out cookies and Rick made hot chocolate. They were trying to make it a celebration.

"How is he doing?" Amy asked as they waited for Rex's bus to arrive.

"Well, he still likes to keep his cape on the chair beside his bed at night. He sometimes talks about Angel, usually to tell us that she would like whatever we're serving him for dinner," Rick answered. He kept his hand on his wife's forearm as he spoke, rubbing softly. Lila's chin quivered, and her eyes filled, but the tears didn't escape this time.

They heard the front door open and slam shut before Rex burst into the kitchen.

"The judge must have decided I can stay, because I smell cookies!"

"You are one smart cookie yourself, Rex." Amy smiled at him.

Rex was taller. He had grown even in the four months they had been waiting for this hearing. He was wearing jeans and a T-shirt that had a picture of an airplane on it. The scared boy who would only wear superhero costumes and capes, imagining they would protect him from terrible forces in his world, had mostly set aside those props now that he was in a home where he truly felt safe.

"Amy, I made something for you. I know this is our goodbye visit, so I wanted you to have something. Just wait here, okay?"

"I'm waiting, don't worry." Amy smiled at him as she packed her notebook into her briefcase.

Rex ran up the stairs to his room and pounded back down the stairs to the kitchen. He had a sheet of paper in his hand, and he held it out to Amy as he ran up to the table. It was a page from a colouring book.

"This is for you."

Amy looked at the picture the boy had coloured. It was a picture of a superhero, with a flowing cape. In his arms, he held a small boy. The caption, in bold print across the bottom of the picture, said "Saved Ya!"

Amy felt tears welling at the corner of her eyes. She blinked and blinked again, in a vain attempt to hold them in.

"I'm glad I met you, Rex. I'm glad you will be safe here. I know your grandparents love you, and they love your mom, too. You all loved Angel, so you will be able to remember her together even as you grow up."

"I know. I can keep her blanket and her doll, so I never forget her, and I keep a picture of me and her on the table next my bed." Rex glanced at his grandfather and Rick nodded.

Rex grabbed Amy's right hand with his own and shook it formally.

"Thank you very much, Amy."

"You're welcome, Rex. You're welcome."

Lila had stood and moved to stand beside the kitchen sink, where she was dabbing her eyes with a tissue. Rick, still sitting at the table, cleared his throat.

"Well!" Rick said, a bit too loudly. "I guess it's time for some cookies and hot chocolate!"

"Yes!" Rex laughed and climbed up into his chair at the table. He reached for the cookie plate as Rick set his plastic mug in front of him, with marshmallows floating on the top.

They shared the snack while Amy asked both grandparents to sign the final paperwork that would allow her to close their file with the agency. She said her goodbyes and drove home. She didn't stop in at the agency. She couldn't bear to face her colleagues with her tear-stained face, and she suspected that she had many more tears to shed this evening.

On the way home, she played a song over and over reminding her that all broken hearts heal, hitting the button that would start it again as soon as the last strains faded. The tears flowed as she nodded her head in time to the beautiful music. Despite the optimistic lyrics, she wasn't completely convinced there was no heart that time couldn't mend.

By the time she got home, her voice was hoarse, and she felt wrung out. She walked with Wiley in the woods, following the paths they had made together, winding around her property as she breathed in the fresh air and tried to let go of the feelings of guilt and pain.

She didn't feel quite as guilty over Felix. It had been the weekend, and the schedule of visits had been set without her. It had been merely her first day covering the file. She was more of a witness to the terrible result of the system's efforts to be less intrusive in a family's life. Her bad luck, that one.

Angel, though. That was on her. She should have been there sooner. She should have insisted on seeing the kids' bedrooms. She should have made an unannounced visit that first week when Amanda hadn't responded to her calls. She knew now that was the week in which Amanda had just stopped her medication. She should have gone to the school the week after the baby died. She would have noticed that Angel was looking scared, with dark circles under her eyes, as the teacher later reported when she was interviewed after the child's death. She would have noticed that Rex was wearing his superhero gear every day and insisted on keeping his shield at his desk.

She should have pushed Rhonda harder. She shouldn't have given in so easily to the direction to decrease her involvement. She should have been clearer about her concerns in court. She should have tried harder to get the psychiatrist to come forward.

"Ha! That bastard," Amy shouted into the woods.

The psychiatrist had been interviewed after Angel's death. He was called into the police station the day after the child had been found in the apartment. Amy watched him arrive, pale and shaken from the news of Angel's murder.

"Amanda has been resisting medication for the past month. She was feeling 'foggy,' she said. She didn't feel like herself, so she was weaning off of it. I encouraged her to complete a daily self-assessment. I wanted her to appreciate that the medication makes her much more functional. If a patient realizes for themselves the benefit of continuing their medication, they are much more likely to take it than if I simply direct it." With this statement, he had glared at Constable Menard.

"What happened next?" Menard had asked.

"Amanda was taking fewer pills. I'm not sure what day she stopped, but by the last appointment she had with me, she had certainly stopped them altogether. She did talk about Angel being in danger and having to do something to protect the child. I talked with her about the importance of protecting children from harm. I…I told her that it is a parent's job above all to keep children safe…" His voice broke. He clasped his hands together and looked at the floor.

Amy had stared at his image on the screen in the video room, unable to believe her ears. The psychiatrist had so prized his patient's confidentiality that he had unwittingly given her encouragement for her actions. Actions that caused her child's death. He didn't know it, but Amanda had even used his words.

"It's a parent's job to keep a child safe," she had said, over and over during her interviews. Amy tried to imagine how he would feel when he learned that fact at the criminal trial. If there was one. She thought she might throw up, the cookies and hot chocolate she'd accepted for Rex's sake at his celebration churning uneasily in her stomach.

Later that night, Amy lay awake on her bed. Finally, unable to even close her eyes, she gave in and sat up. At her computer, she began to research travel. She started with Hawaii, then looked at the Caribbean. She searched for information about South America, Australia, and New Zealand. No place appealed to her.

Amy searched across Canada. Victoria and Vancouver were both lovely, but Amy did not feel drawn there. The mountains held some appeal, but she wasn't sure she wanted to deal with grizzly bears. Amy had always enjoyed Quebec City, but she would not feel at all patient with the Francophone citizens who so often abruptly dismissed her efforts to speak using her high school French.

Amy considered the east coast. Saint John, Halifax, Charlottetown. All lovely places she had enjoyed visiting. Labrador was too isolated and too difficult to get to. Newfoundland and its vast expanse might be the place to go if she had enough money for both a plane ticket and a rental. She had loved Gros Morne National Park. That Fogo Island Inn looked beautiful and a visit there was on Amy's bucket list. But not right now. Not this trip. She could probably only afford a few days there at most and that was without the cost of getting to the remote location. She was going to need more time than that.

Her budget was only going to allow a driving trip if she wanted to rent a place for a long stay, so she'd better look at somewhere in Ontario. She tried another search. All of the tourism packages were for couples and groups. Amy scanned the offers and rejected them all. Muskoka, Niagara, Prince Edward County, the Bruce Peninsula. The places were all resort style, or cottages surrounded by neighbours.

Amy tried searching an online cottage rental service. She had heard colleagues talk about it. Some of the staff had visited some very interesting places around North America through this site, and Amy had enjoyed seeing their photos of unusual rental cottages, apartments, and homes.

Amy scanned the map of Southwestern Ontario. What was that place in Lake Erie, just off the southernmost tip of Ontario? Point Pelee National Park, where Amy had once gone to see the fall monarch butterfly migration. This had been a trip with an old boyfriend who knew about the park because he was also a keen birder. The tip pointed out into the lake toward a series of small islands. Amy looked at the name of the largest one.

"Pelee Island." She entered it into the search engine for vacation rentals.

She found a few listings. Only seven, which seemed like a small number. But the pictures were beautiful. Amy chose a small stone cottage that had two bedrooms. Set on a private, well-treed lot, the listing said it would sleep eight. She didn't need the extra beds, but the cottage looked cozy, and she felt more drawn to it than any others on the site. Pets were allowed, which meant Wiley could come with her. Amy searched for transportation to the island. She found the ferry schedule. The ferry would begin running April first and it was March fifteenth now. Amy sent an inquiry about the cottage's availability for a six-week rental beginning April first. She wondered if the Feltz family renting it was any relation to her colleague, Matt. She thought he'd mentioned being from that part of Ontario.

Amy stayed up searching for information about Pelee Island on the internet. She checked out the weather, the maps, the historical sites, and the seasonal activities. This island might be the perfect escape. She imagined the quiet spaciousness of a cottage on the edge of a great lake, where she might find the peace she needed to mend her heart and mind.

Amy traveled every year. The generous vacation allowance built into the labour contracts for child welfare workers allowed this from the beginning of her career, and now she had five weeks to work with each year. She usually took a week in November to go someplace warm, though she missed that last year in the wake of Felix's death. She took another week in February to go someplace else warm. She had skipped that trip this spring, too, unable to plan a leisure trip as she struggled to deal with Angel's death. Amy had always taken three weeks in the summer during which she and Wiley would make a road trip somewhere in North America. They pulled a tiny trailer behind her car, and camped across the country, always choosing someplace new. Amy couldn't skip her summer vacation. None of her other coping skills were helping her now, and she felt like she was going under. It seemed like the best option was to use the vacation now, when she needed it most.

It was all she could do to keep slogging away, covering her cases, delivering groceries to Faye and Justin. Faye was rallying. Although her last round of chemo had really taken a lot out of her—so much that Justin had sobbed in her arms that one day—it had done the work to reduce the tumour a little bit. The treatments bought Faye more time with her son. At eight years old, that was good. He still needed her. Because he knew he was losing her, he didn't indulge in the usual beginnings of sass toward his mother, but spent his time caring for her and asking her to tell him stories from when he was a baby, because they made his mom smile.

Justin was so perceptive. When she stopped by last week, he was waiting with a card for her. He'd drawn a picture of a woman with features like Amy's, using bright colours on a piece

213

of printer paper folded in half. Everything about the picture was cheerful except for the sad look on the woman's face. He'd written "I hope you feel better, soon. From: Justin" inside the card. Amy hadn't been able to stop the lone tear that escaped as she thanked the boy and told him she would be fine. He looked relieved, and she wished she could believe it so easily herself.

Amy looked at the clock. It was seven in the morning, and she finally felt ready to get some sleep. She called in and left a message for Rhonda. She wasn't feeling well so she was going to take the day off. Amy knew it would be no problem. She rarely missed even a day's work. Once, she had brought in the doctor's note required by her collective agreement. She'd missed five days with the flu. Her supervisor at the time had laughed away any notion that Amy had been faking it. She reminded Amy that usually it was her sending Amy home ill, so she was glad Amy had taken care of herself.

Amy lay down in her bed, where Wiley was curled up at the foot. She drifted off to sleep imagining a cozy stone cottage on a quiet little island in Lake Erie, and for the first time since Angel's death she did not have any of the nightmares that had haunted her since that terrible day.

Chapter 21

Amy woke up just after noon, feeling a little bit better. She wasn't sure if it was the sleep, or the fact that she'd finally made the decision to take a break. She loved her home, but it had become more of a trap than an oasis these past few months. She tried to escape here, but she was unable to stop her mind from revisiting the brutal scenes of death that lurked, just waiting for a quiet moment to hijack her mind.

Amy made a cup of tea and turned her computer on. She was pleased to see that a response from the cottage owner had come in early that morning. Amy held her breath as she clicked on the message, and it filled her screen. She breathed out in relief as she read a notification beginning with the words, 'The cottage is available for the period you requested.'

She skimmed the payment details that followed, and then clicked on the PayPal link and paid both the deposit and the balance, so that the full cost was settled. She smiled as she read the confirmation email and saved it to her travel folder. Amy spent the rest of the day making lists of the various supplies she would need for a six-week sojourn and opened her suitcase to start packing.

Driving to work the next morning, Amy turned the volume up on one of the new playlists she'd made. These ones were harder, edgier. Singing along helped her vent some of her frustration and anger.

Amy walked into the team room, head down. She didn't pause or say hello to Janet, or to Emma, who stood by Janet's desk waiting for Rhonda's door to open. Amy switched on her computer, staring at it while she waited for her email to load.

"Amy, we're planning a team lunch tomorrow," Emma said. "At the Sly Fox. Your favourite."

Amy didn't turn around. "I'm too busy," she said curtly.

"But Amy, we wanted to…"

"I said I'm too busy."

Amy glared at her computer until she heard Emma sigh and walk away.

The morning dragged as Amy sat staring at the screen, her fingers flying over the keyboard. She wanted to get all her paperwork up to date. She wasn't going to leave anything for anyone to complain about if they had to cover her files.

She didn't go into the lunchroom anymore. Instead, she ate alone at her desk reading articles and blogs that mentioned Pelee Island as she planned her trip.

Amy did make the mistake of going into the lunchroom to make a cup of tea one morning, just before lunch. She stood staring at the kettle, waiting for it to boil as she listened to Kiyana and Tanya talking about a client's decision to leave her children unsupervised.

"There's no cure for stupid," Tanya exclaimed.

"Well, it's good for job security, I guess," Kiyana said, and they laughed.

Amy pivoted toward them. Her face was contorted with anger.

"I am so, so tired of hearing that expression around here. You know, it's only by chance that it's not one of you who made a mistake that ended up being investigated." Amy's voice was low and strained. "You both have children. They're not sixteen yet. What makes you think you're any better than any parent we deal with? There but for the grace of God, ladies. The things that happen to these families could happen to anyone."

Amy didn't wait for the water to boil. She stormed out of the lunchroom.

Amy sat at her desk, thinking about bringing an electric kettle in for her desk, and looking at a map of her destination, as though just by gazing at it she might gain the peace of mind she sought.

"Hey, Amy." At the sound of Matt Feltz's friendly voice, Amy turned around to see him walking up behind her, a coffee cup in hand. He was looking at her screen. "That's Pelee Island! What are you looking that up for?"

"Hey, Matt. I'm going to take my summer vacation there. I rented a cottage. Maybe you know the owners? Their last name is the same as yours."

"The two bedroom one online?"

"Yeah, that's it," Amy replied.

"Sure, that's my parents' place. My sister takes care of renting it out whenever the family isn't using it."

"Lucky for me. It looks peaceful."

"The island's pretty special. You'll want to bring as many groceries as you can, though. Especially dry goods, and whatever meat you can carry in your cooler and fit in a fridge. You can order it from the Co-op if you need to. Milk and other perishables, too. But it'll cost more, and you'll have to wait for them to come in on the ferry."

"Good to know. Any other tips?"

"Not really. It'll be quiet there. You're ahead of the tourists, so it'll be mainly islanders. They're friendly enough, though. If you need anything, check in with Sandy. She and her husband, Steve, take care of the place for us."

Amy may have lost all patience with her colleagues, but nothing had changed in her relationships with the families she worked with. Amy made a home visit to the Rhodes family, whose house had needed serious cleaning.

"You're doing a good job. It smells like you just mopped in here," Amy said to Marion Rhodes as she glanced around the kitchen.

"Yeah, I got some lemon scented stuff. That pine stuff you brought us in the fall smelled terrible, even if it did cut through the grime well," the woman replied. She showed Amy through the house and although it might not pass a white glove test, there were no health and safety hazards at the moment. That was enough, and the file would close.

Amy continued to make it her last stop of the day once a week to deliver food and basic necessities to Faye and Justin. She kept up the pretense that the deliveries were from the food bank, and once a month the package actually was put together by the food bank and picked up by Amy for the family. But the food bank was facing its own crisis and the supplies there were sparse most weeks. Faye was eating more than just the expensive soup now that she was feeling better. Amy would have to make some arrangements for while she was away.

She was still being assigned to investigations, but Amy didn't talk much to the police officers she'd once been friendly with. She didn't like the way they looked at her when she came into the room. As if she were fragile—about to crack if they weren't careful. Amy imagined them wondering if she might be in need of a lock-up, herself.

She had once tried to talk to Jacques about Angel's death. As they left the courthouse together one day, she worked up the courage to say she was having a hard time coping and asked how he was doing. He dismissed her curtly.

"Like I said before, you win some, you lose some," he said. "No bones about it; that's the job. If you worry over everyone, you'll drive yourself crazy. You just have to move on. I'm just saying it because I know from experience it's the only way."

Amy had mentioned it once to Will Granger, who was there that day, too. He hadn't dismissed her when she asked him if he thought much about that day. But he had told her that no good would come of dwelling on it.

"You need to be strong to do this job," he said. "It's not for everyone."

She looked at his grey eyes as he spoke, and she could see that he was trying to help. Amy thought about the times she had uttered those same words herself over the years. Sometimes when one of her own co-workers was struggling after a difficult abuse investigation.

Amy longed to talk to Evan, but she was too afraid. What if he thought she was too damaged and backed away? Better to keep it simple.

She did take the time to ask him to make sure Faye and Justin got groceries while she was away. He listened as she reviewed the list of supplies she had been providing and reminded him repeatedly that they were to believe he was picking the orders up from the food bank, who had made a special exception for them due to Faye's illness. Evan agreed to her request easily.

"I'll be happy to do this while you're away. You know, I'm still here if you need anything for yourself, too."

"I'm fine," was Amy's terse reply.

"Amy…"

"I'm. Fine."

Amy stubbornly continued to rebuff Evan's advances despite her longing, convinced it was best for both of them. She refused her co-workers' invitations for lunch or shopping. She really didn't want to give anyone a reason to question her state of mind. Better to let them think she was just a bitch than to let anyone see how hard she was taking this.

She tried to block the memories, but they came anyway. She tried to schedule them, to force them to rise when she had time to cope. It didn't always work. She could sit there and think about the smells and images and let the sadness wash over her when she was alone and in a private place. It didn't work to keep them from coming up when she was trying to interview another little blonde girl. Or when she saw a boy in a superhero cape, climbing the monkey bars at the park.

Perhaps an escape would help her get a handle on this misery. Maybe on Pelee Island she would find her way back to her strength. If not, she might find herself in a locked unit after all.

Chapter 22

Two weeks felt like forever, but April first finally arrived. Amy drove her little car off the ferry and around the island. She passed the winery on her left and turned down the dirt road toward her destination. She found the driveway of the stone cottage easily. It looked just like the pictures on the internet. The painted yellow shutters were a smart contrast against the weathered grey stone. The reflection of the lake danced on the clean windowpanes. Amy sighed with relief as she pulled into the driveway.

"Let's have a look, Wiley. Then we can unload."

Amy turned the key in the lock. The door swung open, and she gazed around the room. A beautiful stone fireplace was on the north wall. Undoubtedly, this had been the heating and cooking centre for the first one hundred years or so this cottage had been used. Now, there were baseboard heaters in each room and modern appliances graced the kitchen. The two bedrooms were cozy, one with two bunk beds and one with a four-poster double bed, just as pictured on the internet.

Amy stood in front of the living room window and looked out over Lake Erie. In the sunshine it looked as if a million crystals danced on the small waves as they wove their way between the shores of the island and the mainland. She wondered what it would look like in a raging thunderstorm.

Amy unloaded her car. She stocked the kitchen cupboards with her supplies, then she unpacked her suitcase, laying her clothes in the drawers of the antique cherry dresser in the room with the four-poster bed. She threw Wiley's dog bed on the floor beside her bed. It was time to try to get back to normal, so Wiley would be sleeping on the floor here. Amy was pleased. In short order she had unpacked everything and settled in.

Satisfied, Amy locked her car door. She called to Wiley, who was testing out the new location of his bed. Together, they walked down the driveway to the road. Amy turned east on the dirt road, and she and Wiley walked toward the south end of the island. They stopped for a while where a break in the rocky shore revealed a small, sandy beach. Amy leaned against a tree, throwing a stick for Wiley to chase before he settled down and sat beside Amy. They stayed that way for a while, with Amy staring out over the lake. It was quiet here. She already felt soothed by the clear blue sky over the deep blue water and the rhythmic sound of waves crashing against the shore. Maybe here she would begin to heal.

Chapter 23

The first week on the island, Amy spent her mornings walking with Wiley. After a few days, they started walking all the way around the island. Amy planned it out—she drove the route she wanted to take and measured the kilometers. She packed a backpack with water and snacks.

Amy was surprised at the number of vehicles that passed them as she and Wiley walked, mostly pick-up trucks with a single occupant. She was even more surprised that every driver seemed to sort of wave at her, raising a few fingers from the steering wheel as they passed by. Amy nodded slightly each time she noticed it, sometimes belatedly waving her own hand. She was afraid that they were mistaking her for someone else, so she began simply ducking her head in embarrassment each time a car approached.

As Amy walked, she contemplated her situation. She could hardly keep working as a child welfare worker if she couldn't find a way to release the horrific images that kept popping up.

She couldn't keep facing the unknown in new investigations, or the anxiety of trying to keep children safe on an on-going basis if she were reliving the shock of finding Felix, dead. Of finding Angel, dead. She couldn't continue to suspect every client of having some major mental health problem, worrying that they might be the next one to have some kind of break, ending in another child's death.

Amy knew that she had to find a way to make peace with the deaths. To be able to live with Angel's heartbreaking end, and her part in it. She needed to accept what had happened and move on. Like Menard had done, and Granger.

Amy walked, usually stopping to share her packed lunch with Wiley on some rocks by the beach on the east side of the island. The first day, she'd set out with the intention of having lunch at the West Pier Pub and dinner at the Boathouse Inn. After the first day, though, she decided not to return to the restaurants after all. The food at both restaurants was fine, although in both cases she had eaten less than half. She still didn't have much appetite.

If she were honest, Amy would admit she avoided the restaurants mainly because she just didn't want to talk to anyone. She suspected they wouldn't want to talk to her either if they knew.

No one would understand a child welfare worker who was running away from her responsibilities, trying to cope with the fact that children had died on her watch. Undoubtedly, no one here wanted to meet a child welfare worker anyway, even without knowing she had let children die. Amy was sure of that, because no one she'd ever met was pleased to learn she worked for CAS. She thought about the waitress from the Sly Fox. Amy didn't want to face that stigma here on this island where she was trying to escape, to sort herself out and decide her future.

Chapter 24

Amy and Wiley walked daily, following whatever route Amy had mapped out. It usually took between three and five hours, and when they got back to the cottage Wiley dropped into his bed and was quickly snoring.

Amy started writing in a fresh journal she had purchased just for this trip. After Phil had mentioned it, she'd done some reading about the value of writing about trauma. It was worth a try.

All her fear, shame, and guilt poured out through the tip of her pen and spilled across the pages. All the things she had not said out loud to anyone, though she desperately wished to share her burden. After each walk, she wrote until her stomach was rumbling.

On her fifth day in the cottage, she closed the journal when her hunger pangs grew too strong to ignore. She made a sandwich and put it on a plate with a bunch of green grapes. She took it to the table and ate it all. It must be the walking and that fresh lake air, she thought. It had been almost six months since she had cleaned her plate.

She fell into bed and listened to Wiley's heavy breathing from where he lay on his own bed. Amy drifted off to sleep even though it was only five o'clock in the afternoon. Just as she had the night she had discovered this cottage on the internet, Amy dreamed of sandy beaches, rocky break walls, and blue skies. Amy generally slept well here. She still woke up with her heart pounding most nights, but she was falling asleep more easily. The lake air seemed to be working its magic.

Amy and Wiley settled into a comfortable routine. Up around eight, some eggs for breakfast, and a walk around the island. Each day of the week she chose a slightly different route. The purpose was the same. She mulled and pondered and reflected. As her mind travelled back, Amy was able to move beyond just the scenes of those horrible days. Amy remembered her years as a young, fresh social worker hired to do child protection work. She thought about her early lessons in self-protection and the gradual hardening of her shell.

Writing every day, Amy reflected on her choices over the years. She left out names and details that would make it possible to identify anyone but herself if the journal were found. She wrote, purging herself of all she had kept inside for so long.

Amy wrote about work. About memories of her most difficult cases and the fears and anxiety she had carried. She wrote about successes, as well. The families she thought maybe she had helped. It was that feeling that kept her there, putting in long hours and trying to show up in a way that enabled people to accept help even if it came from CAS.

The job always came first. Work had become the only constant, and now she was flinching even thinking about it.

One day when Amy was walking the route around the island that had become her favourite, she noticed some activity at an old stone church that had become one of her favourite sights on the island. The doors were propped open. She crossed the church yard and peeked in, gazing up at the beautiful stained glass in the windows before looking across the pews to find it empty. In the entryway she read a plaque that said the church was the oldest on the island. Taped on the wall beside the plaque was a handwritten sign that welcomed visitors to stop and rest in the sanctuary. A sticky note on the bottom of the sign read "Please leave doors open. The church is being aired out for spring."

It was chilly inside, with no heat source evident, but the chill was refreshing and a gentle, warming breeze blew through. It was peaceful. Amy sat in a wooden pew and imagined the families of the island who had sat here over the centuries. She wondered if this was the church Matt's ancestors had attended, but there were a handful of churches on the island, and she had no idea if his family even went to church. From that day on, she took up the habit of stopping at the church almost every day. The quiet moments she spent in the serene refuge became the part of her day that she most looked forward to.

Amy sat in the church one morning at the beginning of her second week on the island. Her thoughts drifted over her career choices, as usual. It was easy to think, sitting here in quiet solitude and gazing at the back of the wooden pew in front of her, or up at the high ceiling beams.

A throat was cleared behind her. Amy jumped in surprise, then looked at her hands in her lap. She kept her head down, hoping the intruder would take the hint that she did not desire company. Amy was disappointed and startled when the throat was cleared again, only this time right at the end of the pew she sat in. Amy looked up to see a woman standing there.

"Hello. Welcome to Pelee Island." The woman smiled and the lines at the corner of her eyes crinkled up. A shock of blonde hair stood straight up with spiky tufts aiming in various directions away from her scalp.

"Thank you," Amy said, eyeing the woman. "It's a beautiful place."

"It is." The woman paused. Her eyebrows lifted and her lips worked a moment before she asked the question Amy could see forming.

"Why don't you wave?" The woman asked, a bit brusquely.

"Pardon me?" Amy's brow furrowed in confusion.

"On the island, we wave. You've been here several days. You're renting the Feltz place, the stone cottage with the yellow shutters. If you're going to be here a while, you should wave back. You know, tourists don't always bother to wave back. They're in a hurry." The woman raised her eyebrows in amusement. "Ha. Like anything on this island is going anywhere. Like they might not be able to see it all in a couple of hours. But you, you're here for a while. You want to be part of the island for a while, you should wave."

Amy stared at the woman. Having said her piece, she stood with her arms crossed and her lips pursed, waiting.

"I didn't realize people were waving at me. I thought people were mistaking me for someone else," Amy explained.

The woman tipped her head back and let out a loud guffaw.

"Well, that's an answer I haven't heard before. Honey, we're all waving at you. We're trying to welcome you to our island."

"I didn't know. I'll start waving back."

"That'd be good." The woman dropped herself into the pew across from Amy.

"So, where are you from, Amy?"

Amy's eyebrows raised when the woman said her name.

"Laurie Feltz always lets us know who's renting their place. We keep it up for them over the winter and in between rentals." The woman stuck out her hand across the aisle.

"I'm Sandy. I do the housework and my husband Steve does the yardwork."

Amy shook Sandy's hand. She smiled weakly, a little overwhelmed by the whole exchange.

"I'm from Green Valley. North-east of Toronto, about two hours."

"Ah. City girl, then?"

"Not really. I live in the woods out in the country. There's no city in our county."

"Hmmm. Well, if you live in the woods, why'd you come here to get away from it all?" Sandy asked.

"I suppose because I have no memories here. Pelee Island is a blank slate for me."

"I see." Sandy leaned back in the pew, with her arm stretching across the back of the bench as she sat angled toward Amy. Her eyes narrowed slightly, but she didn't ask any more questions.

"Well, our tourist season doesn't start for a while yet. We've got a few things that go on around here though, and if you would like to join in, you'll be welcome. Especially if you start waving."

It was Amy's turn to laugh.

"Oh, I'll be waving. Now that I know I don't have some long-lost twin on the island that I'm being mistaken for, I'll wave back, for sure."

"Good. If you want to join us, a few women get together on Tuesday nights. After supper, around six thirty. Bring some knitting, or some other kind of craft to work on."

Sandy paused, and inspected Amy carefully.

"Do you do any kind of craft?"

"I paint a little," Amy said.

"Ah, good. Bring your paints. We meet at my place. I'm in the big green farmhouse where Howard's Road meets Smuggler's Run. You come on up any time after six. If you're early, you can help me make the tea."

"Okay." Amy watched the woman leave the church. She turned back to the front of the sanctuary, her smile fading. She supposed she had better brace herself. If Sandy was any example, people were going to want to know what the hell she was doing here on their island.

Amy finished her walk, making her way back to her temporary home. When a dusty blue pickup truck approached her, Amy noticed that, as usual, the driver lifted three fingers from the steering wheel in her direction. This time, Amy raised her hand in a return wave. The driver smiled broadly and nodded to her as he passed.

Amy smiled as well.

Back at the cottage, Amy prepared some thawed perch she'd bought on a whim from the little fish shop on the mainland dock. She had spotted the sign for fresh fish as she waited to board the ferry.

Amy dipped the perch filets in egg, dredged them in flour, and then fried them in a pan of sizzling hot oil. While the fish cooked, Amy put coleslaw dressing on some packaged shredded cabbage and carrot mix and stirred it up.

After dinner, she got out her journal. Sandy's conversation had her thinking about acceptance and friendship. Things that don't come easily to someone in her line of work.

A CAS worker knows that the most awful, horrible, frightening things you can imagine happening to a child can actually happen in real life. And when you are a child protection worker, no one else wants to spend a lot of time with you. Maybe they don't think about it too much before they have kids, but they are definitely aware and not interested in spending time with you when their babies are here. They're worried you might report them even though they are really excellent parents, at least, that's what Amy thought.

Amy thought about her one-time very best friend, Rachel. When Amy started work at the CAS in downtown Toronto, Rachel went to work for a corporation in the north end of the city. They stayed close, meeting up for dinner once a month. They double dated. Eventually, Rachel got married and Amy was her maid of honour. A grand wedding it was, too, at the Old Mill. Fancy. Amy could still remember the feeling of sitting beside her friend at the wedding dinner. Rachel, in the centre of it and so happy in her dress, surrounded by family and friends. Amy had stayed close-by throughout the day, ready to help with whatever Rachel needed. It felt like those moments had sealed their friendship.

Amy wrote about their shared dreams and joys. She wrote about how, for a while, Rachel had worked so hard to set Amy up with all of Stewart's friends and acquaintances. None of them seemed that interested in her, although she did have a stand-by date with Stewart's co-worker, Sam. He was fun, until he got serious about another woman he met at a work event and no longer needed the entertainment an occasional double date with Amy offered.

Amy wrote about how things had changed when Rachel got pregnant. Rachel and Stewart were thrilled. Amy was thrilled for them, too. At her baby shower, Rachel thanked Amy for organizing it. She mentioned what a good friend Amy had been, helping her get a job in university, helping her study for exams, helping her on her beautiful wedding day, and now helping her welcome her first child. Rachel made a fuss over how much Amy meant to her, and Amy joked that she would be left in the baby power dust when the baby arrived. Rachel swatted her friend lightly on the arm and vowed not to let that happen. She said she wanted them to always be close, and that nothing would change. Amy believed her. Amy had laughed as Stewart fretted about Rachel's aches and jumped to serve his pregnant wife's every whim. Rachel had laughed as well, though she admitted to Amy that she loved the pampering.

But then the baby arrived. Jane Ann, who would be called Janey. Amy learned how to quilt, and her first project was a pink and white baby quilt, a welcome gift. Amy arrived to deliver the quilt on a Friday after work.

"You look tired," Rachel said as they sat down on a comfortable leather couch with the baby in a reclining bouncy seat on the floor in front of them. Amy set her bag on the floor.

"Well, I came from work," Amy said. "But I'm so happy to be here. I don't feel tired."

"I don't know how you keep doing that job," Rachel said. "I mean, I know it's your career, but it just seems so...awful."

"Sure, it's hard sometimes, but I love my work, Rachel. It's what I do. Anyway, it's the weekend now, and I'm here to visit you, not to talk about work. I brought something for you and Janey." She tugged the quilt out of the bag at her feet and passed it over to her friend. Rachel seemed pleased to have it, although Amy noticed Rachel's fingers worked over the few spots on the quilt that weren't perfect before she set the gift aside on the end table.

After that visit, Rachel's invitations to visit came further apart, mainly because Rachel never came into the city and Amy worked late so often, she had trouble making it up to Rachel's place. So, when they did get together, Amy would drive to Rachel's neighbourhood, where they would walk to the local play place, and sit with the other moms that lived nearby.

The very last visit was the hardest. Amy pulled into Rachel's driveway, parking to the side as usual. Rachel came out of the house, holding the baby. Amy was shocked, because it was clear Rachel was quite pregnant, and she hadn't told her friend. Rachel looked equally shocked to see Amy there.

"What are you doing here?"

"Uh…we had plans for tea," Amy said.

"Didn't you get my message? I can't go."

"When did you call? I had my ringer off and didn't check my phone when I was driving."

"I called twenty minutes ago. Well, I'm sorry you drove all this way." The little one squirmed in her arms, but Rachel turned her body each time the baby tried to look at Amy.

"Well, congratulations on your pregnancy, anyway. Can I at least say hello to Janey?"

Amy approached Rachel's side, just as the child turned toward her. Amy saw a red line on Janey's cheek with a fresh bruise forming around it.

"She just fell. Nothing else happened," Rachel bit out. "She's just starting to walk, and she fell forward into the coffee table this morning."

Amy stared at her friend, then glanced at the baby's face again.

"It looks like she hit the table pretty hard, poor thing," Amy said.

"Are you going to report me?" Rachel turned to face Amy, a mixture of fear and defiance dancing across her face.

"No, Rachel. I'm not going to report that your baby fell and bruised her cheek on the coffee table while she was trying to walk this morning. Is that why you called to cancel?"

"Well, you do work for CAS. How was I supposed to know what you'd do? I know you have a duty to report suspected child abuse."

"Rachel…"

"Amy, I really need to get going. I'll call you and we'll reschedule."

But Rachel had never rescheduled, and Amy had been too hurt to make the call to her old friend. She didn't want to see that look on Rachel's face again.

Amy closed the journal. Maybe writing this all out wasn't such a good idea. She was definitely churning up old hurts. Things she thought she put away a long time ago.

Amy brewed a pot of tea and took it out with her to drink as she sat on the rocks. Wiley came with her and stretched out beside her on his favourite flat rock.

She had just over four and a half weeks left. She would go on Tuesday to satisfy Sandy. Maybe, in the company of the women of the island, Amy would find some relief or direction. Maybe.

Maureen Pollard

Chapter 25

Tuesday morning dawned bright. Amy walked with Wiley on their usual route. She'd been waving back for four days now, but none of the islanders had stopped to chat. Other than Sandy, and the woman who ran the store where Amy got her milk, fruit, and vegetables, she hadn't had a conversation.

As she approached the cottage from the road, Amy could see a package on the porch. Wrapped in brown paper, it leaned against the door of the cottage. She could see her name printed in bold block letters.

AMY MALLOY
PELEE ISLAND, ONTARIO
CANADA

Shaking her head, she picked the package up and looked for a return address. Her heart beat faster when she found none. Very few people knew she was here. Who would send her a package?

Rhonda wouldn't bother. Her hands would be full trying to make sure the others covered both Amy and Leigh Ann's caseloads. Six weeks was a long time for a worker to be off when the team was already short staffed.

In fact, Amy couldn't think of anyone at the agency who would send her something. If they thought of her at all, they were probably cursing her absence as they worked late again. Or they were relieved they didn't have to deal with her in her unpredictable emotional state.

"What do you think, Wiley? Should I get the cops to check it out?" Amy held the package out to Wiley, watching his reaction. The wolfhound sniffed it and nudged it back toward her with his nose.

"Hmm. Safe enough, eh? Probably just as well, since the one cop on the island is likely already busy." Amy was glad the dog hadn't reacted to the package, but she still eyed it nervously for several moments before deciding to go ahead and open it.

Amy slid her finger under the corner of paper that had torn while the package was in transit. She ripped the paper open, shaking her head again at the fact that the package had arrived, addressed that way, with such limited information given about where she was.

As the paper peeled away, Amy saw a business sized envelope, and two books.

The title of the book on top was about mindfulness-based stress reduction, and contained a series of short, focused activities to try. The second was about trauma recovery. Who would send her these things? Maybe someone from work, after all?

Amy picked up the envelope. It wasn't sealed and when she lifted the flap there was a single sheet of lined paper folded within.

Unfolding the paper, Amy didn't recognize the handwriting. She scanned the page and saw the signature at the bottom. Paul Shields. She thought about the times she'd worked with Paul on the abuse investigation involving that young boy, Timmy, and at the scene of the baby's death. She liked him. He'd transferred up from Hamilton and had a lot of experience. He was smart, sharp, and witty, and he was thorough. A good combination in a cop. Better yet, he wasn't one of the ones who seemed to dismiss every social worker as a bleeding heart who couldn't separate facts from emotion in an investigation. He respected her input and that put him high on Amy's list of police officers she appreciated working with.

Hey Amy,

I stopped by the agency the other day to talk to you about a case. Maeve said you were on vacation for six weeks and said she'd be surprised if you even came back at all. Tanya said she hadn't seen anything like it, the way you just stopped caring and crawled inside yourself only coming out to snap at people.

Well, I hope you do come back. I know you didn't stop caring. In fact, I bet that you are there on Pelee Island, caring a whole lot right now. About the baby, about little Angel, about Timmy. About Tom and his mom Faye.

Evan said Faye had a setback, but she's rallying again.

I am sending two books. A few years ago, a friend went through a bad stretch after a child died in Hamilton. My friend met a great therapist. Part psychologist, part Buddhist is how my friend described him. Anyway, that guy recommended reading these books to help deal with the trauma. They helped my friend, and maybe they'll help you.

There is no way you could see what you saw and be the same again. But you are strong. You care. You can find your way back.

When you do come back, I'd like to talk to you about a case. There's no rush, no crisis, but I'm interested in your thoughts. I know you'll be back. You care too much to stay away.

Take care of yourself on that island. Don't let the wine get you. Don't let the pheasant hunters get you, either. They shouldn't be out until fall.

Paul

Amy re-read the letter. He was right. She hadn't stopped caring. She cared so much she didn't understand why she didn't die right in that room with little Angel. She felt almost like a part of her had.

Amy held the books and looked at them each in turn before deciding to try the one about trauma recovery first. It was definitely a relevant topic. She put the one about mindfulness-based stress reduction on the bedside table. It felt like so much time had passed since she had taken that mindfulness training through work. She still used the breathing exercises, but it would be a good idea to focus on some of the exercises in this book. She remembered how much it had helped before when she needed to calm her mind.

Cup of tea in hand, Amy sat on the rocks and the sound of the waves crashing against shore served as a backdrop while she read. She looked up after chapter four and realized it was later in the afternoon than she thought. She called to Wiley, who raised his head off the flat rock he was sprawled on and stood up.

As she got ready to go to Sandy's, Amy thought about what she had read. Maybe she needed to find someone to talk to about her experiences. Writing was helping, she thought. But maybe it was time to add therapy.

She looked over her things and chose a canvas, then readied her easel and the art box that held her drop cloth, paints, brushes, and palette.

Amy loaded her gear into the car and drove the short distance to Sandy's place. She glanced to the west and saw the sun starting to dip low over the horizon as she turned into the driveway marked by a mailbox painted with a beach scene.

Sandy and Steve owned an old farmhouse. The siding was painted bright green with white trim. Amy looked up at the chimney, built from fieldstone. There was no smoke curling from the top on this warm spring day. The cement walkway was cracked and uneven. It led to a porch built from the same type of fieldstone as the chimney.

Before Amy reached the porch stairs, the front door swung open. Sandy stepped out on to the top step, one hand ruffling her already spiky hair.

"Well, hello there! I'm glad you came. Come in, come in." Sandy took the easel and led the way into her home.

The main floor was open, with partial walls at critical places to support the upper story. Sandy set the easel up by the window on the west side of the living room.

"You'll have the best light here. The sun'll go down but when it gets too dim, there's a lamp there, behind you."

"Perfect."

"The others will be along shortly. Come on into the kitchen with me."

"What can I do to help?" Amy looked to Sandy, who was in front of the sink.

"Everything's ready. Just letting the tea steep."

Sandy checked the tea pot and used a spoon to scoop out two soggy bags. She poured two cups and looked up at Amy.

"What do you take?"

"Just a bit of milk."

"Sure. I'll let you pour it." Sandy nodded in the direction of a dainty china creamer on the round dining room table. Amy did as she was told and stirred her tea as she admired the grain in the dark stained wood of the table.

"Yep. They don't make them like this anymore, either." Sandy touched the tabletop.

They moved into the living room. Around the perimeter was a mix of chairs and loveseats in various styles. Every chair had fabric in some shade of blue, but that was all that was similar about them. There was a wingback chair, a rocking chair with an upholstered seat, and an overstuffed armchair. There was also a small, austere loveseat with no arms, and a Victorian style one with delicately carved woodwork and round cushions. Amy sat on the loveseat, across from Sandy, who sat in the armchair. Sandy gazed out the window toward the setting sun for a moment before speaking.

"We've seen a lot of people come across the water to this island for lots of different reasons," she began, turning to look at Amy. "What are you running from, Miss Amy Malloy?"

Amy raised a startled eyebrow at the question, but Sandy continued. "We see all kinds. Once in a while we get one like you. Looking to run away from the world. So, what are you running from?" Sandy settled back into the armchair.

Amy perched on the edge of the loveseat with no arms, feeling exposed. She wished she'd chosen a seat she could sink into.

"Well, it's a long story."

When Amy didn't say more, Sandy leaned forward.

"Honey, I can see that you're scared, and that you're sad. I know it was bad. In fact, I haven't seen anyone come through looking as bleak as you, yet. But you're safe here. So, what are you running from? A violent husband? A spurned lover? Some kind of tragic death?"

Amy stared for a moment, then started speaking.

"I'm a child protection worker. A baby died in October, and I was the worker responsible for the file when it happened. Then, about a month later, another child I was supposed to protect died." Amy's voice cracked, and she was embarrassed to find her eyes filling with tears in front of a stranger.

"Ah. Tragic death, then. Well, yes, that's pretty bleak." Sandy's eyes softened. "Honey, you can tell me about it if you want. I've been around a while and heard some sad stories. Some bad stories. Before we moved here, I was a nurse. Lived in Windsor and worked in an emergency room across the river in Detroit. I can handle it."

Sandy sipped her tea and waited. She didn't have to wait long. No one had asked Amy to tell her story yet, and she was ready.

"I was supposed to protect her. No one else thought the risk was that serious. My supervisor thought I was being intrusive and controlling. She said we couldn't run around imposing court orders on people because of…" Amy paused as the tears started flowing freely, "because of my gut feelings."

"Mmhm," Sandy nodded, but remained otherwise silent in her armchair, sipping her tea.

"Then, it was horrible. So horrible. I couldn't stop seeing them. Everywhere." Amy swiped her eyes with the back of her hand. "I couldn't eat. I still can't eat anything red. I couldn't sleep without waking up screaming. I couldn't do my job without feeling like my heart was going to jump out of my throat every time a door I knocked on opened. And nobody understood. They stopped talking to me. Probably because I couldn't stop snapping at them. But they just wouldn't stop whining about meaningless things!"

Amy wiped her eyes again, then took a sip of her tea.

"That sounds pretty bad. No wonder you wanted to get away," Sandy said.

"I needed to get away. I've dealt with bad situations before. Heartbreaking stories and even death. This time, I just couldn't do it. I couldn't look at myself in the mirror knowing that I had a hand in allowing that poor, beautiful child to die. I couldn't get away from that thought. Even my house didn't feel safe, and home has always been my haven."

"Well, honey, you're probably in the right place. This island makes a rather good refuge. That's for sure. The birds and the butterflies have always thought so, too. They all stop in to rest here on their migration routes."

"I'm sorry. I'm going to be a mess when the others arrive."

"Don't worry about that. I told them all to come at seven tonight so you and I would have time to talk." Sandy went into the kitchen and poured some more tea into her cup.

"The powder room is over here by the back door if you want to wash your face. There're some face cloths under the sink."

Amy went into the small bathroom and did as Sandy suggested. She pressed the cool cloth against her eyes and held it there. When the cloth became warm, she ran it under the icy well water again and repeated her actions.

"Well now, that's better." Sandy smiled at Amy when the younger woman emerged.

"Thank you. I'm sorry." Amy smiled back weakly.

"No need to apologize, honey. We all need to let our pain out sometimes. Now, if you want to give me a hand, you can wash these berries while I whip the cream."

Amy did as she was asked. The two women worked silently in the kitchen for several moments as the hand mixer whirred.

"I got some books in the mail today," Amy said when the cream was whipped, and Sandy turned off the mixer.

"I heard," Sandy said.

"You heard?"

"It's a small place."

"I guess. It was from one of the cops I worked with a few weeks before this happened. One is a book about trauma recovery written by a therapist. The other one is full of mindfulness exercises."

"Well, that's an interesting combination. Especially coming from a cop. All the ones I met in that Detroit emergency room would have given books like that the side-eye. They were tough." Sandy paused a moment, looking thoughtful. "Had to be."

"Yeah, I was a little surprised, too. He sent a letter with it. Said a friend had a similar experience and found that these books helped the most. He said he knows I'll be back because I care too much to walk away, but I need to take care of myself first."

"Well, he's not wrong. I don't know you well, but from what I've seen so far, I have to agree with him."

"Maybe. I guess part of why I'm here is to figure out if I can go back. I can't live the way I have been for the last few months. That much I know. What I can do about it isn't clear yet, though."

"I guess you've got some reading to do, then."

"I guess so."

"Listen, Amy," Sandy said quietly. She wiped her hands on a tea towel and reached over to grip Amy's hands as she spoke. "You can do this. Take it from an old battle axe. You are good enough. You are strong enough. You will get through this. I want you to remember that, Amy. You are good enough. You are strong enough and you will get through this. I believe in you."

There was a knock on the door. Amy looked at the clock on the wall above the kitchen sink. It was shaped like a rooster with the clock face on the round, puffed out chest. Seven o'clock. Well, Sandy had her timing down. Amy wondered how many other wounded souls Sandy had invited to come by early for a cup of tea.

"Come on in, Jenny. You know you don't need to knock here." Sandy waved a short woman with shoulder length curly red hair through the door.

"Well, I wasn't sure if I'd be interrupting a conversation or something. I saw the car out front." Jenny's cheeks were pink as she answered her friend.

"Well, you're not interrupting anything. Come on in and help me get out the drinks."

Jenny put her bag down beside the wingback chair and went straight to the fridge. She brought out a bottle of white wine.

"Ah, the Riesling. Good choice. This will go well in the mix."

Sandy opened a cupboard and brought out a large glass punch bowl. She put the ladle on the counter and gave the bowl a wipe with a damp dish cloth. Jenny emptied a can of strawberry flavoured frozen concentrate into the bottom of the bowl. She poured a jug of pink lemonade over the slush, then added the bottle of wine. She took a wooden spoon, stirring until the last of the frozen concentrate dissolved in the mixture. Then, after licking the end of the wooden spoon and dropping it into the sink full of soapy dishwater, she set the ladle into the bowl.

While Jenny mixed the punch, Sandy handed jelly jars to Amy and told her to set them on the dining table. As they worked, the front door flew open, banging against a dining room chair that had been pushed back.

"Oops! Sorry, but could I get a hand here?"

Amy rushed to the door and the tall woman handed her a cake box.

"Hi. You must be Amy. I'm Irma. That can go in the kitchen for now. Counter's fine, it doesn't need the fridge."

Irma flicked her head in the direction of the kitchen and her long silver hair swished around her face in response.

"Good, you got it. I didn't know if I called in time for them to put it on the ferry." Sandy eyed the cake box. "Did you check it yet?"

"No. Ian said it looked good, though. He said the guy who delivered it made him look before he put it in the snack bar fridge."

Sandy laughed.

"Good old Dirk at the Lake Bakery on the mainland. It sounds like he delivered it himself instead of sending one of his staff. It'll be right, then. You get out the veggies, dip and cheese when you put your bags down."

The women continued to work together, setting out snacks, moving the punch bowl to the place of honour beside the jelly jars on the dining table. They absorbed Amy into their group and included her in their chatter.

The door opened again, and a woman breezed in, tendrils of her wavy brown hair clinging to her face with sweat. She tossed her bag onto the Victorian loveseat and spun around in the centre of the living room.

"Oh, I love Tuesdays! Is the punch ready? I could really use some punch. The wind was against me on the way over. With my luck, it will shift and be against me on the way home again, too."

"Amy, this is Laura. She bikes here. Comes up Centre Dyke Road and thinks it's windy. She won't bike along the shore, where the wind really blows." Sandy introduced the newest guest.

"I'm it for tonight. Susan can't come because James has got some stomach bug and Wally won't deal with puke. For a fisherman, that Wally's got a mighty delicate stomach." Laura ladled punch into a jelly jar, gulped her first glass down and filled it again.

"Well, girls, let's eat." Sandy passed out plates and the women loaded them with cut veggies and cheese and crackers. They each filled a jelly glass with punch. Laura was on her third glass. No one noticed as Amy set her glass to the side, untouched. The punch was red.

The women sat and talked about the weather, and about who was doing what this week. The fishermen were getting the boats ready. The farmers were getting the fields ready. People were getting the cottages ready. Summer was coming and everyone had something to get ready now that the ferry was running again.

When the snacks were done, the women pulled out their crafts and the talk turned to politics and religion. The Mayor of Pelee Township was apparently a single man, and the object of pursuit by more than one woman on the mainland. The Anglican priest was back for the summer, but his wife was staying in Windsor this year. Just as well, since she'd been too stuck up to join their Tuesday night meetings. That basically exhausted the talk of politics and religion.

"We like to keep it light on Tuesdays. We've got the rest of the week to talk about the heavy nonsense if we want," Sandy explained to their guest as she changed the subject.

Irma was hooking a beautiful rug in the shades of a Pelee Island sunset. Amy could almost hear the rhythm of the waves as she looked at Irma's work.

Jenny was knitting a delicate baby sweater. Her first grandchild was due in the fall and so far, she had knit three blankets, two sweaters, three hat and bootie sets, and a teddy bear. The other women laughed as they rhymed the list off for Amy's benefit. Jenny just kept knitting.

Sandy worked with clay on a portable pottery wheel. She shaped a square piece of clay into a deep, beautifully shaped bowl. Her foot worked the pedal and her hands moved intuitively over the clay, never missing a beat as she gossiped with her friends.

Laura had set up jewelry making supplies on a low table in front of her and worked with her beads and wires while they talked.

Amy's easel was set up on her paint splattered drop cloth to gain the full benefit of the sun through the window, and when the room got a bit dim as the sun set, she turned the light on, just as Sandy had suggested. At that angle, no one could see her work, as she mixed her acrylic paint and brushed it onto the canvas. She smiled as she worked, and the scene developed under her hand. She didn't join in the conversation much, just let the flow of laughter and lilting voices roll over her as she painted.

Finally, Sandy stood up. She went into the kitchen and washed her hands.

"That's enough for tonight, I guess. Show and tell time." She looked around the room. "Who wants to go first?"

Amy held her breath. She hadn't realized they would show off their work at the end of the night. She would have chosen another subject to paint. The other women took turns, holding up their work as everyone admired the crafts, including Sandy's bowl.

They all turned toward Amy. She took a deep breath and turned her canvas toward the room. The women looked at it in silence for several long moments.

On the canvas was a painting with four figures painted in broad strokes. A woman with long silver hair sat in a wingback chair holding a sunset in her lap. Another woman, with blonde spiky hair sat in a wooden dining chair, her hands hovering over a piece of clay. A figure with wild red curls sat with a baby sweater half made on the knitting needles in her hands. A head full of wavy brown hair was bent over a small table, with wires, beads, and pliers in her hands. There wasn't a lot of detail, but the picture had the same gentle glow as the real room that held these friends as they came together in their weekly ritual.

"Amy! You should be famous. That's beautiful." Laura was the first to break the silence.

"You've got some talent, that's for sure," Jenny agreed.

"It's just something I play with. Painting helps me think. Without letting me think too much, I guess, if that makes any sense," Amy said.

"Honey, it doesn't have to make sense at all. If it makes beauty, that's good enough," Sandy said, patting Amy's hand. "Okay! Well, that's enough of that. Now, let's have cake!"

The women moved quickly, putting away their craft supplies. Sandy directed Amy to the bathroom to wash her paint brushes. When Amy came out, the cake was on the table and the women were standing around waiting for her.

"We always let the guest of honour cut the cake unless she's too drunk on the punch. We just spiked it with wine tonight, and you don't seem drunk, so it's your job," Laura said, beckoning Amy to the table.

Amy approached and looked down at the cake. A round cake with white icing, the words were piped on in bright blue. "Welcome to Pelee Island Amy Malloy," it said.

Amy was surprised that tears welled up again. She fought to keep them from spilling and Sandy chuckled.

"Oh, honey, go ahead and cry. It's just a way to release all the big feelings," Sandy said.

"Yep, we all take a turn crying on Tuesdays. It's half the reason we get together," Irma said.

"The other half being the punch," Jenny chimed in.

The women laughed, and Amy took the knife that Laura held out. She cut the cake in half.

"Just cut it into six pieces. That's one for each of us and one for my breakfast," Sandy said.

When the cake was reduced to crumbs and the tea pot was empty, the women packed up their things and headed home. Each woman stepped up to Amy, wrapping her in a hug, and whispering in her ear. "Don't mind the others, now. Be sure you come back next week." Each woman said the same thing, until she got her hug from Sandy.

"You read those books. You paint another picture. You come here for supper Friday night," Sandy whispered as she held Amy a moment longer.

"I will," Amy whispered back. She loaded her art supplies into the back seat, closed her car door and headed home, smiling through the tears rolling down her cheeks.

Amy had finished both books by Friday. She found the first one surprisingly easy to read, and even found herself making notes as she worked her way through the eight keys the author described. Amy began to recognize that she had more to process than just the two most recent deaths. She thought she had done a lot of work over the years. She liked to joke that every day of her life was therapy, but reading this book underscored how little she had realized she needed it. Waves of old guilt and pain surprised her, crashing against the fresh pain of a starved baby, and a battered little girl.

Amy skipped her walk for a few days. She journaled furiously and she journaled pensively. She returned to the books for another prompt and then she journaled some more. By the time Friday was here, she felt all journaled out after three days of writing.

Amy got up early on Friday. She wrote intensely all morning, then ate a quick bite of lunch before taking her journal out to the rocks. She pored over the pages full of her scrawled mixture of facts and emotions. Yes. She could see some threads of connection. She could see where Angel's death, and Felix's, reminded her of her worst fears. How they reminded her of her helplessness. But she wasn't actually helpless. The books were also showing her ways to take control of her reactions. Maybe she would be able to untangle this mess after all. She was going to need a good therapist.

Maureen Pollard

Chapter 26

Amy fed Wiley his supper early. She grabbed the bottle of wine that was chilling in the fridge and headed over to Sandy's. She was glad she had agreed to go to dinner tonight, she needed the change of scenery. She hadn't been further than the rocky shore just a few feet from the door of her cottage since Tuesday morning.

"Come in! It's never locked!" Sandy called from the back of her house.

Amy went in and headed back to the kitchen. She offered the bottle of wine to Sandy.

"Well, now. You didn't need to do that." Sandy put the bottle in the fridge. Amy saw a whole shelf of bottles from the Pelee Island Winery. "We're never low on wine here. Milk sometimes, but never wine."

Amy laughed. It felt good.

Sandy handed Amy a chopping knife.

251

"You can cut up the cucumbers for the salad. They're not local, but this time of year this is it. You should be here in late July—everything is fresh out of the field then and the taste— oh—the taste! For now, though, we get hothouse and we're happy enough to have that."

Amy began to chop the vegetables.

"So, no walks since Tuesday this week. Are you taking care of yourself?"

The knife stilled in Amy's hand.

"It's all right, you know. We all go through times when we just need to retreat."

"Oh."

"What have you been doing with your time, then, if you weren't walking?"

"Reading the books and writing in my journal."

"Your friend will be pleased you read them. What are you writing?"

Amy didn't answer.

"Well, that's okay. Even a nosy neighbour doesn't need an answer to every question." Sandy smirked and took the chopping board that held the cucumbers and tomatoes.

"I've been writing about my memories."

"That's a good place to start. You know memories are just our interpretation of what we experienced, right? You know that if three people witness the same event, you will get three different versions of what happened when you ask them later what they saw."

"I do know that. I investigate child abuse and have to figure out what really happened all the time," Amy said, only noticing the sharpness in her voice as the answer left her lips.

"Good. Don't forget. It applies while you're writing about your own memories, too."

Sandy set the salad bowl on the table, then pulled the oven door open and took out a baking dish with bubbling cheese on top of rolled forms.

"Southwest, for our island in the lake, off southwestern Ontario. Chicken enchiladas—I hope that's okay."

"It looks fabulous." Amy was suddenly aware that she had eaten very little in the past three days. Mostly peanut butter sandwiches because they were quick and easy to hold in one hand while she kept writing.

"Sit. Dig in." Sandy set them on the table, then slid a lifter into the dish and moved two enchilada rolls to Amy's plate. She served herself, then sat down at the table. "It's just lemonade in the pitcher tonight. You can have wine if you want, but the second cop's over for the weekend, and they'll have the RIDE program set up somewhere on the island tonight."

"Lemonade's fine."

They ate in silence for a few moments. As she chewed, Amy paid attention to the sensation of the spicy meat and creamy cheese rolling over her tongue.

"Amazing. This is wonderful," she managed to say between bites.

"Would you like me to tell you something about the island?"

"Sure. It seems like an interesting place."

"It is. There's a local fellow who's written a bunch of booklets about our history. Like the story of the original winery here on the island. It was one of the first ones in Canada."

As Amy ate her salad and enchiladas, Sandy regaled her with tales of the early settlers on the island. The little stone church Amy loved to visit on her walks was built in the late eighteen-hundreds, the first of the group of churches that would eventually serve this isolated community.

While Amy finished her meal, Sandy wrapped up her stories.

"Well, that's probably more than enough history for tonight."

"This island has a lot of stories," Amy said.

"It's true, it does. There are still a lot of descendants of the first settlers here. We take care of each other on this island."

"Yes, I guess so, if your Tuesday circle is any example."

"It sure is." Sandy laughed. "Well, six weeks is a good stretch of time. Enough to sink into the tempo and the rhythms of the island life. By the time your visit's done, this place will be in your blood."

"Maybe so." Amy gazed out the window across the fields.

"You know, Amy, what you went through is rough. I don't need to know all the details to know that. And when a body goes through something that rough, well, it has a way of dredging the bottom. Just like the fishing boats that drag a trawling net along the bottom of the ocean. The fish that they're after aren't the only thing that get stirred up. It's a messy process. It causes some collateral damage, and it takes time to settle out again."

Amy didn't say anything. But with her belly full and her eyes dry, having spent all of dinner thinking about the history of this island instead of her pain and her responsibility for the pain of others, she was listening intently.

"They say that the dredging they do for fish has stirred up ancient ocean bottoms, as well as the more recently dropped layers of pollution from phosphates. So, these plumes of suspended particles float in the ocean, causing disturbance with the way they hang in the water, and causing disturbance again when they land far away from where they were stirred up."

"And?" Amy leaned in a little.

"Well, the way I see it, our feelings and memories are kind of like that. When a terrible thing happens, it stirs up things we thought were settled for good. It moves things and now they're not where we expect them to be. Sometimes they cause more pain while they're moving. Sometimes they change our emotional landscape when they settle again. Either way, we sort of have to ride the waves and see what happens with the tides."

"Huh. You know, Sandy, that's a decent analogy." Amy sat back in her seat and smiled. "And it just about sums up how I've been feeling."

"Well, sure. The really bad ones set us all off, one way or another."

They turned the conversation to the influx of tourists the island would see over the coming weekends. The weather was getting warmer, which would bring folks to visit the winery. Amy headed home feeling the satisfaction of a good meal and, maybe, the beginnings of a new friendship.

Maureen Pollard

Chapter 27

Amy was sitting on the rocks in front of the cottage watching the waves lap against the shore. It was a calm day, and the sound was gentle. The sun was overhead as it neared noon. She had been sitting on these rocks for an hour after her walk every day this week. She was amazed at how different the lake was each day when you looked at it so closely, and over such a long period. The height of the waves. The angle at which they hit the shore. Whether there was any driftwood, or maybe some foam being pushed relentlessly against the rocks. The occasional fish darting by in the shallow water.

She focused on her breath and tried to clear her thoughts as the mindfulness book suggested. When her mind began to race again with harsh memories like the bloody scene of Angel's death, she treated it like an errant child and beckoned it back, reminding herself to focus on the rhythm of her breath.

Wiley had gotten used to her new routine of sitting on the rocks. He tended to lay sprawled on the grass behind her, sleeping and sometimes twitching as he chased the rabbits or whatever else ran through his dreams.

Last Tuesday night's session had been so much fun. They spiked pink lemonade with wine and raspberry vodka, now that the newbie had been initiated with last week's comparatively tame wine-spiked punch. Amy allowed herself to become tipsy, softening the sharp edges of her memories and slowing her reflexes. She had driven over to Sandy's, but she walked home, deciding she would get her car the next day.

The women had crafted and gossiped about celebrities. What started in Amy as restrained giggling soon progressed to rowdy laughter from deep in her belly. It was fun. She thought it might have been some of the most fun she'd had in years. And between the raspberries and cream and the punch, she found she was finally able to swallow red foods again.

Amy drew her mind back to her breath, but the smile lingered as she coaxed her thoughts to disentangle from images of the women who had befriended her so she could be present in this moment.

A sudden bark from behind her burst through the silence. Amy's eyes flew open as she turned to see what Wiley had barked at. He rarely made a sound, and it startled her. She could see a man walking toward her from the driveway. She didn't recognize the car.

As he approached, Amy shielded her eyes from the sun. Finally, he was close enough that she could make out the features of his face.

Amy sat very still, her breath lodged in her throat unable to sink into her lungs or push out through her nostrils. She waited for him to speak first.

"Hey, Amy. How are you?" Evan sat down on the rock beside her. She noticed that she felt calm with him beside her, even though she sensed the worry within him and knew he must come bearing news from home. She saw that he had an envelope and some folded papers in one hand.

"I'm okay, Evan. Still working some of it through, but I think I'm going to be okay." Amy turned her face toward him, as she had earlier turned toward the sun.

"That's good, Amy. I'm really sorry to come and interrupt your retreat." Evan looked out over the water, his lips pressed together in a tight frown.

"My six weeks is up at the end of this week, Evan. You're not interrupting." She laid her hand over his. "I'm glad to see you, even though it looks like you've brought some bad news."

"Amy…"

"What is it, Evan?" she squeezed his hand now. "It's okay. I'm ready. Just say whatever it is that's brought you here on the first ferry of the morning. You must have driven half the night."

"I did, actually." Evan looked into her eyes. "Amy, I'm really sorry to be the one to tell you, but Faye passed away last night. Justin came home after school and made her soup as usual. She didn't have the strength to come to the table, so he brought it to her on a tray. He said she tried eating but stalled early and couldn't finish. I'd stopped in with some groceries. I'd started dropping in with smaller loads more often because she didn't seem to be doing that well. She looked tired, so I asked if I could take Justin out for ice cream. She said yes. When we got back…"

"Oh, Evan." Amy's free hand flew to her mouth, even as she tightened her grip on him with the other.

"When we got back, Faye was looking weak. Still breathing, but just barely. Justin looked scared, and he asked her if she was going to finish her soup. She said she didn't think so. She took his hand and held onto it. She said she loved him very much, he was a good boy. She told him to be good for you."

"What?"

"That's what she said. 'Be good for Amy.' She closed her eyes and stopped breathing then." Evan's voice cracked and a tear escaped the corner of his eye.

"Oh, Evan." Amy took a deep breath. She didn't bother to wipe the tears that fell. "Where is Justin now?"

"He's asleep in the back seat. He stayed awake for most of the drive, but shortly after we got off the highway he finally conked out."

"He's here? You brought him here?" Amy stared at him.

"Well, after O'Driscoll's funeral home took the body, there wasn't anyone to look after him. I kept him with me, because there was no one else for him to stay with, and he couldn't be left alone, of course. He showed me the kitchen drawer where his mother kept her important papers and said there was something in there for you. In the drawer, I found Faye's will and a sealed envelope addressed to you."

He handed her the paperwork. Amy opened up the papers and scanned the handwritten will.

In the event of my death, I name Amy Malloy, social worker, to be the legal guardian of my son Justin, who needs someone who will be strong and gentle at the same time. Amy has always been that.

Amy's tears flowed as she opened the envelope with her name on it, a mixture of sadness and anxiety rising into her throat as her finger slid under the flap and tore the paper. She paused to wipe her eyes because she was having trouble reading.

Dear Amy,

I know we didn't get a chance to talk about this. I'm sorry for that. I can't imagine how you must feel. It all happened so quickly when the treatment stopped working. I don't have anyone else who can do this. Justin needs you. And I think you probably need Justin.

Please take care of him. He thinks he's grown and knows it all, but he's still just a little boy really, and when I'm gone, he'll need a good substitute mom. I can't think of anyone better than you.

There's not much left but take what we have and use it to help take care of him. Never let him forget that I loved him with all my heart.

Faye

Amy looked at Evan. She handed him the paper and wiped her eyes as she looked back out over the water. The landscape looked the same, but Amy knew everything had just changed in her life. Again. Justin was in the car. Asleep. Her responsibility now, willed into her care. What in the world was she going to do about that?

"Does he know?" Amy asked as she waved the will in front of Evan.

"He knows. He said his mom talked to him about who he would want to take care of him. They agreed on you. He told me last week when I dropped off the groceries."

"Oh sure, thanks for the heads up." Amy's attempt at sarcasm failed when her voice broke and her tears began to flow again. "I'm not sure I can do this. I'm just barely getting my own self together right now."

"You don't have to do this. You didn't know about it, and you didn't agree to it. You can say no."

Amy looked over at Evan's car. Justin had reclined the seat and his forehead rested against the window, his mouth hanging open in sleep. She pressed a hand against her chest, rubbing the area over her heart, which felt crushed by the weight of it all.

"How can I say no to that boy? Look at him."

"Sure, him and a hundred other kids just like him," Evan said. "You can't help everyone. Sometimes you have to help yourself."

"Now you sound like Menard. He's turned his heart as hard as a rock."

"Yeah, I did, didn't I. Trying to be devil's advocate, I guess." Evan took her hands in his and softened his tone. "Look, Amy. You don't have to know what you're going to do about everything right now. It's enough to take it one day at a time. See what happens and see what feels right."

"I'm just so worried about what could happen. Take one grieving almost-nine-year-old boy with a history of fighting and getting suspended. Mix him in with a foster family, any foster family. Let him start to show some anger because he's grieving. When the anger gets big, because the grief is, and, well, because he'll hit puberty soon enough, let the foster parents react to protect their home and family. That's the recipe for how kids end up moved from place to place, hauling a few changes of clothes in a garbage bag, getting angrier and bigger until they end up in group homes or detention centres. That's not a path to adoption. Teenage boys grieving the loss of their primary attachment figure are not nearly as desirable as a beautiful wee infant you can rescue and raise up in your own ways."

"Well, you know the system better than I do."

"You know exactly what you're doing, don't you? Of course, I have to take care of him. He's such a good kid at heart. The bigger he gets the less people will be able to see that, if he stays on the path he's been on."

"It's up to you, Amy. I'm just the messenger."

Amy blew her bangs out of her eyes. She jerked her head toward the cottage and started walking toward the door.

"Well, you might as well come in. I'll make some lunch. You must be starving after your drive."

"What about Justin?"

"Let him sleep a bit longer. He's safe enough here."

While Amy put together a salad with spring greens, tomato, and cucumber, they talked about what needed to happen next. There were no arrangements for a funeral. No money either. O'Driscoll's had agreed to hold Faye until Evan returned with Amy. Amy would have to decide what to do.

"Did Justin mention what he wanted to do?"

"No, he didn't really say much at all."

"Okay, well we'd better see what he's thinking before we make any plans."

"What who's thinking?" Justin asked. He stood in the doorway, rubbing his eyes with his fists.

"Well, well, speak of the devil," Evan said.

"Come on in, Justin. Welcome to Pelee Island." Amy smiled. The dog ambled over to Justin and sniffed his ankles. "Justin, meet Wiley. He's my buddy."

"What kind of dog is he?" Justin held his hands up and stepped away from the big animal.

"Wolfhound. He's big, but he's gentle."

Justin hesitantly stepped forward and rested a hand on the dog's big head. Wiley, sensitive as always, sat perfectly still, staring at Justin from deep soulful eyes. After a long moment, Wiley shuffled closer to Justin, who knelt beside the dog and lay his head against the beast's neck. Amy watched the pair, and her own eyes welled up with tears as she remembered the times Wiley had been her biggest source of comfort, too.

"He's a friendly dog," Justin said. "I can just tell."

Amy set out the salad, some sandwich buns with cheese and sliced deli meat, then mixed a pitcher of lemonade that she set on the table. Evan and Justin sat and filled their plates. The trio made small talk while they ate. Amy knew Justin needed to eat and get used to his surroundings before they talked about anything big. When they finished, Evan got up to clear the table and start the dishes. Amy asked Justin if he wanted to go sit on the rocks outside with her. Wiley followed and stretched out on the grass behind them as they arranged themselves facing the water.

"I'm sorry about your mom. I know how much you loved her and what a good job you did taking care of her. She was proud of you. She loved you so much."

"I know. She told me all the time." Justin stared out at the lake.

"Did you two talk about what kind of funeral she wanted?"

"Not really. She said there wouldn't be any money for a funeral. She said not to worry about her body because she would always be with me in my heart."

"Well, she's right." Amy paused. She glanced at the boy sitting still on the great flat rock he had chosen. "If money was no issue, what would you like to do for her?"

"Well, I don't know. I don't like to think of burying her body in the ground. I read on the internet about these cool Eco burial pods, where you can be planted under a tree that will grow over your body, but it's expensive. And you still have to put the body in the ground." Justin heaved a big sigh before continuing. "So, I guess I would have her cremated, and I would choose an urn and keep her with me wherever I end up living."

"Well, we can probably arrange that, Justin. Would you like me to get in touch with O'Driscoll's and plan it?"

"You don't have to, Amy. I know my mom didn't talk to you about any of this. I think she hoped you would just take over. Probably because you kept buying groceries and bringing them by and even made it so Evan would come when you were away. She said you care a lot, and you wouldn't just turn that off."

"Well, Justin. Your mom was a pretty smart lady. I do care a lot about you. A person doesn't just turn that off. She was right." Amy turned to face Justin and waited for him to look at her before she continued.

"I'm not sure what kind of parent I'll make, Justin. I have no family, really. I try hard to do the right things, but I make mistakes all the time in my own life. I work hard, and I get bogged down by it all sometimes."

"You don't have to take me in, Amy. I know I can go into foster care." Justin lowered his eyes to her knees.

"That's true. But if you're willing to put up with me trying my best, even if that means that sometimes my best isn't that great, then I'm willing to give this a try. I do care about you, Justin. I think you are smart, caring, determined, and talented."

Justin ducked his chin against his chest, looking at the ground.

"Some people miss those things about you because they believe the tough act you were putting on when you wanted to stay home with your mom. I know better. You think that if you act tough enough and strong enough, people will leave you alone. They won't try to hurt you or push you around."

"Well, acting tough does work, sometimes," Justin huffed.

"Sure, sometimes. Listen, if I'm going to try, I'm going to need you to try, too. Because that act is going to hold you back if we don't figure out a way for you to be strong without it. So, people can see the real Justin. The one who took such good care of his mom. The one who is a kind and caring person."

Justin had turned to stare at the lake again and tears were rolling down the boy's cheeks. His shoulders shook silently. Amy waited until he was still once more.

"I'm willing to give it a try if you are. Who knows, Justin, we might make a great team. It seems like your mom thought we would."

"I'm willing to try." It was all Justin could do to push the words out as he started to choke up once more.

"Good. So, we shall try." Amy put her arm around the boy, and he leaned into her shoulder.

At the sound of Evan clearing his throat behind them, Amy turned to see him standing there. He sat down on Justin's other side, reaching his arm around Justin, and resting his hand on Amy's shoulder.

"We shall all try, and I bet we'll be good at it. Neither one of you are alone in this, you've got me, too," Evan said.

They sat there, wrapped up together on the rocks, encouraging Justin to tell them stories about his mother until Wiley whined at the door of the cottage, reminding them it was time to eat.

Amy and Evan tucked Justin into one of the bottom bunks after dinner. Wiley lay down on the floor beside the boy's bed. Amy took Evan's hand and led him outside, back down to the flat rocks by the water.

"Listen, Evan. I want to apologize."

"You don't need—" Evan began.

Amy put her hand up to stop him.

"Let me speak. I'm sorry for pulling you to me and taking advantage of you the night I found Felix. It wasn't fair to you when you were honest with me about your feelings. I should have sent you home instead of opening my door."

"You didn't take advantage of me. I'm a grown man, Amy, and I made a choice to come out there and offer you comfort. I knew the risks. You were honest with me, too." Evan blew out a breath as he ran a hand through his hair. "I'm not sorry we slept together. It was amazing, just like I knew it would be, to be with you and then hold you all night while you slept. I don't regret that at all."

"Fine. You're right. It was pretty comfortable," Amy conceded. She glanced at him and saw that he was smiling.

"But I'm still sorry for being so difficult in the months afterward. That was uncalled for."

"You were a bit harsh," Evan agreed. "The trouble was that you were much harsher with yourself than you ever were with me."

"What?" Amy stared at him.

"Amy, I have seen a lot of people who have investigated some grisly deaths. It is not uncommon to cut yourself off from your supports when you are reeling from the trauma. Everything you have been going through is a completely normal reaction to finding yourself in the centre of two criminal investigations where children you were working with died."

"How do you know? How do you know it's normal?" Amy asked.

"Because it's almost the same thing I went through after my first murder investigation. The victim was the same age as my kid sister, and it messed me up for a long time. You may have noticed we only go out for tea and dessert, and never a drink? I don't drink anymore. It's a long story, for another day."

"I didn't know." Amy said.

"Nobody in Green Valley does, except my Sergeant. I told him the day I started here that this was going to be a fresh page for me. You know, I got a second chance after getting into trouble as a teen, and I had to find my way out of a rough patch again as an adult because I wanted to keep being a cop. I'm a good cop. So, I trusted him with my past and asked him to give me a chance. He did."

"You are a good cop," Amy agreed. "I'm glad he gave you that chance."

"You're a good child protection worker. One of the best. You can come back, Amy. If you want to, it's possible."

Amy looked toward the cottage where Justin lay asleep. She turned her gaze back toward Evan.

"I guess I have to give it a shot."

"Good. I'm still here for you." Evan sat with his hands in his lap. "I meant everything I said."

"Okay, Evan. I'll take it under advisement. Let's go inside," Amy said. "But I think maybe it's best if you sleep in one of the bottom bunks in Justin's room tonight."

Evan didn't argue.

Maureen Pollard

Chapter 28

Amy was up early, showered, and making pancakes in the kitchen when Justin woke up and stumbled out of his room. He rubbed his eyes as he made his way toward Amy. Wiley trailed behind the boy, laying down at Justin's feet when he sat in a chair at the dining table.

"Good morning!" Amy said.

"Morning. What are you doing?" Justin asked.

"Making pancakes. Do you want some?"

"Do you have any chocolate chips? I like pancakes with chocolate chips."

"Sure." Amy reached into the cupboard for the package of chocolate chips and added some to the batter.

"Can I have coffee?" Justin asked.

"Did your mom let you drink coffee?"

"No. She said it would stunt my growth."

"Well, then my answer is no. It will stunt your growth," Amy said.

"That's what I thought."

"Hey, what's this? Are you two planning a feast without me?" Evan stepped out of the bathroom, dressed in fresh jeans and a T-shirt.

"Oh no, you're invited, too," Amy said with a smile. "Chocolate chip pancakes."

"I guess you're going to let him have coffee," Justin grumbled.

"Yes, and when you are eighteen, you can drink coffee, too."

"I was sixteen when I started drinking coffee," Evan said.

"And look at you. You're incorrigible."

"Maybe, but I don't think that's because of the coffee."

"So, maybe I can drink coffee when I'm sixteen?" Justin asked.

"Maybe," Amy replied. "We'll see."

They kept up the light banter over breakfast. Evan asked what she normally did with her days here on the island. She described her routine, including the daily walks, the painting, the quilting, and her Tuesday evenings crafting. When they finished eating, Evan shooed her out of the kitchen.

"You go for your morning walk. The men will take care of the dishes. It's the least we can do since you've fed us lunch, dinner, and breakfast now."

Amy packed her snacks and water bottles. She hadn't planned a route today, but she knew the island roads well enough now that she didn't really need to. She set out down the road toward the church. It seemed like a good day to reflect on the new developments, and the peaceful sanctuary drew her in. She sat down and closed her eyes.

"Hey! I thought I might find you here." Sandy's now familiar voice interrupted Amy's meditation. "So, who are those two handsome men visiting you?"

"Well, one wants to be my boyfriend, I guess. The other is my... I don't know what to call him, but his mother just died and left me as his legal guardian."

"Holy shit. No wonder you're over here praying. You went from being all alone in the world to having a ready-made family."

"I guess so," Amy said, a smile tugging at the corners of her mouth. Leave it to Sandy to get to the heart of the matter. "And I'm going to take on the little boy, but I'm not so sure about the boyfriend."

"Taking in one person at a time seems reasonable," Sandy agreed. "So, this is it. You've only got a few days left."

"Yes, well, I'm going to have to cut it a bit short. Justin's mom died two days ago, and the funeral home is holding onto her until we can get back there. She left me in charge of everything."

"Are you ready to go back?" Sandy asked, studying Amy.

"I think so. I feel a lot stronger than I was when I got here, that's for sure."

"The island's a special place. Its rhythms have a way of bringing peace if you're seeking it."

"Oh, and I was seeking it," Amy agreed.

"Well, if you're not leaving today, it's Tuesday. You can still come over tonight. If your men will let you out."

"Oh. They'll let me. They're not going to have any choice. I wouldn't miss my last night with you ladies for anything."

"Good. See you at seven, then." Sandy grinned and waved as she strode out of the church, leaving Amy to return to her private reflections.

When she grew restless in the pew, Amy left the church and walked over to the ferry office. She asked about the schedule for the next day.

"Well, you're already booked at eleven o'clock on the Jiimaan. Your friend and his kid stopped in to reserve a space for his truck and your car about half an hour ago."

"Good," Amy said. She had just come in the day before to see when she should plan her trip back to the mainland, although she hadn't booked anything then. She couldn't decide whether to leave in the morning, or to spend as much of the

271

last day as possible soaking up the island's healing energy before heading back to Green Valley.

"No problem. That Wiley's fickle, eh? As soon as the men show up, he's on their team just like that."

"Well, they do say dogs are man's best friend," Amy quipped. The ticket clerk laughed as Amy turned to walk back down the road toward the stone cottage.

Amy walked through the door to find Evan and Justin working in the kitchen. They whirled around when they heard the door.

"You're just in time," Evan said.

"We made lunch for you!" Justin chimed in.

"Hey. Sit down," Evan said as he turned back to the stovetop.

Amy sat and waited as the two put the finishing touches on their creation. They presented her with an omelet, neatly flipped and filled with tomatoes, spinach, mushrooms, and cheese. She clapped and grinned at them. Her grin grew wider when she saw their servings, consisting of two piles of broken omelet on each plate.

"We needed some practice, but we got yours just right!" Justin said.

"You did, indeed. It's almost too beautiful to eat. But I am too hungry to save it, so I'm going to eat it anyway."

As they all tucked into their lunch Amy explained she had a meeting to attend that night.

"Thanks for booking us on the ferry tomorrow. I know we need to get back and take care of Faye. I'm going to go to the meeting tonight, though, to say goodbye to the friends I've made here. They've been very good to me."

"It's been good for you here, by the look of those paintings you've done," Evan said, gesturing toward the canvases leaning against the living room wall. "Don't worry, we'll hold men's night while you're out. Maybe we'll take a long walk with Wiley and explore the shoreline."

"Sounds good," Amy said. "I wouldn't mind getting out for another walk myself. Why don't we go over to lighthouse point this afternoon?"

"What's that?" Justin asked.

"Just a path through the woods to a beach where the old island lighthouse is. It doesn't work anymore, but several years ago a group got together to raise money to rebuild it. It was just crumbling until they restored it. It's the one place on the island I haven't walked yet. Do you guys want to go?"

"Sure," Evan said.

"Okay," Justin agreed.

They took Amy's car, with Wiley and Justin sharing the back seat. She parked in the lot near the trail's entrance, and they walked down the road, into the woods, following the path until it came out on the beach. Justin and Wiley ran ahead of Evan and Amy. Evan reached out for Amy's hand, but she pulled her hand away and shook her head no.

"Evan, I don't want Justin to get the wrong idea."

He shrugged and nodded as they kept walking.

Justin explored the beach, poking at a dead fish that was washed up on the shore, picking up shells and rocks. Evan showed him how to skip the flat smooth stones, making them jump over the water's surface. When the breeze picked up, they agreed it was time to head back to the car.

Amy got her paint supplies ready to head over to Sandy's. She watched Evan and Justin by the water, Justin still trying to perfect the angle for skipping a stone.

"I'm on my way, guys. See you later," Amy called. They both turned and waved to her before returning their attention to the task at hand.

Amy was surprised to see that she was the last to arrive. She was usually the first one there and helped with making the punch. She carried her supplies up to the house and walked in as she was now used to doing.

"Surprise!" her four new friends shouted at her as she walked through the door.

There was a cake on the coffee table, four gift bags, and a bowl of punch, of course. Amy felt the tears welling up and didn't bother to try to stop them.

"Well, what are you standing there for? Shut the door and come on in!" Sandy called from the kitchen.

It was a glorious meeting, but no crafting was done. Instead, they ate cake and drank punch as the four women shared their impressions of Amy throughout her stay on their island. Each woman had prepared a gift for Amy, and when the cake was eaten, they presented their offerings in turn.

"This rug is for you. It has the shape of our island on it so that you can bring a piece of us wherever you go. Hopefully, it will bring you the peace of mind we've watched you find over these past several weeks," Irma said.

"I made you this necklace from beach glass," Laura explained. "Tossed by the waves, pushed into the stones and sand, the glass is worn soft and smooth on the surface. It's not broken, just changed in shape after all its trials. Like your spirit. You're not broken. You've only shifted your shape to accommodate your trials."

"I knit you this," Jenny said, holding out a beautiful sea green baby sweater.

"A baby sweater?" Amy asked. "I don't have a baby."

"I think you will," Jenny said with a smile.

"I made you this mug. The heart on the mug is yours. When you are lonely and afraid, fill this mug with a hot drink and let it fill your heart with warmth and love. Embrace it, as we would embrace you if we were nearby when you needed us." Sandy handed her the ceramic vessel.

Finally, they gave her a small wooden frame that held a card with handwriting on it.

You are good enough.

You are strong enough.

You will get through this.

Amy found herself crying again. She wiped away the tears, even as she smiled widely.

"I'm going to miss you all very much," she managed to choke out.

"We're going to miss you, too. Which is why you must come back to visit regularly. The ferry runs from April first to December every year, you know."

"Yes, I do know that. Just try to keep me away now that I know what's here!" Amy laughed.

When the goodbye party was over, Amy ended up walking home. The punch had been powerful tonight. She carried her gift bags into the cottage. Evan was sitting up in the living room, reading a novel. He came to help her, taking the bags and putting them on the table.

"Hey, you've been crying," he said as he wiped her cheek with his thumb.

"I'm going to miss those women," Amy cried. "Look. They gave me gifts."

"I see that. They gave you punch too, huh," he said.

"Yep. Strongest punch I've had yet. Must've put some extra raspberry vodka in tonight. To go with the cake."

"Well, who doesn't like raspberry vodka with cake?" Evan asked, laughing.

"Nobody I know, I'm sure." Amy pulled out the little green sweater. "Look. Look what Jenny made me. She said I'm going to have a baby."

"Did she now?" Evan asked.

"I don't know if I'll be a very good mother," Amy sighed. "Do you think I'll make a good mother?"

"I think you'll be an excellent mother," he replied. "After the raspberry vodka wears off, anyway," he said as he led her to the bedroom, undressed her, and tucked her into bed. She was snoring before he closed the door to her room and headed to his bunk in Justin's room.

The sun was bright the next morning. Amy felt surprisingly well, with just a mild headache that got better when she drank several glasses of water. She packed up her belongings and loaded her car. Evan and Justin didn't have much to pack, so they were ready first. Amy stood for a long moment, staring at this cottage where she'd gathered her strength again.

The ferry ride was shorter and smoother on the M.V. Jiimaan since it was a bigger ship than the Pelee Islander and it travelled faster. In what felt like no time at all, Amy was in her car and headed back to Green Valley on the highway, following behind Evan and Justin in Evan's truck. When she finally turned in the driveway of her own personal refuge, she sighed.

Yes, she was home.

Yes, she would try again.

Chapter 29

Justin stood beside Amy, dressed in brand new clothes. Black dress pants with a sharp crease, a grey dress shirt with the buttons done up all the way to the neck, and a black tie with a grey diagonal stripe. He wore shiny black dress shoes as well. He and Amy had gone shopping when he said he wanted to wear something special for his mother's funeral.

He held his chin up high, trying to blink back his tears. Evan stood on Justin's other side. With his hands clasped in front of him, Evan looked as comfortable in a suit as he did in his uniform.

Faye had been prepared for cremation, and the trio were there to see her off. The soft strains of Amazing Grace played in the background over the sound system of the crematorium. A tall, thin man in a black suit stood beside the plain wooden casket that held Faye. He raised the lid and beckoned Justin over. Amy nodded at the boy.

Faye was dressed in her favourite warm sweater. She was always cold, and Justin wanted her to be comfortable. She was wrapped in a brightly coloured quilt that Amy had made for her about a year ago. The quilt gave the small body a soft, cozy nest inside the otherwise stark box. Justin looked at his mother's face. The frown lines and wrinkles that had been ever-present with her pain in the last six months were gone. She looked even more peaceful than she had in her sleep, which had been difficult and fitful at the end.

Now the tears fell freely, and Justin didn't bother to wipe them away. He reached out and his hand hovered over his mother's cheek. He looked at Amy, who nodded. He rested his fingertips lightly on her cool, firm skin. Amy put an arm around him, and he rested his head on her shoulder. Evan approached on his other side, nodding at Amy over Justin's head. Amy and Evan each took one of Justin's smaller hands in their own and squeezed. Justin nodded his head, and the man closed the box again, and waited silently for them to leave the room so he could nudge it toward its final destination.

They drove in silence to Amy's house. She checked on the stew she'd left simmering in the crockpot that morning. She put a batch of biscuits in the oven while Evan and Justin hiked through the woods with Wiley.

She looked at the calendar, at the square for that day. It was Friday, and she'd written "last day of vacation" in blue ink back on a day that now seemed like a lifetime ago. Amy picked up the phone and dialed.

"Hello, Maeve. It's Amy. How are you doing?"

"Oh, Amy! I'm fine. How are you?" Maeve asked. "We've missed you. You wouldn't believe the rowdy scene we had in here yesterday. Here I was with my finger hovering over the police call button and wishing you were here to calm everyone down!"

"I'm sure someone handled it just fine." Amy smiled, then braced herself for what she was about to say next. "Listen, I'm back to work Monday. Can I speak to Rhonda for a few minutes? I want to talk about a plan."

"Well, Rhonda's not here anymore."

"What? What happened?"

"She took a job as a Director of Service over at York Region CAS. So, your team has a new supervisor. She's from up north."

"What's her name?"

"Marie Koostachin."

"Okay, can I speak with Marie, please?"

"Sure thing, Amy. I'll put you right through."

Amy waited, listening to the extension ring once, twice. It was picked up before the third ring.

"Marie Koostachin speaking." Her voice was strong and smooth.

"Hi, Marie. This is Amy Malloy. I've just been on vacation for several weeks. It sounds like I missed a few things there, so welcome to Green Valley Children's Aid Society."

"Thanks, Amy. I've been looking forward to meeting you. You're back on Monday, yes?"

"Yes. I'm calling to talk about my return. I guess by now you've heard I wasn't doing very well when I left."

"I know you found two children dead during two different home visits about a month apart. I imagine how you were doing was related directly to those experiences."

"Well, yes. I was pretty irritable and hard to be with before I left. I…"

"I can understand how that is. Several years ago, I was involved in an investigation where two children died in a murder-suicide. I was irritable and difficult for a time as well. It was one of the hardest times I've ever been through, and I certainly wasn't myself."

"That must have been awful."

"It always is, every time it happens to one of us. You don't have to apologize for struggling with your feelings about it. Now, how are you feeling about coming back to work on Monday?"

"That's what I wanted to talk about. I guess I'm as ready as I'm ever going to be, but I'm hoping to take a few days in the office to settle back in. I need to catch up on what's happened with my families and readjust to being there."

"I think that's a good idea. Put your toes in first to test the water before you jump in all the way."

"Something like that. Is that okay with you, then?"

"Yes. In fact, I think it's the best way. When you come in Monday, we'll speak in person. What time will you be here?"

"I'm usually in about eight o'clock."

"Okay, well when you get here and get settled, come on into my office."

"I will. Thanks, Marie."

"No problem. I'll see you Monday morning, then."

As she ended the call, Amy looked out the window to see Evan and Justin following Wiley back into the yard from one of the trails. She smiled and took the biscuits out of the oven.

Evan left late that night, after a game of Monopoly Junior. After he left, Amy tucked Justin into bed in the guest room that would become his.

"You don't have to put me to bed, you know. I'm big enough."

"I know you are. I'd like to tuck you in though. Is that okay?"

"I guess so. When are you and Evan going to get married?"

"What?" Amy stared at Justin.

"Well, he's your boyfriend, isn't he?"

"We're very good friends," Amy answered.

"You should get married. Then he would stay here with us every night. We would be a family."

"Well, it takes time to make a decision to get married. After all, we're friends first."

"My mom said she thought Evan would be good for you. He talked about you a lot with her."

"Really? Hmm. I hope it was all good!" Amy joked.

"Oh, it was. I heard them sometimes. They both love you."

"Oh, Justin. Well, we'll see what happens together, I guess."

Chapter 30

Monday morning was sunny and warm for the middle of May. Amy hoped this was a good sign as she drove the familiar route into work. She had a new play list. Renewal, she called it. She sang along with one of her favourite songs about redemption through making your own choices in life. It was by a reggae band she'd once seen open at a popular rapper's concert.

It was early, not quite eight o'clock by the time she dropped Justin off at school and pulled into the parking lot at work. She hefted her leather briefcase over her shoulder and picked up the box that held three plastic containers filled with fresh, warm muffins. A peace offering of sorts. She left two containers in the lunchroom with a note propped up between them.

Happy May!
Amy

The third container she took to her team room and set out with butter and a knife and another note.

With apologies for not leaving sooner.
With hope we can move forward as a team.

Amy

Amy hung her briefcase on its hook and looked at her desk. Nothing had moved since the Friday she walked out six weeks ago. Maybe nothing had changed here, but it still felt different somehow. She flipped on her computer so it would be ready to go after her meeting with Marie.

Amy walked over to the supervisor's office. The door was open, and she could hear soothing instrumental music playing at a low volume in the room. Amy was surprised at the transformation from Rhonda's sterile desk and shelves filled only with documents, reference books, and training manuals. Amy could see a small round container with sand, pebbles, and a miniature wooden rake sitting on the corner of the desk. A colourful wall-hanging depicted children in a playground. Amy knocked on the metal door frame.

"You must be Amy. Come in, come in. Sit down." The middle-aged woman had long black hair, streaked with grey. She stood up, and Amy saw that she was tall and broad shouldered. She wore khakis and a ruby-red turtleneck sweater.

"And you must be Marie. Hello." Amy extended her hand, and her new supervisor shook it with a warm, firm grip.

"So, how was your time away?" Marie asked. "What did you do?"

"I spent six weeks on a little island in Lake Erie. Pelee Island."

"What did you do there?"

"I walked. I read some books. I wrote in a journal. I painted. I made some friends."

"That sounds perfect. I hope you were also able to begin to forgive yourself. I've reviewed your work. You did the best you could, Amy. The deaths of those children were not your fault."

"Thank you." Amy swallowed the lump in her throat.

"So, Marie. How are you settling in here?"

"It's only been about two weeks, but so far so good, I think."

"I'm sure you'll be a welcome addition to our team." Amy smiled.

"Well, thank you. I hope so. Now, you mentioned that you wanted to catch up on your families. I think that's a good idea. When you have had a chance to read up on the files, we can chat again, and you can fill me in on your next steps. Does that sound good?"

"That sounds fine. Thank you."

"No problem. Let me know if you need anything while you're settling back in." Marie stood and looked at Amy. "I mean that. An ear to bend, a shoulder to cry on, or a hug. No extra charge."

"Okay, thanks." Amy said, relief washing through her as she left the supervisor's office.

Amy sat at her computer and opened her case files, one after the other. She began to read the notes that were made by the covering workers. Nothing much had changed here either. The Rhodes family with the dirty house had managed to keep the housework up even in her absence, proven by an unannounced visit. They were ready to close. The Somani file had been closed again after a brief flare up of the same parent-teen conflict they had been struggling with last summer.

Timmy Rankin was still placed with Donna. His injuries had all healed and he had come out of his honeymoon phase a few months ago. The notes said he was stealing from the foster home. Not money, but trinkets. Amy read that his foster father's watch, his foster mother's leather gloves, and Logan's favourite video game had all been found under Timmy's pillow when he was at school. The covering worker had recommended they call the police and ask an officer to have a chat with Timmy about the consequences of stealing. Amy would have to call Donna. She looked at the clock—it was not even eight thirty yet, so she would wait. The kids would be on the bus by nine and it would be easier for Donna to talk then.

She noticed that Jane's file was still open. Thinking back to the farm at harvest time, Amy considered the time that had passed. It should have closed last month when the six months of voluntary service was up. She was about to open the case notes when she heard a shout.

"Muffins? Amy must be back! The Amy we all know and love, not that crabby woman who was masquerading as Amy for a while there. That one never brought us muffins!" Janet's voice carried over the cubicle walls.

Amy sighed. It was time for the reckoning, she supposed. She left the relative safety of her cubicle to meet her co-workers at the table where the container of muffins sat. Amy was surprised when she was greeted by her whole team, smiling at her. She had not expected it to be this easy.

"Welcome back, stranger."

"We've missed you. You're a hard act to follow."

"All your families wanted to know where you were and when you were coming back."

"We've missed your muffins!"

Amy smiled, surrounded by her teammates. She noticed Marie standing in her doorway, nodding as she watched the reunion. Amy suspected the welcome by her colleagues would have been frostier if that office still belonged to Rhonda. She was just as glad Rhonda was gone, and she didn't need to know.

Amy held out the muffin container to Marie, who took one and joined the group around the table. Before long, the phones started ringing, and it was back to business as usual.

Amy sat at her desk once more, with her phone on 'do not disturb.' She opened Jane's file and was about to begin reading when Janet came around the corner of her cubicle.

"You're wanted at the front desk, Amy. Maeve said there's a police officer here to see you."

Amy sighed. Jane's file would wait a bit longer. She headed out to the reception area, where she could see Constable Menard waiting in the lobby. He was in uniform and held a sheaf of papers in his hand. He didn't smile when he saw her.

"So, you're back." He handed her the papers. "It looks like there is going to be a trial after all on that murder case."

"Are they done assessing Amanda then?"

"Looks like it. Trial dates are set for next month. You'd best clear your schedule." He wouldn't meet her eyes.

"Sure. That was fast."

"The trial won't be, though. Criminal court never moves fast," Menard said.

"Right. Have a nice day, Jacques." But she was speaking to his back as he strode across the lobby and through the door.

"He's all hard and prickly, that one," Maeve said.

"Yes. I imagine he thinks I might be contagious," Amy said.

"Well, if you were contagious, I don't know what we'd do with all the homemade muffins around here."

Amy laughed and headed back to her desk.

Finally, she was able to open Jane's file. She saw that the covering worker had scolded Jane for keeping Josh home from school for two days. There was no note about why he was home, just a recommendation that the file be kept open for another six months. She was going to have to go out and see just what had happened there. Amy wondered if Jane was keeping him home to help with the planting or weeding.

Amy read through her other case files. Not much had changed in six weeks. Two files were ready to close, but the covering workers had left the paperwork for Amy's return. One recording was due this week and two were overdue by three weeks now. She could catch those up if she had another day in the office this week.

At nine, Amy refilled her coffee mug and sat down to call Donna. They talked for about half an hour and Amy caught up on Timmy's antics. Donna hadn't called the police as the covering worker suggested.

"Oh, Amy, this little boy isn't stealing. He's hoarding. He's trying to feel connected to us. So, we took back our belongings, but we each gave him something we didn't need every day in its place. I gave him a scarf I don't wear now that the weather's warmer. Darryl gave him a book, and Logan gave him a sweatshirt that's gotten too small for him anyway. Now Timmy keeps the scarf and the book under his pillow instead and wears the sweatshirt to sleep in. He knows we're happy to have him feel connected to us."

"And that, Donna, is why I knew your house was as perfect for him as it gets. Thank you."

"No need to thank me. I get all the reward I need seeing these kids getting stronger as they grow and figure out they can do things differently."

Amy ended the call and checked the time. She walked over to Marie's open door and knocked on the frame once more.

"Come on in and have a seat." Marie finished typing something on her keyboard and turned to face Amy over her desk. "How is the re-entry going?"

"Not bad. I was served court papers for the criminal trial, but that's the worst of it so far, and I was more or less expecting that." Amy paused. "Whatever you said to the team to ease my return, thank you."

"Ah, they were ready to hear it. When I came, the whole team was fragmented. There wasn't a sense of community in here. We took a half-day team retreat my second week in to talk about how they were feeling, and what they wanted to feel in this room instead. Your Monday Muffins were one of the things that made them feel connected. It was quite perfect that you brought some in this morning."

"Well, it was the first time in a long time I felt like bringing some muffins in. I guess that's a good sign."

"All around, I'd say," Marie agreed. "Now, give me a run down on your files."

Marie listened and took a few notes as Amy reviewed each file. When she finished her recitation, Marie nodded.

"That all sounds fine. I'd like you to see Jane first. Find out what's up and whether we really need to spend another six months or not."

"Okay. I'll call her now to see if I can come by," Amy said.

"Today? It's your first day back."

"I'd rather get it looked after. I feel all right. Surprisingly well," Amy said.

"I'll get the two overdue recordings finished first, then tomorrow I'll work on the one that's due this week, and my paperwork will be all caught up."

"Do you want to talk about court?" Marie asked.

"No. Not today. There'll be time for that later on. The first trial date's not until next month."

"Okay, that's fine. When you're ready, we'll book some time with the legal department to review your evidence."

"Sure. And I guess you should know that I'm going to be coming in at nine forty-five on Wednesdays." Amy glanced out the window as she spoke, avoiding eye contact.

"I've set up therapy and the earliest appointment I could get was at eight thirty, after I drop Justin off at school. I usually work late often enough that making up that hour shouldn't be a problem."

"I've seen your records, Amy. I'm not worried about your time. You've got a history of taking care of your work. I'm glad to hear you're going to take care of yourself, too."

"Okay. Good." Amy stepped toward the door, then turned back toward her new supervisor. "Marie? Thanks."

"Anytime, Amy."

On her way back to her desk, Amy heard Maeve paging her to come back to reception. She sighed. It couldn't be more court papers. The young parents whose baby had starved pled guilty to the charges of failure to provide the necessities of life, so there would be no trial in that case.

Amy stepped into the reception area and noticed a colourful bouquet of spring flowers on the desk. Beside it was a gift basket, wrapped in yellow tinted cellophane.

"Is it someone's birthday? Those are beautiful," Amy said, nodding at the gifts.

"Nobody's birthday today," Maeve said, her eyes twinkling. "Those were both just delivered for you!"

"What? For me?"

"For you. Look at the cards."

Amy read the card attached to the flowers first.

There's no heart that time can't mend. You will be stronger in your broken places. Welcome back to where you belong. You have been missed.

Amy stared at the bold print on the card. Evan. It wasn't signed, but she knew it. She smiled as she read the words again. He was probably right. She did belong here, for better or for worse. She didn't suppose she was good for anything else at this point.

"Don't forget this!" Maeve pushed the basket toward her.

Amy opened the card. She didn't recognize this handwriting, but she did recognize the words.

You are good enough.
You are strong enough.
You will get through this.

We've got your back, and just so you know, we're coming to see you the first week of June. It's the last time we can get away before the summer tourist rush begins. We've been wanting to take our act on the road for a while now. Thanks for giving us our first destination!

With Love and Wine Punch,

Best Interests

Sandy, Irma, Laura, and Jenny.

Amy looked in the basket. There was a bottle of Pelee Island wine, strawberries, grapes, and a chocolate bar labeled "IN CASE OF EMERGENCY: Unwrap and eat one delicious square at a time. The world will wait."

Amy laughed. She carried her gifts back to her desk. There she was able to begin the task of reading her backlogged emails with a smile on her face.

Maureen Pollard

Chapter 31

Amy headed over to Jane's house. They'd agreed to meet at three thirty. That would give them about half an hour to talk before the bus came and then Amy would have a chance to talk with the children as well.

She pulled into the now familiar driveway and looked around. The garden was planted with the hardiest vegetables, though it was still too early for most plants because there was a risk of a hard frost until the end of May. Jane was waiting at the front door, and let Amy in. The tangy scent of simmering tomatoes filled the house. They walked to the kitchen together, and Amy sat at the table while Jane stood at the stove stirring spaghetti sauce that she told Amy she was going to freeze.

"So, Jane. Tell me what happened a few weeks ago. Josh missed some school?"

"He did." Jane pursed her lips.

"What happened?"

"He was sick," Jane said.

"He was sick? Did you explain that?"

"I did. He had a temperature, and he was throwing up. That woman at the school didn't believe me, and neither did the one they sent out to check on us when you were gone."

"Did you take him to see the doctor?"

"No. He was better by lunch time the second day. Kept some chicken soup down and his temperature was lower. Just gave him tea and let him sleep."

"Ah, so you took care of your boy when he was ill, and no one believed you. Did anyone talk to Josh?"

"Yeah, he tried to tell them. They told him he didn't have to protect me." Jane kept stirring the sauce.

"Okay. Well, Jane, when the kids come home, I'd like to talk with each of them, like I usually do."

"Sure. I've never stopped no one from talking to the kids."

"I know. So, what are you planting this spring?"

"Well, the potatoes are in this week. The tomatoes and peppers are started and we're putting them out on the back porch to harden off during the days. They'll go in the ground in about another week. Then the cucumbers, beans, corn, squash, and pumpkins will get planted, and this year we're going to add sunflowers. Chelsea asked for some."

"Sounds like it will be another good garden. You do a good job with it."

"Not much choice. That farm stand keeps us in oil."

"I know it. How did your probation go? You're finished with it now?"

"Yes. They got me doing some community service hours down at the food bank and over to the women's shelter. I'm teaching cooking and canning lessons, both places. They're gonna let me keep it up even though I finished my hours." Jane stood taller.

"What a great idea!"

The bus stopped at the end of the drive and Amy watched Josh, Tyler and Chelsea come into the yard past the cedar hedge.

When they saw her car, the younger children started running, but she watched as Josh hung back.

"Amy! Amy! You're back!" Chelsea cried as she burst into the kitchen. "We didn't like that other woman."

"Hush, child. That's not polite."

"Well, it's true," Chelsea said.

"We don't have to go around shouting the truth out all the time. It can hurt people's feelings."

"Well, anyway. We missed you."

"Hey, I missed you, too. Who wants to talk to me first today?"

Chelsea volunteered to go sit in the front room first with Amy. They chatted about school and home and Amy had no concerns as Chelsea rattled off their recent activities. Chelsea said everything had been good except when Josh was sick. He was puking and she even had to empty the bucket for him once because her mom was out working in the garden.

Tyler was next. He wasn't as bubbly as Chelsea, but he covered a similar list of recent activities, including having to pitch in to empty Josh's puke bucket more than once when his mom was busy.

Josh went last. He came into the room with his head hung low.

"Hey, Josh. How are you doing?" Amy asked.

"Fine." He didn't raise his eyes.

"I heard you weren't feeling well a few weeks ago. It sounds like it was pretty terrible."

He looked up at her under bangs that were a bit too long and shaggy. His eyes narrowed as he considered his response.

"It was terrible. I missed school for two days. Couldn't stop throwing up."

"I heard even Chelsea had to empty your bucket once when your mom was out in the garden."

Josh turned red and nodded.

"Well, I'm glad you're feeling better. Did anyone else come down with it?"

"No. I think that's why they didn't believe me. Tyler and Chelsea didn't get sick at all."

"Ah, well, sometimes people are suspicious. I'm sorry they didn't believe you, but I do."

"You do?"

"Yep. So, I'm going to go back to the kitchen and talk to your mom a bit. Can you take the little ones outside for a while?"

"Sure. We need to clean up the dog sh…uh…dirt anyway."

"Thanks."

Amy didn't sit down again when she reached the kitchen. She stood beside Jane, who was still at the stove minding the simmering tomatoes. She told Jane she was sorry for the misunderstandings that happened while she was away. Amy believed that Josh had been sick. The file would close as planned.

"You don't think the new supervisor's going to be a stickler and want to keep it open? That's what the other one said."

"No, I don't think that will be a problem. I'll close the file this week, and you'll get a letter from me in the mail to confirm it."

Jane's grip on the wooden spoon eased as she continued to stir the sauce, absorbing Amy's decision.

Amy checked the time. She'd better get going. It was time to pick Justin up at the after-school program, and she didn't want to be late the first day.

Chapter 32

Justin settled into the back seat of the car and started digging around in his backpack as Amy drove out of the school parking lot.

"Amy! Look what they gave me!" Justin held up a small silver angel figurine. "And a card signed by my whole class. Even the principal signed it!"

Amy pulled over and took the card, already bent at the corners from handling. She read the condolences offered by Justin's eight- and nine-year-old classmates. Mostly they wrote things like "Sorry about your mom," and, "We missed you."

"That's so nice, Justin. The angel will be a forever reminder of your mom."

"I know. I'm going to put it up, so it doesn't get wrecked."

"Good idea. What else did you do at school today?"

Justin talked the rest of the way home about his classes and what happened at recess, filling Amy in on what seemed like every detail. When they pulled in the driveway, Wiley was there to greet them.

"Justin, take your angel and put it on the kitchen counter for now. We can put it in a safe place and put the card up with it. There's a shelf in your room that would work. Maybe this weekend we can clear my things out of that room and move your things in."

"So, I'm really going to live with you and Wiley?"

"I think so. I need to meet with a lawyer to make sure it's all done up properly, but I don't see any reason we can't get started on settling you in."

"Wiley!" Justin threw his arms around the wolfhound's neck. "We're going to be brothers!"

Amy laughed and shooed them off to play in the yard while she made dinner. Amy hummed as she sautéed snow peas, carrot slices, and yellow peppers with some garlic and olive oil while she grilled four pork chops. The rice cooker was bubbling on the counter beside the sink. She knew she'd need plenty of food for this growing boy, and he didn't mind leftovers either.

Her humming was interrupted by the door slamming open. Justin tumbled in, followed by Wiley.

"Amy! Evan's here! I didn't know Evan was coming."

"Me either." Amy set down the spatula she was using to turn the vegetables in the pan and faced the door.

"Hi. I brought some things for Justin. I couldn't reach you on your cell phone when I tried." He waited on the door mat.

"Well, come in. We're almost ready for supper if you want to stay." Amy looked at her cell phone. "Battery's dead. That's why you couldn't reach me."

"Ah. Here, Justin. Take this box to your room and then come to help me with the other ones." Evan waited for Justin to leave the room. "Faye asked me to help Justin pack up the house in her last few days. There wasn't much. Three boxes of his things, a suitcase with his clothes and one box with things that belonged to his mother that he wanted to keep. Everything else went to Salvation Army."

"I was just telling him that this weekend we can clear all of my things out of that room to make space for his. So, your timing is perfect," she said.

"Is it? Is my timing also perfect to—" Evan began.

"Okay, that box is on the floor by the window. Amy, is it okay if I stack them there until we clean the room out?" Justin asked, coming into the kitchen.

"Sure. That sounds just fine," Amy said as she stared at Evan, wondering what he had been about to ask.

Evan and Justin brought in the boxes and the suitcase. They stacked them neatly under the window in Justin's new room while Amy put dinner on the table, with place settings for three. Dinner conversation was easy. Justin answered their questions about school and his friends. They kept away from talking about Evan's work and Amy didn't mention hers either, other than to say her first day back went well, and she thought she was going to really like the new supervisor.

When dinner was over, it was still early. Amy supposed that was what happened when you worked on a child's schedule.

"We have about two hours before you need to start getting ready for bed. Did you have any homework?" She asked Justin.

"No. The teacher said there would be time for me to catch up what I missed later."

"Do you want to work on your room, then?"

"Could we?" Justin's eyes lit up.

"Sure. We might even get most of my stuff packed up tonight. Do you want to change the paint colour in there before we organize your things?" Amy asked. The walls were painted cobalt blue and the trim was a jade green.

"No! I like the colours." Justin hesitated, then said, "I would like sheets that don't have flowers on them, though. Maybe for my birthday?"

"Oh, I think we can manage that. Maybe for a welcome gift. How about if I pick you up at school tomorrow afternoon and we can shop for some new sheets and a comforter you like."

"Really? Really?" The boy's eyes were wide.

"Really." Amy turned to Evan, who was clearing the table and running water to do the dishes. "Evan, can you go to the basement and bring up three of the empty plastic bins with lids? I think that will hold what I have stored in Justin's room."

"Sure." Evan turned off the water and went to the basement stairs.

"Let's get started, Justin." Amy led the way to the bedroom. By the time she had opened the closet, Evan was there with the bins.

"I'll clean the kitchen while you work."

"Thanks, Evan."

"No problem."

It didn't take Amy more than an hour to empty the closet and dresser. She had two storage containers under the bed, but they were easily moved to a new home in the basement. Amy would have to figure out where to store her painting supplies, but that would probably be easy enough the next time she had the urge to paint. She left Justin sorting through his boxes after helping him place the silver angel and the sympathy card in a place of honour on the shelf above his bed.

The kitchen was clean, and Evan was sitting in the living room reading. Amy felt her heart squeeze when she saw him there. Was this what it felt like? Being in love with someone? This fierceness and tenderness all tangled up inside? No wonder people did crazy things.

Amy came around the end of the couch and sat beside him.

"Your thoughts were interrupted earlier. You were about to ask me if it was the perfect timing for something?" Amy prompted.

Evan put his book down and turned his body toward Amy.

"I was. I was hoping it might be the perfect time to ask you if I could spend the rest of my life coming home to you and Justin, like today. Although not with a bunch of boxes and a suitcase every time." Evan smiled nervously.

"Are you asking what I think you're asking?" Amy stared at him.

"I am." Evan reached for her hand, enveloping it in his. "I don't have a ring, but will you marry me, Amy?"

"I guess so, Evan." Amy paused, her eyes searching his face. "The question is, do you really want to marry me? I mean, are you sure? I'm just not convinced I'm cut out for marriage."

"I'm sure, Amy. I've never been more sure of anything."

Amy sighed. "Even if I insist we take a vacation in a little stone cottage on Pelee Island every year?" She smiled tentatively, and felt his hand squeeze hers.

"I will. If you'll have me, I'll go anywhere with you every year for the rest of my life."

"Yes!" Justin shouted. They turned to see him standing in the doorway to the living room, a fist thrust triumphantly in the air.

"Well, I guess that settles it. It looks like we're going to be a family," Amy said.

"We're already a family. We're just going to make it official," Evan corrected as he bent down and touched his lips to hers to seal the promise.

Amy's Playlist Picks

Happy Birthday Playlist

Forever Young - Joan Baez
Forever Young - Rod Stewart
Forever Young - Alphaville
At my Funeral - Crash Test Dummies

Life is Good Playlist

Let It Go - Great Big Sea
Let It Go - Michael Franti and Spearhead
Never Alone - Jim Brickman (feat. Lady Antebellum)

Rhythms of Youth Playlist

This Is The Day - The The
I Got the Message - Men Without Hats
Kiss Off - The Violent Femmes

Renewal Playlist

I Believe - SOJA (feat. Michael Franti)
Never Surrender - Corey Hart

Favourite Songs from the Concert

Ode to a Broken Heart - The Once
We Are All Running - The Once

Acknowledgements

I am fortunate to have had many generous, kind and supportive people in my corner on the creative journey to where I am today: published author of a memoir and a novel, and a songwriter, too. My deep gratitude is extended to:

Bob McLean, for always believing in me, and for reminding me on an October day twelve years ago to write more than just reports and affidavits, which led me to find Firefly Creative Writing.

Firefly Creative Writing, where the idea that I could write a novel was nurtured into bloom by Chris Kay Fraser and her fabulous team, and all the other Fireflies around the table who encouraged and inspired me. I'm especially grateful to Britt Smith for her insight and input on the earliest draft of this project.

Michelle Walker, for so many things, but in the case of my creative endeavours - for telling me when she thinks it's good, and when she thinks it's not, too. But in a nice way, because she loves me.

Shawn McDonald, for writerly companionship across a library table over BLTs, and also for connecting me with wonderful editors for my writerly projects.

Eric Wong, for providing a developmental edit offering keen insights and thoughtful suggestions, along with some gentle but firm nudges where the middle draft needed it most.

My Editorial Woman of Mystery, for helping me bring it all home with delightful enthusiasm for this project, wise guidance and skilled editing.

Angela Johnson, who cheerfully and skillfully helps me manage so many of my projects, in this case for excellent proof-reading and for a delightfully fun author photo shoot.

Jennifer Bogart, for insight and a bit of polish to make it shine, along with lending her skill in formatting for publishing.

Ana Chabrand, for a brilliant cover, from concept to finished product.

David, Noah, Lauryn, Jenna and Sophie, for being interesting company and adventurous explorers of this life we're living, for cheering me on in my creative projects and for taking good care of one another while I write.

Mom, for listening to my stories endlessly and loving me always.

*Special note to all the people I have worked with. This isn't about you. Or me. It really is entirely fiction. I solemnly affirm it.

About the Author

Maureen Pollard is a registered social worker, an author, and a songwriter. Born and raised in the part of Canada that's south of Detroit, she now works and lives in the part of Canada that's a little bit east of the fabled centre of the universe; her whole life spent on stolen land.

She worked primarily as a front line child welfare worker for the better part of 20 years. *Best Interests* is her first novel.

Made in the USA
Columbia, SC
02 July 2021

41319538R00166